QUEENDOM OF THE SEVEN LAKES

A B Endacott

Cover designed by Marcus Moltzer
Cover illustration by Ellen Liu

This book is a work of fiction. Names, characters, places, and incidents either are products of the author's imagination or are used fictitiously. Any resemblance to actual persons, living or dead, events, or locales is entirely coincidental.

ISBN-978-0-6481875-1-6

Books by the same author

Coming soon

For my parents.
My mother,
for teaching me to be
the ruler of my own Queendom,
and my father,
for helping me build it.

The mind of a queen is a thing to fear.
A queen is used to giving commands,
not obeying them;
And her rage once roused is hard to appease
-Euripides, Medea

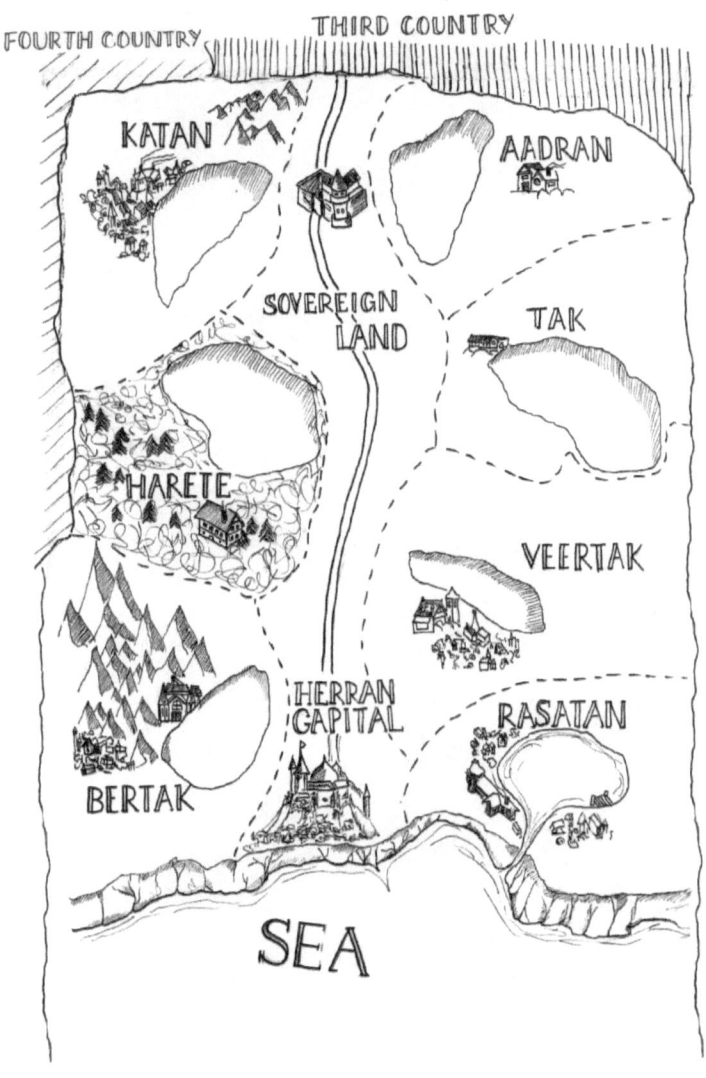

The Second Country

ONE

"I will take you to the Queen." The servant looked at the assassin then shifted her gaze uneasily to the pile of blades on the table.

Elen-ai had been required to remove her weapons before she was permitted to see the Queen. She had almost snickered aloud when the request was made. Surrendering her blades was a far cry from disarming her, although she felt the weight of their absence. For as long as she could remember, she had always carried some kind of weapon.

No less than two Royal Guards walked on either side of her as she followed the servant along the corridor. Had she not felt so acutely out of place, she would have been fighting laughter. It was an almost sweet naiveté to think that two guards could subdue her.

The Palace corridors alone were indisputably beautiful. The walls were covered with the most exquisite tiles, each tile painted by hand and arranged in a visual feast of geometric design. Delicate light from the midmorning sun coming in through the windows filled the corridors with a haze of colour. Despite the beauty she walked through, Elen-ai was not comfortable in the Palace. The absence of her weapons was disconcerting, but not the cause of the itch at the back of her neck. Her discomfort was caused by the fact that she was walking so openly, so observably. It felt deeply unnatural to Elen-ai who was most at home blending into shadows, slipping surreptitiously along an unnoticed path rather than walking in the open where everybody could see her. Unfortunately – unusually – today she had no choice in the manner of her passage.

Elen-ai counted twenty-three doors as they walked, wondering why she couldn't detect the sound of movement or voices behind them. It was an unfounded suspicion, but she couldn't help but feel she was being deliberately taken through parts of the Palace that were empty. Somewhere from far away, the faint sound of a training drill being called reached her ears. It seemed members of the Palace Guard were practicing.

Elen-ai's escort halted in front of the twenty-fourth door. It didn't look any more or less special than the preceding twenty-three, but the guards and the servant stood a little straighter before the servant smartly knocked on the door and opened it.

From her place just outside the lovely sitting room, Elen-ai looked around at the interior, noting the shadows, hiding spots, entry and exit points, and what could or could not be used as a weapon. The room was a veritable death trap for anyone who was unfortunate enough to be the name on an assassination contract. But then again, most rooms were if a member of the Family had been engaged to kill someone.

"Your Majesty, Elen-ai of the Family." The servant bowed low, all but prostrating herself before her ruler.

The Queen of the Second Country, known also by its inhabitants as the Queendom of the Seven Lakes, rose from her chair, her skirts rustling with the movement. Elen-ai was conscious of the plainness of her own simple tunic and trousers in contrast to the ornate skirts and bodice of the Queen. However, each woman had a role to play, and the job of Her Royal Highness Latana was to look like someone who wielded a vast amount of power. Elen-ai's was to kill people. So while the Queen had her beautiful skirts and long, intricately braided hair, Elen-ai wore simple trousers and shirts and kept her dark brown hair cropped close to her head.

"Thank you." The Queen addressed the guards who had escorted Elen-ai. They hesitated, clearly unhappy with the prospect of leaving their ruler alone in the room with Elen-ai, but the Queen's tone held a clear directive: leave. To disobey would be intolerable insubordination.

"Ah, Lord Silius asked me to remind you about the, uh." The servant who had led the way glanced at Elen-ai uncertainly, clearly uncomfortable with the prospect of completing her sentence in front of Elen-ai.

"Yes, the matter of the justice appointment, I know. Please tell him that I will make my final decision once I have finished with Elen-ai and our visitors from the Third Country." The Queen did not seem to share her servants' discomfort with discussing anything in front of Elen-ai. In fact, in her tone there was almost the suggestion of a rebuke for her servant's conspicuous concern.

Only when the doors had closed did the Queen turn her attention to Elen-ai. "Please, come and join me," she invited the assassin, indicating the seat opposite hers with a wave of her hand. The Queen had not so much invited Elen-ai to be seated as subtly commanded it. Elen-ai obeyed.

The two women sat regarding each other in silence for many moments. The Queen's eyes were the colour of liquid gold, set in a face of delicate beauty. Not all of the Queens who had ruled the Second Country had been beautiful, but Latana was, a fact which inhabitants of the Queendom knew well. However, few were given the chance to see this beauty for themselves, and even fewer this close. Elen-ai had entered a group of highly privileged people without even trying. Her gaze was drawn to the thick gold collar that encircled the Queen's slender neck. While it may have looked like a simple piece of jewellery, Elen-ai knew better. It was worn to prevent her throat being cut by someone sneaking up from behind. A quick glance confirmed that the Queen wore matching cuffs on her wrists. Perhaps they would be effective against a hired sword, but they would never stop a member of the Family.

"Would you care for a drink?" the Queen offered.

Elen-ai had been trained in a great many arts, but the nuances of court etiquette did not number among them. "Yes please, your Majesty," she replied, wondering if instead of accepting she was supposed to refuse to fulfil some elaborate ritual of manners.

"I have juice here, or I could call for something else if you would prefer?" The Queen indicated the pitcher and two glass vessels set on a small table by her side. Elen-ai had never drunk from glass before. Cups and goblets crafted from the material were fiendishly expensive. She wondered if the juice would taste different from glass rather than the vessels from which she normally drank.

"Juice would be fine, thank you," Elen-ai said.

With deft movements, the Queen poured from the jug, handing the drink to Elen-ai. The gold at her wrists flashed as she moved. As she sipped the juice – which was exquisite, Elen-ai reflected that she would much rather return to the quiet simplicity of the Family's home rather than be in this ornate, beautiful room being served juice in glass vessels by the Queen. The distant sound of the training drills had faded, leaving a conspicuous silence broken only by the clink as the Queen poured herself a drink and set down the pitcher.

Queen Latana picked up her own glass and drank. "Now. To business." The quiet firmness of her manner was now entirely focused on Elen-ai. "I presume you are wondering why you are here?"

"Not particularly. The Family offers only one service. Who would you like me to...remove?" Elen-ai chose a euphemism at the last moment in deference to whom she was sitting opposite. Normally she took a small delight in being blunt with people who asked for the services of the Family. She liked to remind them of what they were asking her to do.

4

"I presume you have heard the rumours of my infertility?" Instead of answering Elen-ai's question, the Queen asked one of her own.

This was not uncommon behaviour. People often felt a need to explain their motivations for seeking the removal of another person. What they didn't realise was that provided they paid, no explanation was necessary. Elen-ai had learned, however, that it was easier to let her clients justify their request. So she simply nodded. The whispers that the Queen was barren had been present at every level of society for many years now. While the Queen had given birth sixteen years ago to a healthy son, no other child had followed, leaving the Queendom without an heir. With every year that passed, the whispers became more agitated and seemed to have more truth behind them than mere speculation. Soon the Queen would definitely be too old to bear children, and that would mean disaster for the country, especially as the Queen's only sister was far too old to be recalled from her marriage to take the throne.

"Regretfully, they are true," the monarch said without any apparent concern for the significance of what her statement implied.

Elen-ai looked at her Queen with polite curiosity. Why this was being confided to her she had not the slightest idea. It wasn't as though she could kill every person who spoke of this. It would leave the Second Country with very few inhabitants indeed.

"Which leaves me with a problem," the Queen continued.

Elen-ai did not speak but was certain that her agreement with that conclusion was evident on her face.

"However, I have a solution. My son will take the throne when I die," the Queen said.

Elen-ai froze. No man had ever taken the throne of the Second Country and for good reason. A Queen could have a child without the father's identity being known. A man could not. The delicate power balance between the Queendom's seven most powerful families was preserved by virtue of the fact that the monarchical line remained free from any marital allegiance. It ensured that however many power games were played by members of the seven clans, the Queen would always be able to make rulings that were free of any familial obligation. Marriage was a powerful weapon, and the Queen was not somebody's tool to be used for their own power. What Queen Latana was proposing would shatter that precise balance. The Family was not particularly invested in the power politics of the Second Country, but its members were citizens of the Queendom, accustomed to tradition and perhaps more importantly, not immune to the turbulence that such a radical departure from tradition could create. Horror crawled its way across Elen-ai's mind as she considered the Queen's proposal and its implications.

"I know what you are thinking," the Queen spoke calmly, not giving Elen-ai the opportunity to wallow in her shock. It would seem that was something she would have to explore at her own leisure. "My own brothers have voiced their objections enough times. But my mind is made up and I will announce the decision at the Summer Council."

Elen-ai was not surprised to hear that the Queen's advisers – brothers who were trained from birth to serve the Queen in an advisory capacity – objected to this proposal. It was madness and certainly could not have either the best interests of the Queen nor the Second Country at heart.

"Despite the fact that the Queen's word is law, there are always those who would seek to break the law. Especially when they do not like it. My son will make an excellent ruler. Of this, I have no doubt. However, I fear the actions of those who may use this decision to advantage themselves. I fear for his life."

Elen-ai did not offer her own opinion on why someone may attempt to kill the Prince. Nevertheless, she could easily understand why someone may, out of anger at the Queen's decision to spit in the face of hundreds of years of history, be moved to an extreme act. Even she felt a hot flash of rage somewhere deep inside her at the impudence of the Queen to think that she was above her country's history. Somehow she did not think that the Queen would appreciate the contribution. Instead, she asked a question. "Begging your pardon, your Majesty, but I'm unsure what this has to do with me?"

"I seek the services of one who knows best how to slip through shadows and kill undetected. Because of your specific skills, Elen-ai, you are best placed to protect my son's life. The Royal Guard may keep the Palace secure, but I need the skills of someone who can do more than simply patrol. You know from where an assailant would come, how they would come. That is the best way to preserve my son's life, to know from where someone would strike, and pre-empt them before they reach him."

Elen-ai chose her words carefully before speaking. "Your Majesty, I take life. I am not certain that my skills actually extend to preserving it."

The Queen arched an eyebrow, her beautiful face otherwise unmoving. "And with whom do you suggest I trust with the life of my son? The Katan clan? They already have my sister through a marriage. It-" She stopped herself and shook her head. "No," the Queen continued. "The Family's reputation is built upon the fulfilment of its contracts and its discretion. And your unwilling-ness to kill the Queen or her family members. I would trust one of you with the safety of my son over anybody else, even members of my own Royal Guard." It almost seemed as though she was about to say more, but instead, the Queen stayed silent. Perhaps the words that she almost followed that statement with were "I can't be certain that there won't be someone in the Royal Guard who would seek to kill my son for my decision".

"I haven't accepted the contract yet," Elen-ai cautioned. Members of the Family had the right to refuse any contract put before them. Even one from a Queen. She seriously considered refusing this request.

In wordless response, the Queen pushed a piece of paper across the small table that sat between them. Elen-ai leaned forward to pick it up. Her eyes widened at the amount written on it.

"Perhaps you should tell me more about who you think may harm your son," Elen-ai said cautiously. It would be impossible to turn down such a sum out of hand.

The Queen gave a satisfied half smile, and settled back into her chair, hands curling around the glass full of juice. "I'm not sure what else I can tell you. Once I announce this, I do not doubt that any of the seven families would attempt to take his life if they deem it favourable for their fortunes. Although I do think the Veertak are the least likely to attempt such a thing."

Elen-ai nodded. Everyone in the Queendom knew of the political allegiances and loyalties that existed between the seven powerful families of the Queendom. Even the Veertak, who were the least politically inclined due to their preference for the acquisition of knowledge, had their own quiet ambition to broaden the scope of their power. However, as a rule, the Veertaks were known to avoid violence where possible, instead of using their wits to increase their wealth and standing.

"Aside from that, each family, regardless of their outward loyalty, has members who perceive things differently and would seek to embark upon the course of action that sees my only child dead. I cannot allow that to happen." For a moment a look that was decidedly un-Queen like crossed the monarch's face; the look of a mother terrified for the safety of her child.

"That's not much to go off," Elen-ai noted.

"I know," the Queen admitted. "It's why I've approached the best."

"Flattery won't get you very far, your Majesty," Elen-ai said with a slight smile.

"You don't have children, Elen-ai." The Queen did not ask so much as make a statement. Elen-ai nodded her head in confirmation. No member of the Family had children. If they wished to marry or have children, they had to leave the Family.

"I love my son with everything that I am," the Queen told her. "I didn't think I would. I thought that having a child was a necessary part of my position. Especially..." she trailed off as she searched for the exact words. "Especially given the manner in which royal heirs are produced. However, I loved him from the moment I first felt him kick inside me. And I would do anything to protect him." There was a faint plea in her voice.

"What are the terms of the contract?" Despite the fact that she knew the display of emotion was almost certainly a calculated slip to manipulate Elen-ai, it was uncomfortable seeing her ruler's vulnerability. It seemed that the Queen had known exactly what to do in order to push Elen-ai towards accepting the contract.

"You will become my son's shadow. Wherever he goes, you go. You are not to leave his side. Once it is deemed that there is no longer a significant threat to my son's life, the contract will be completed. He is my only child, Elen-ai. I need to know that he will be safe from any threat." The Queen's voice dropped, a quivering note of fear creeping in.

Elen-ai exhaled slowly, using the time to filter through the facts, discarding the emotion that her Queen was attempting to rouse in order to influence her decision. At the end of her breath, she nodded. "I'll do it."

A genuine smile crept across the face of Queen Latana, touching her golden eyes. "Thank you," she said.

"I assume I start right away?" Elen-ai asked.

The Queen nodded. "I will take you to him. He should be in the middle of his lessons now." She rose, her regal composure absolute.

Elen-ai carefully placed the glass on the table next to the piece of paper on which the Queen had written the Family's fee before she too got to her feet. "One more thing," she said.

The Queen gestured for Elen-ai to continue in place of speaking.

"I'll need my weapons back."

TWO

Elen-ai followed the Queen through the Palace. Neither the Queen nor Elen-ai spoke. Elen-ai was lost in her thoughts, trying to look beyond her instinctive reaction of horror at the prospect of a man on the throne and consider whether the Queen's son would even be a good ruler. She certainly had her doubts. For most of his life, he would have been taught how to advise an unborn younger sister rather than to rule. Not that the Queen's advisers didn't have considerable authority in their own right. But to lead required far more than simply having authority conferred upon you.

As they walked through the Palace, Elen-ai reflected once more that its corridors really were magnificent. She saw several tiny gardens through the windows that they passed and wondered who sat in those lovely, carefully tended outdoor spaces. None of them had any occupants. Elen-ai had been in many different dwellings built from stone or wood, the homes of both poor and rich. No room that she had been in came close to the wealth that she could see merely in the Palace's corridors, let alone the room in which she and the Queen had sat drinking juice.

After several minutes the Queen paused before an open door that led into a larger courtyard. Elen-ai could hear the sound of strikes and heavy breathing coming from outside. She watched the Queen as she looked out into the yard, the corners of her eyes and lips softening at what she saw outside. The

Queen took a breath and turned to the assassin, beckoning for Elen-ai to join her at the doorway. Taking a step forward, Elen-ai looked out into the yard in which a young man was sparring with an older, clearly more skilled opponent. Two other men sat on a nearby bench. They appeared to be watching the bout in front of them, but Elen-ai could see the way their lips moved almost imperceptibly. They were talking, and from what Elen-ai could see, they were talking about something that pleased neither of them. She had a strong suspicion that their subject was the Queen's heir.

The Queen lingered in the doorway a moment longer then stepped out into the yard, her appearance arresting the attention of its occupants. The fighting ceased, and the two men on the bench stopped their surreptitious communication and stood.

"Latana," one of the two men on the bench greeted the Queen. Elen-ai presumed that he was one of her three brothers. Surely nobody else would dare address the Queen by her first name, and certainly not in such a brazen fashion.

"Good morning Nikalus," the Queen said, her voice warm with affection. She walked over to him and embraced him, then his companion.

Looking at them together, Elen-ai felt sure all three must be related. The Queen had the same nose as the one she had called Nikalus, while she shared her liquid gold eyes with the other. Beyond that, something about the mannerisms of all three was similar in the way that could only be familial.

"Elen-ai, may I present to you Nikalus and Kaine. My two younger brothers." The Queen turned from her brief conference with her brothers back to Elen-ai. Elen-ai bowed to both of them.

"Nikalus, Kaine, this is Elen-ai of-"

"The Family." The young man who had been sparring cut off the Queen, coming over to embrace her. His opponent had discreetly exited the courtyard at the entrance of Elen-ai and the Queen. The boy was more broad in the shoulders than Elen-ai had initially judged, and already a full head taller than the monarch. He was half a head taller than Elen-ai too, and she was quite tall. Elen-ai judged him to be in the middle of his teenage years, although the way he carried himself made him seem older than he actually was. He fixed a cold look at Elen-ai.

"This is my son, Gidyon," the Queen said, looking fondly at her child. It was a more restrained expression of the one that had crossed her face as she had watched him sparring in the yard.

Elen-ai bowed to the boy - the Prince. "Your Highness."

He continued to regard her with an expression of mild distaste.

"Latana, I must again voice my objection to hiring an assassin to protect our nephew." Kaine spoke directly to the Queen, as though Elen-ai wasn't there.

"Why, Kaine? Do you think that she won't be able to protect my son? That she will not be discreet about her identity?" A look of vexation crossed the Queen's face as she turned to address her brother. His hesitation was all she needed. "You and Nikalus and Sil have all have raised objection to this course of action. You are all telling me what to do, yet none of you is proposing your own solution!" A frustrated note crept into the Queen's voice.

Elen-ai recognised the tone; it was one she heard in her own voice when she was squabbling with her brothers and sisters. There was something profoundly shocking about hearing her ruler speak in a manner that was so terribly ordinary. Then again, Elen-ai had seen her share of supposedly dignified people behave in ways that were profoundly undignified. That came with her job.

"Are you really certain this is something to be discussed in front of our guest?" Kaine leaned around his brother to speak more clearly to their sister, his tone pointed. He was quite handsome, Elen-ai could not help but notice.

The Queen glared at her two brothers, clearly outnumbered but unwilling to back down. "I have made my decision and that is all there is to it. Would you like to stay and complain about something else, or do you have somewhere to be?" she snapped.

Cowing to her authority, the Queen's two younger brothers bid her and their nephew farewell and left the courtyard without so much as a backward glance at Elen-ai.

"Mother, is this really necessary?" Gidyon asked once his uncles had departed. Evidently he did not wish to lend weight to their argument within their earshot. As rude as he was being by speaking about her as though she were not there, Elen-ai had to credit him with his obvious unwillingness to voice his objection in front of anyone other than his mother.

"Gidyon, I believe there is a real possibility of someone trying to hurt you. Just this week our agents heard new reports of things that leave me gravely unsettled. Elen-ai will keep you safe. Of that, I have no doubt." The Queen raised a hand to gently brush her son's cheek. Unlike many boys of his age, he made no move to stop her, instead smiling fondly down at his mother. They had the same smile.

"But there are guards everywhere. They can keep me safe. And I can defend myself."

Elen-ai considered what she had seen of the Prince's sparring practice. He was somewhat competent, but he needed far more practice and tuition before he would be able to fend off someone who was actually skilled with a sword.

"My darling, please do this for me," the Queen asked her son, taking one of his hands in both of hers and bringing it to her lips. There was something fundamentally intimate about the bare display of love for her son. It seemed as though the Queen had forgotten that Elen-ai was there. Not that Elen-ai believed that for a second. It was more likely that this was yet another calculated display to ensure that whatever Elen-ai may think of the Queen's decision, she would still protect this boy. As much as Elen-ai hated to admit, it was effective.

The Prince relented with a shake of his head and a something that could have been a small smile. "Promise me that it won't be for long, though."

"I promise," she told him. "But for now, Elen-ai must stay by your side wherever you go. Only then can I be sure that you will be safe. I'll leave you two to get acquainted. I must attend to our visitors from the Third Country." She smiled fondly at her son again before casting Elen-ai a quick nod of thanks. Then she exited the courtyard, leaving Elen-ai and the Prince alone together.

Elen-ai let the Prince break the silence. She always let her clients speak first.

"I don't want you around me, assassin," he told her bluntly, all the tenderness that he had displayed toward his mother gone.

"I gathered." She wasn't offended by his distaste for her nor was she surprised that he didn't want her to be constantly by her side, even if it was in the name of safety. Members of the Family were often considered unpalatable company.

"Your kind should not be allowed. My first act when I take the throne will be to outlaw the Family," he informed her rudely.

Instead of giving him the satisfaction of any response she kept her face totally neutral. "I'm sure that when that happens, myself and the other members of the Family will be quite dismayed," she told him in a polite tone.

Uncertain at her lack of response, he glared at her. She couldn't help but notice that unlike his mother's liquid gold eyes, his were vibrant blue, like the colour of water on a sunny day. It was quite arresting. "Just don't get in my way. I can take care of myself," he snapped.

Elen-ai already regretted her decision to accept the contract. She had far more worthy things to do with her time than look after someone who shouldn't even be in line for the throne. If he was going to behave like this for the entirety of the time that she was to protect him it would a very unpleasant experience indeed. The petty thought made its way across her mind that maybe someone would want to kill him because he was so obnoxious. "If you think you can take care of yourself, then why don't you prove it? You and your sword against me unarmed," she suggested.

He considered the offer for a moment then nodded, the arrogance clearly written across his face. It was amusing that he thought he might be able to best her.

She took a step away from him to give him the space to take his stance and bring up the sword he still held in one hand. After that, she gave him to the count of three before she knocked him off his feet and pointed his own sword at his throat.

The Prince looked around, bewildered. His expression suggested he was vainly attempting to understand exactly what she had done. She offered him the hilt of his sword then held out a hand to assist him getting back to his feet. He accepted both, the hostility with which he had initially treated her had gone, replaced with a slight wariness and, oddly, curiosity.

Elen-ai still said nothing. She had proved the point easily. To say anything would simply humiliate him further. He returned her silence, a slight colour creeping into his cheek, which made him look his age. Without uttering a word he turned and stalked out of the courtyard, his back rigid with anger and bruised pride. Elen-ai followed him, her feet making no noise even on the gravel that covered the courtyard. There was something immeasurably satisfying about knocking this boy who would be ruler to the ground. The outrage at the travesty his ascension to the throne would represent was still within her, but the sharp edges to it had been dulled. Perhaps it was petty of her to take such delight in using her unfair advantage to humiliate him, but it had made her feel a bit better.

She followed him through the Palace. They wound their way along a new set of corridors, all as stunning as the first through which she had walked, past more doors and court-yards, and into what she could only assume was one of the Palace's residential wings. Here they passed servants who scuttled to and fro, all of whom averted their eyes as Gidyon and Elen-ai passed them either out of discretion or discomfort, Elen-ai couldn't quite discern which. She wondered whether they were aware of the Queen's plan to make him their heir. Servants did have a way of knowing things that were supposed to be secret. Elen-ai made a note to look more closely at the servants. A careless word from a servant to the wrong person would easily make a threat to Gidyon's life plausible.

The Prince stopped at a door, flinging it open with ill-mannered force. Clearly, he was still smarting over the humili-ation Elen-ai had delivered to him.

The only word to describe the Prince's living quarters was luxurious. Elen-ai had to work hard to keep from gasping as she gazed around his private sitting room. The walls were adorned with beautiful tapestries and the space furnished with exquisite items. Elen-ai followed the Prince through the sitting room and into his bedroom which was dominated by a bed that looked as though someone could be lost within its massive confines. Pillows practically overflowed on it. A small bed had been brought in and placed along one of the room's walls. The Prince stood still in the middle of the room, staring at the sec-ond bed.

"That shouldn't-" He stopped and turned to Elen-ai, re-alisation dawning on his face. "Surely you don't have to sleep in the same room as me," he protested.

Elen-ai said nothing, the sarcastic suggestion of course that nobody would ever try to sneak in during the night to kill him remaining wisely unspoken.

Gidyon gave a sigh of anger and frustration and took off his shirt. When Elen-ai made no move to leave the room he glared at her. "Do you need to watch me bathe, too?" he demanded.

She knew that she probably should remain by his side as he bathed, but she couldn't quite bring herself to see him in such a state.

"Let me check the rooms, then I'll wait outside while you bathe," she told him, settling on a reasonable compromise.

He continued to glare at her as she looked around the bedroom, efficiently going through every corner, hiding spot, and shadow to ensure that the room was free from any threat – even a sharp corner on which the Prince may fall and hurt himself. She finally checked the window to ensure nobody had managed to sneak up to the second floor of the building. In the middle of the day, only a member of the Family rendering themselves invisible could do it, but Elen-ai would never allow anyone to accuse her of not being thorough.

"Are you quite done?" the Prince snapped as she moved into the adjacent bathing room - similarly luxurious to the other parts of his suite. The floor and walls were tiled with dark stone that had been polished until it shone. A huge tub sat in the middle of the room. It was filled with water from which peals of steam rose. Another bucket of water, presumably for rinsing, sat next to it. With only one tiny window to allow the steam to escape, Elen-ai could see no serious threat in the room unless someone was hiding in the tub, which they definitely weren't.

She went back into the Prince's bedroom. "I think you should be safe," she told him, enjoying his sigh of exasperation.

While he bathed, she went back into the sitting room. She took the time to herself to examine the room in more detail. A writing desk was on one side. It was clearly used often if the small ink spots on it were any indication. A well-thumbed text on the Queendom's legislation was placed to one side.

She paused her inspection for a moment to make sure that Prince was still alright. The sound of contented splashing reached her ears. Reassured that there was no immediate danger unless he somehow contrived to drown himself, she resumed looking around the room.

Her survey was cut short by the entrance of a Palace servant.

"You're Elen-ai?" he asked. Elen-ai straightened and nodded, unfazed by his clear uncertainty. She wondered if he knew exactly who she was. It seemed likely that the Queen would seek to hide that she had hired a member of the Family from even the Palace staff. But servants did have a way of knowing things they weren't supposed to.

"These are yours," he told her brusquely, jerking his head towards the items that filled his arms.

Elen-ai crossed the room and took the proffered items from him. He all but ran away from her once she had taken it, leading her to suspect that he knew more about her than he should.

Shaking her head, she examined what he had brought her, although the feel of the bundle gave away the fact that her weapons had been returned to her.

THREE

Under the cover of darkness, Elen-ai slipped unseen through the halls of the Palace. Long ago, the lives of gods and humans had touched. In that time, the powers of the gods bled across to their mortal companions. Women and men were able to perform feats that rivalled the gods themselves if legends and myths were to be believed. However, the gods had receded from the mortal realm and the fantastic skills that knowing them brought had been all but forgotten. Yet some still remembered what faith could offer – the Family who had guarded their secrets and followed the way of the Shadow God with dedication, was among the small group of people in the world who still had skills of which most could and would only ever dream. Elen-ai used those forgotten skills now as she concealed herself from anybody who may have seen her, blending her lithe form seamlessly into the shadows of the corridors. Only the most astute of observers would have noticed the slight displacement of air as she passed by them, and even then it was a far more subtle sensation than a person's passage would normally make.

She was completely unnoticed as she passed the patrolling Royal Guards. If she had wanted, she could have killed every one of them before they even had time to realise that their final breath was wheezing out of them. Elen-ai almost felt sorry for them; these men and women were some of the best fighters in the land. But against Elen-ai and the secrets of the Family, the assassin's death would touch them long before they would be able to use the training they had received.

The sprawling complex of the Palace took her through winding twists and turns. In addition to the earlier corridors along which she had been taken that day, Elen-ai passed through several new corridors, adding as she went to the map of the Palace in her head. She quickly moved through the servant's quarters and their far less opulent corridors and stairways. Soon she had the measure of the Palace's design, understanding how the many corridors fitted together in the plan of the architect - or architects - who had envisaged the great building's construction. She passed through the kitchens, empty and scrubbed clean in anticipation for the work that would be recommencing in only a few hours, long before most of the Palace's inhabitants would awake for the next day. She saw the pantry, stocked high with a variety of foods, some so costly that an enterprising thief could make a small fortune from their liberation.

From the kitchens, Elen-ai stole through the dining halls - a grand banquet hall that could seat at least three hundred people and a smaller more intimate dining room which was where she presumed the Queen would normally eat. That evening the Queen had been dining with the dignitaries from the Third Country, so the Prince had chosen to eat in his quarters, saying no word to Elen-ai who had sat on the other side of the room to him eating in her own comfortable silence.

The dining halls led Elen-ai into a series of sitting rooms. She examined those rooms carefully, finding several little spaces in which one could conceal themselves and listen to the room's occupants unnoticed. She presumed the sitting rooms were where the Queen entertained various visitors and charmed them into giving her what she wanted. Indeed, Elen-ai had been in one of those rooms that very afternoon and had capitulated to the Queen's desires like many before her. Each room was different, furnished and designed to create a particular atmosphere and a different message. After moving through all of the sitting rooms, Elen-ai understood that the one in which the Queen had received her was selected to convey neutrality and calmness. The room with the blue walls and dark wooden cabinets was clearly one that held a hint of urgent authority. The room with walls the colour of fresh cream and large soft sofas with pale pink cushions was for seduction. As she moved from the Council room, identifiable by the round table with fifteen chairs, through to the grand throne room where the Queen received petitioners, Elen-ai reflected that the many faces the Queen needed to have must be exhausting. She wondered who the Queen actually was behind the many masks she wore.

After a moment of hesitation – this was her ruler after all – Elen-ai made her way into the Queen's rooms. Her purpose in exploring the Palace so thoroughly was to ensure that there was nothing that could surprise her if an assailant were to make an attempt on the life of the Prince. The first thing drummed into all children of the Family was that knowledge was the most valuable tool an assassin could have at their disposal, more valuable than any weapon. She could still remember one of the Mothers walking through the fish market with her when she had been quite young, only nine or ten years old.

"Look, Elen-ai. That man over there buying the sea eels is a servant of clan Tak. What does it tell you?"

"That someone has disgusting taste in food," Elen-ai responded immediately.

Her dry humour earned her a severe look. "Perhaps. But think about the price of sea eels. They are cheap. It tells you that nobody is in their house in the capital except for servants and that their servants are not well treated. Or perhaps that the Tak family is encountering some financial difficulty. Find out which and suddenly a world of possibility is open to you. Poverty breeds much desperation, an empty house is a perfect place in which to hide, and a disgruntled servant is worth their weight in jewels." The Mother's eyes gleamed as she spoke.

It was a lesson that Elen-ai had never forgotten, especially as her first kill had been a member of the Tak family. One of the Tak's lesser sons had impregnated a girl and refused to acknowledge the girl or his child. The girl was heartbroken, believing that he had truly loved her. Even if he had loved her, she was a laundress and of no worth marrying. Her father, furious at the pain inflicted on his beloved daughter had come to the Family and spent nearly all his savings to exact revenge on the man who had hurt his daughter. Elen-ai had learned of the Tak man's habits by drinking one evening with one of the Tak family's servants. The servant, a man who had little fondness for his employer as a result of their unwillingness to pay their servants well, told Elen-ai of her target's penchant for swimming each morning. The next day Elen-ai had followed him to the stream in which he swum, slipped into the water after him, and held him underneath with the tenderness of a lover. It had been deemed a sad accident. The true skill of the Family lay not in their ability to take life but to make it seem as though that life had not been deliberately taken. Death was useless to most of the Family's clients if it was clearly intended. That was why the Family was so expensive; nobody ever knew if a death was the work of the Family or simply an unfortunate part of life. The Tak son was missed by few, although many other contracts that Elen-ai had fulfilled had been far less just. It seemed the Mothers and Fathers had been gentle for her first time.

The modesty of the Queen's apartments surprised Elen-ai. The seduction, power, or gentle reassurance of the sitting rooms were completely absent, giving nothing away about who the Queen was when nobody was watching. The elegant simplicity of the writing desk, couches and tables was understated despite the significant amount of money they certainly would have cost. Unable to resist the Family's maxim to acquire knowledge whenever the opportunity arose, Elen-ai rifled through the papers on the Queen's writing desk. To her chagrin, there was nothing of particular interest aside from some polite correspondence between the Queen and the heads of the seven families that unsurprisingly, said nothing of any substance.

The sound of voices in the corridor outside reached Elen-ai's ears. She recognised one of the voices as the Queen's. Elen-ai wove the shadows around her more tightly as the Queen and someone else entered the room, clearly in the midst of a disagreement.

"I still don't see why you need to hire a member of the Family to protect him, Latana. If someone finds out, the uproar would be tremendous," the man told her, irritation in his voice.

"You may be older than me, Silius, but that doesn't mean you know better than me," the Queen bit back.

"I've been trained since birth to advise you, to consider everything. You've merely been trained to rule," he told her. He sounded slightly smug.

"That may be so, but you aren't in my position. You've not seen what I've seen, you don't know what it's like to rule. You don't have enough information to have an informed opinion on the matter," the Queen said, sinking down into one of the couches in the room. From her position, Elen-ai had a perfect view of the Queen's face. It was obvious that this Silius was the brother to whom she felt the closest. Elen-ai could see it in the way the Queen's shoulders did not hold the same slight tension as when she had spoken with Nikalus and Kaine, nor did she seem to be in a state of cautious anticipation for what he was about to say. Even her speech was more casual, less considered.

"You're right, I don't know everything on the matter. Because you aren't telling me everything." His voice was soft but firm as he addressed his sister.

"Silius there are some things that you just can't understand unless you experience them yourself." The Queen sounded almost amused, if not slightly tired.

"Were the circumstances in which Gidyon was conceived really that bad?" Silius asked, clearly awkward at asking the question.

His sister threw back her head and laughed in response, clearly delighting in that discomfort. "How long have you wondered if that was my reason for all this?" she asked.

He made an awkward gesture in place of a response.

"Well if you must know, the circumstances of Gidyon's conception were quite fun actually," the Queen told him, a slight smirk on her face. Elen-ai knew that sort of look. It was the look of one sibling delighting in tormenting the other. On the Queen, it was disconcertingly normal.

Silius again did not reply. The Queen's smirk broadened. "There's nothing wrong with enjoying the more physical pleasures in life," she told her brother.

He gave a slight sigh that had her laughing again.

"In the name of the Divine One, you're such a prude sometimes, Silius. Oh honestly, sit down, will you?" she said, sounding slightly exasperated.

He did as she bade, sitting next to her. "Latana, please try to explain it to me," he said gently.

The Queen sighed, her flawless brow furrowing as some private emotion made its way through her. "You know the paternity of the royal line is unknown." She stated a basal fact. Because it was of the utmost importance that the Queen did not become beholden to any one of the seven families through marital ties, she was not allowed to marry. However, the necessity to promulgate the line remained. The solution had been in existence for as long as the Queendom had existed in its current form. Celebrations populated by eligible men from the seven families, following a thorough examination by a doctor, were regularly held, often spanning a few evenings at a time. The Queen would invite the men who caught her fancy back to her bedchamber, but there was a strict understanding that she must take at least two different men to bed with her over the evenings. If a child eventuated, it would be unclear who the father was, offering all the families an incentive to remain loyal to the throne given that it may be one of their own who held it, while also ensuring a reasonable neutrality on the part of the Queen.

Silius nodded curtly to her question, even though a response wasn't strictly necessary.

"I never thought much of it, really. It was something that every queen must do - a duty to produce an heir. And I was given the opportunity to have my pick of eligible and handsome men. I thought that having a child would be necessary. I never thought-" she stopped herself, recollecting her thoughts before she continued. Elen-ai couldn't be certain, but it seemed as though the Queen had caught herself about to say something else.

"I thought that having a child would be easy, that it wouldn't affect me. And then I actually fell pregnant with Gidyon. The first time I held him in my arms my entire world shifted. Suddenly there was this little being that something within me - something so innate, wanted to protect with everything that I was. It made me feel so powerless. I, a Queen, Silius, rendered utterly powerless by a tiny infant. And to think that he was this miraculous product of -" the Queen abruptly stopped speaking, biting her lip and looking down at her lap.

However, if her behaviour was unusual, Silius did not seem to notice. His demeanour had softened completely.

"You know, I felt a similar way when you were born." He reached out a hand to gently place on top of one of hers.

She raised her head with a questioning look on her face. He nodded in response. "It's true. I was brought in to see you right after you were born. You were this tiny wrinkled little thing, so fragile and so delicate. I'd never seen anything more lovely. I think even if I had never been told that it was my duty to look out for you, I would have anyway. I do understand what you mean, Latana. Do not fret."

"He means more than you could ever understand, Sil," the Queen whispered. Elen-ai could see the tears glistening in her golden eyes.

"And you're certain there is a threat to his life?"

"I can't be completely sure. You are the one who hears the whispers, after all, but I do honestly believe someone is going to try and take his life."

"Do you really think that this assassin will be able to keep him safe?" He asked, giving her hand a gentle squeeze.

"I think that if anybody can, she can," the Queen returned.

"And do you think we can keep the fact that we have engaged the Family a secret?" he persisted.

"I think we have no other choice," she replied.

"Alright then, I'll tell the others to stop being so difficult," he relented.

A smile curved the lips of the Queen of the Second Country as she looked at her older brother. "You always were a soft touch, Sil," she teased, although there was no malice in it.

He shrugged, a smile of his own crossing his face in reply to hers. When he smiled Elen-ai could see a strong resemblance between them, and the depth of love he bore for his sister.

"Alright. Bed," Silius said firmly, getting to his feet. There was something humorous about the Queen being instructed to go to sleep like a small child, especially as she nodded obediently and rose to her own feet.

Elen-ai waited until Silius had departed the room and the Queen had gone into her bedchamber before exiting the room, noticing that it appeared the Queen had no servant to help her undress. That fact alone did not surprise her. From what she had seen, the Queen placed a high value on her own privacy. However, something about the exchange she had witnessed made the absence of any servants to wait on the Queen odd.

She slipped out of the Queen's room through an open window, a frown on her face. She had no doubt that the Queen was telling the truth about the depth of her love for her son and the desperation accompanying it to protect her child whatever the cost, but Elen-ai had been watching the Queen's face very closely, and she couldn't shake the suspicion that there was something the Queen had not told her brother. Something that linked to the lack of attending servants. Without any evidence, Elen-ai did not know what it was, although the Queen's certainty that Gidyon's life was in danger seemed too adamant to be simple paranoia. Elen-ai resolved to find out what the Queen had kept from her closest brother. After all, information was the most important thing to any member of the Family.

She found herself in the stables that were almost directly below the Queen's room, the musty smell of straw and feline tickling her nose. Curious, despite the knowledge that she should return to the Prince, she peered into the large area where the kittanae slept, thoughts of the Queen's secret banished for at least the moment by sight of the magnificent creatures. The five giant felines were curled together, an overlapping of paws and heads that looked blissfully comfortable. One was still awake. The sleek animal looked at her with an unblinking ferocity.

Only every ridden – never used to pull a cart, for they would not tolerate such indignity – the kittanae were magnificent animals owned only by the most wealthy of people. The reclusiveness with which they inhabited the depths of forests such as those on the Harete lands or the fringes of the Katan and Bertak lands, combined with their ferocity made them almost impossible to successfully catch. Elen-ai had never ridden one, they were far too obvious for one, but riding the large cats were supposed to be an experience like no other, especially as crossing the country on a kittanae took less than half the time in a carriage pulled by the lumbering hearat.

It was an act of transgression for her to touch the animal, but curiosity overtook her. Elen-ai leapt noiselessly into their pen and stretched her hand out to the one that was still awake. With something approaching trepidation, she placed her hand on the side of the kittanae's neck. Its warmth against her skin was a shock, almost as much as the softness of its fur. Elen-ai ran her hand down the animal's neck, feeling it lean slightly into the pressure of her arm. The beginnings of a purr rumbled in its throat. She stayed petting the animal for a few more minutes, then remembering herself and her task, she left the stable as noiselessly as she had entered it.

On her way back to her mattress in the Prince's bedchamber, Elen-ai detoured through the other residential wings of the Palace, finishing with the one reserved for guests. In the only occupied bedchambers in that wing, Elen-ai found two people. From the clothes strewn on the floor of the room and their possessions, she concluded that they must be the foreign dignitaries from the Third Country the Queen had mentioned in the courtyard and dined with that evening. For a moment, Elen-ai stood in the bedroom watching the two entangled forms as they slept. There was a profundity to the absolute absence of any reserve between the two sleeping people in the way their limbs were entwined that captured her gaze for an extra few seconds. The woman stirred in her sleep, her long dark hair spread around her. In response, the man drew her closer to him. His face nestled against hers, so close it looked almost as though they were two parts of the same whole. Elen-ai looked for a moment longer before she slipped out of the guest wing and back to her contract.

FOUR

While Elen-ai could say many unkind truths about Prince Gidyon, she had to admit he was no slouch. He awoke early and began his day with a light breakfast that was immediately proceeded by a series of lessons. Elen-ai wordlessly followed him wherever he went without once receiving any acknowledgment of her presence from the Prince. She might have thought she had inadvertently rendered herself invisible but for the fact that a servant came and mutely handed her a plate of food at the breakfast table. However, the Prince's animosity toward her did not overly trouble Elen-ai. Her duty was to protect him, not to be liked by him.

The Prince's teachers were a collection of severe individuals, all experts in their respective fields. As far as Elen-ai could tell, none of them posed any threat to the Prince other than possibly boring him to death. She listened as the finer points of mathematics, lawcraft, and economics were imparted to him, trying to keep from tapping her fingers or toes in boredom. Although, while Elen-ai may have been profoundly disinterested in the rates at which various items were taxed, Gidyon was a diligent and interested pupil, listening to his instructors with unwavering attention. As far as Elen-ai could tell, these lessons had been a part of Gidyon's life for as long as he could talk, separating him from any other children who may have lived in or around the Palace. She regarded the Prince during the hours of lessons with a certain curiosity. Seeing someone who had been so abrupt with her display such courtesy and deference to others was quite disconcerting, especially knowing what a solitary upbringing he must have had. That alone occupied her attention during the hours of tedious lessons. Perhaps there was more to this Prince than just youthful arrogance.

Lunch was taken with the Queen in the small dining room that Elen-ai had slipped through the previous evening - apparently, the Prince would often dine there with his mother and uncles for both lunch and dinner. Elen-ai was given a seat at the table rather than being relegated to a corner of the room as she had been at breakfast - the Queen's doing she could only assume.

Gidyon and Elen-ai arrived first, sitting and staring awkwardly at each other across the beautifully set table. The glass wine and water vessels which were placed on the table caught the light, almost blinding in their delicate beauty. The Queen swept in a few moments later. It was a welcome relief. The Prince's surly silence with her was starting to wear thin.

"Good day Elen-ai." The Queen graciously greeted her, a deceptively open smile on her beautiful face. Elen-ai's discovery of the fact that the Queen was guarding a secret seemed at complete odds with that lovely, open face.

"Your Majesty," Elen-ai responded, bowing.

"How are you finding life in the Palace so far?" the Queen asked as she sat.

"So far, very safe," Elen-ai responded politely, sitting once the Queen was seated, and taking up cutlery once she saw the Queen do so. She noted that the delicate plates upon which the lunch was served were from the Katan region's artisans. Even everyday lunch was imbued with wealth here in the Palace.

"Do you hear that, mother?" Gidyon demanded from the other end of the table. "Safe. I am fine. We do not need her."

Elen-ai, however much she found the Prince's attitude toward her distasteful, wholeheartedly agreed with him.

The Queen turned to her son, the charming smile fading from her lips. "Gidyon, how could you speak about Elen-ai in such a tone and in front of her? Elen-ai, I am so sorry for my son's rudeness." She turned back to Elen-ai, extending a hand briefly in an apologetic gesture.

"Honestly your Majesty, there's no need for you to apologise. The Family is not often well regarded," Elen-ai said, throwing a somewhat pointed glance at the Prince who was glowering into his food.

"Others may behave in a manner that a member of the royal family may not," the Queen replied, her comment clearly directed at her son more so than in response to Elen-ai.

Elen-ai recalled the Queen's candour with her brother the previous evening. The responsibility on the shoulders of any leader would be tremendous, even more so one who was attempting to change history. Elen-ai felt for the Queen, trying to balance her roles of ruler and mother to prepare her son to be lead a country that did not want a man to be their monarch. In the Family, all Mothers and Fathers were tasked with only one duty: to prepare the children of the Family to enter the trade of killing. Life was simpler there. Elen-ai thought wistfully of the Family's house with its dark corridors and shadowed halls. She missed the simple quiet and understanding of her brothers and sisters. If she were lunching there, she would probably do so out on the roof. Perhaps she would be joined by her favourite sister, Mari-am. They would often sit in companionable silence on the roof of the Family's house, looking out over the city's rooftops. Elen-ai loved the jumbled collection of houses and chimneys that spread out as far as the eye could see, with the Palace looming on the hill to one side and the glitter of the port on the other. Most days an acute ear could hear fragments of conversation from the street. Sometimes Elen-ai would overhear banter that left her chuckling to herself. It was a far cry from this beautiful room with the Queen on her left and the Prince on her right.

"I want to go to the market tomorrow," the Prince announced, ignoring his mother's reprimand.

"Absolutely not," the Queen replied without even pausing to consider.

"But I go to the market every week," Gidyon objected.

"There is too much risk," his mother told him firmly.

"Isn't that why I have my assassin?"

"What did I just tell you about your manners when speaking to Elen-ai?" The Queen put her hand down on the table with a bang.

He didn't reply but the resentment was obvious in his expression.

"Apologise to Elen-ai," the Queen ordered. "Now," she added when he said nothing.

The Prince breathed in through his nose sharply then looked directly at Elen-ai; the first time he had done so that morning. "I apologise for my rudeness, lady Elen-ai. It was remiss of me to address you in such a manner and I will do my utmost to ensure that it does not occur again."

His overly formal language and the sickly sweet tone were a clear jibe of themselves. It did not escape his mother's attention.

"I do not know what is causing this, but you are utterly insufferable, Gidyon. I did not raise you to be like this," she snapped.

"If I'm so insufferable then I shan't impose my presence on you any longer," he replied, standing and storming out of the room.

Elen-ai wondered whether she should pursue him, but decided against it. She instead sat quietly with the Queen who propped her elbows on the table and buried her face in her hands. After a moment she raised her head from her long, elegant fingers. "I am so embarrassed that you were witnessed that," she said.

"It's alright," Elen-ai told her, shrugging slightly and taking another mouthful of food. Being a guest of the Palace did have some perks. The meal was a delicious medley of fresh vegetables cooked in a rich sauce accompanied by meat so delicious that it could only have been one of the Tak family's lows. She had never eaten anything so fine.

"No, it is not. My son cannot be a good ruler if he is going to be rude to those he finds unpalatable for whatever personal reason," the Queen despaired, rubbing two fingers on each temple in small circles.

Elen-ai didn't reply to that - the Queen was correct. "Does he often go to the market?" she asked instead.

The Queen nodded. "Every week. He likes to talk with the people there. He says that it helps him better understand the lessons that he learns from his tutors." She sounded tired, like a parent at the end of her tether rather than a Queen.

"Let him go tomorrow. I'm sure I can keep him safe from anything that may occur." Elen-ai surprised herself with the offer. She didn't want to do anything to make the Prince happy, but after only one day within the Palace, she was desperate to be among the fuss and noise and mess of the city outside this world of perfect rules and behaviour. In some ways, the Queen's horror at Gidyon's rudeness was more unsettling to Elen-ai than the actual rudeness. She lived in a world in which insults were exchanged on a daily basis. People would frequently treat her rudely if they knew her origin. The Family was often feared but rarely well loved.

"I really do not think that is a wise idea," the Queen objected. "Any hired hand could be waiting for him there."

"I promise no harm will come to him," Elen-ai assured her.

The Queen looked down at her plate of barely touched food and sighed. She made no effort to disguise her discomfort and unhappiness. "Are you certain?"

"On the honour of the Family," Elen-ai promised solemnly.

"Alright," the Queen relented, picking up her cutlery and moving a piece of food across her plate.

"I'll go and find him," Elen-ai told her, taking one final mouthful of the delicious food before regretfully leaving the remains of her meal so she could go and find the Prince.

He was in the practice courtyard, moodily stretching before his fencing lesson. At some time between when he had left the dining room and when he had gone to the courtyard, he had changed his clothes.

"What do you want? For me to apologise to you again?" he demanded when he saw her.

"I convinced your mother to let you go to the market tomorrow," Elen-ai said, not even acknowledging his question.

He stopped and straightened up. "What? Why?"

"Does it matter?" Elen-ai stepped toward him linking her hands behind her back.

"Yes it does. But thank you." It sounded as though he actually meant it.

"There are a few things, though. Your mother seems to think that there is a real likelihood that someone is trying to kill you. I promised her on the honour of the Family that I wouldn't let you die."

"Go on," he said, his expression was guarded but not hostile, which was something.

"You go with guards?" she verified.

"Two."

"There will be five tomorrow. If you speak with someone, you are to stay this distance apart from them at all times." She stepped forward to demonstrate how far she meant.

"They're people from the market. I know them," he protested.

"No, you don't," Elen-ai countered. "And if someone wants to kill you, from any closer than where I am from you now they can do so before anybody - even me - could stop them."

The disbelief showed in his eyes.

"The longest kind of blade that someone can conceal on themselves is this long." Elen-ai drew one of her own concealed weapons to demonstrate. The Prince started at the sudden appearance of the blade in her hand. She continued as if he hadn't reacted. "Look, I hold it out like so," she extended her arm, "and I can't reach you. Any closer and..." She took a half step forward and in another movement that was too fast to see, she had flipped the blade so that the hilt was facing him and brought it to rest in front of his heart.

He took an involuntary step back, clearly perturbed.

"You'll keep that distance, then?" she asked.

He nodded, his eyes on her blade.

The Prince's afternoon was just as tedious for Elen-ai as the morning. She watched as he engaged in a range of combat exercises, silently evaluating the technique of Gidyon's teacher. For someone who wasn't a member of the Family, his teacher was quite good, and she certainly put the Prince through his paces.

After the exercise, Gidyon bathed and met with his mother who had requested his presence in one of the sitting rooms. Wondering how the Prince would behave given the exchange with his mother over lunch, Elen-ai followed him to the sitting room. The Queen had chosen the room that Elen-ai had in her mind dubbed the seduction room. With the afternoon sunlight coming in through the windows, the space was warm and inviting. She imagined that the blue sitting room at this time of day would be far less cosy and much more intimidating as the cool of the deep blue was given an extra intensity by the light.

Perhaps she was beginning to get the measure of the court's ways after all.

The Queen had changed her clothes to compliment the room. She wore a dress of soft gold the same colour as her eyes. It was a simple design but the simplicity somehow seemed to heighten her aura of authority, especially given the gold she wore at her throat, wrists and now also in a thin chain encircling her head. Against the midnight black of her hair, the gold gleamed. Whatever she might have been hiding, she was unquestionably magnificent.

"Mother." Gidyon paused at the door and greeted the Queen in a formal tone.

"Thank you for coming, Gidyon," she replied, a smile just touching her face. Elen-ai reflected that the thanks were not really necessary. The Queen had asked her son to do something. His mother or not, she was still the Queen.

"How may I be of service?" Gidyon asked with just a touch of reserve. He too was clearly aware of the fact that he couldn't really have refused the Queen's summons.

"I thought it appropriate that you meet our friends from the Third Country," the Queen informed him, extending her hand in a gesture that clearly indicated she wanted him to come to her side.

The Prince stepped forward, his back stiff even considering the formal doublet he wore. Clearly, he had not forgiven his mother for her rebukes at lunch. Elen-ai slipped into the room unobtrusively and took up a place near the wall. Mother and son stood awkwardly side by side until footfalls in the corridor announced the imminent arrival of others.

The man and woman who Elen-ai had seen entangled in sleep the previous evening entered the room.

"Your Majesty." The woman greeted the Queen first, smiling with what Elen-ai thought to be genuine warmth. It seemed the Queen's charm had worked its magic on these dignitaries.

"Ah, Councilwoman Kuch and Councilman Hart. I'm so delighted you could join us. I'd like you to meet my son, Gidyon. I have yet to announce this to the Second Country, but he is to be my heir. Given the severity of the matters our two countries share, I thought it appropriate he hear at least some of our discussions, given that he may also have to manage these matters." The Queen sharing her appointment of heir before making the knowledge public was a brilliant display of trust that would make anyone willing to call the Fourth country an ally. Noting the uncertain glances directed toward Elen-ai, Latana added "and this is Elen-ai, a trusted advisor." No further explanation was offered or requested.

"Let us continue our talk over some refreshments," the Queen continued. She called out to a waiting servant who immediately brought in a tray of cakes and drinks and placed it on the room's main table. The Queen invited her guests to sit with a gesture, perching herself on the edge of a deeply cushioned chair. "Elen-ai, can we tempt you with a cake?" The Queen turned to address her.

With a small shrug, Elen-ai stepped forward to take one of the delicate deserts laid out on the tray, murmuring a word of thanks to the Queen. She was sure that she should have politely declined, but she had no time for court games, and the cakes looked too delicious for politeness. She bit into the cake as she returned to her position on the room's edge. It was even more delicious than she had thought it would be, a miracle of some clever chef's mastery of sugar, cream, and candied fruit.

"Councillors, I've heard quite a few tales about the beauty of your capital, Oranis – are they true?" The Prince leaned forward, his attention completely focused on the two foreigners and a disarmingly charming smile on his face. Elen-ai tried not to stare at this engaging young man. She wondered where the surly brat that she had followed around all morning had gone.

The man, Councilman Hart, leaned forward in reply. "I daresay it is. Although no story can truly capture the beauty of Oranis."

"Especially at sunrise or sunset." Councilwoman Kuch's eyes lit up as she spoke, her love for the city clear.

"Is it more beautiful than Herran?" The Queen asked, a hint of mischief in her voice.

"Begging your pardon, your Majesty, your own city is very fair, but truly nothing can match Oranis. From the approach when it simply seems to rise from the plain, there's something about it that commands the awe of anyone who sees it, be they a native of the city or a visitor." Councilman Hart spoke with an easy charisma of his own.

"I'd love to see it." A wistful expression crossed the Prince's face.

"Maybe one day you will." Councilwoman Kuch smiled at him.

"Is it true that you were both part of the uprising that occurred three years ago?" Gidyon asked with eager curiosity.

The Councillors exchanged a brief glance. "I didn't realise that so much was known about what happened within the Third Country," Councilwoman Kuch said. "The fact that we are here, as far as I understand, is quite unprecedented. The history of the Godkissed Continent is not one in which the four countries have had much official contact with each another at all."

"You are quite correct, Councilwoman, even many of my teachers do not know of the recent events in the Third Country. I learned it from the merchants and traders, here in Herran's markets. They're terrible gossips." The eloquence of the Prince's speech surprised Elen-ai as did the breadth of his knowledge. Despite the Family's extensive awareness of events within and beyond the Second Country, the knowledge of the Prince actually exceeded her own in this instance. She had never taken a contract in The Third Country. The country itself was reasonably small, but it while it might not have been some-where particularly special, the best routes to much of the Fourth Country ran through it. Wealth and significance flowed in off the levies incurred by traders crossing the territory. Yet despite this, the people from the Third Country were curiously insular. All traders from there kept to themselves, even when they were far from home. Elen-ai had heard only vague men-tions of rebellion and counter-rebellion taking place. Whispers of legendary figures had accompanied the accounts she'd heard, but such things were more often than not embellish-ments to make a good story, so she'd paid them little heed.

"How admirable. A young man with a desire to learn of the world around him." The slight emphasis on 'young' by Councilwoman Kuch was not lost on Elen-ai, nor did it seem, the Prince.

"One is never too young to learn, Councilwoman. For in-stance, I just learned that you are indeed the Councilwoman Kuch who is the subject of several reverential stories," Gidyon replied smoothly.

The expression on the woman's face made it clear that the Prince had unnerved her. It seemed that despite her apparent place within legend, the Councilwoman was not as adept a politician as the Prince or his mother. Hardly surprising, really. The delicate feuds of the Queendom's seven families required leadership that was well versed in the art of discourse and in-ference. The Third Country did not have such requirements, as far as Elen-ai knew.

"I'm hardly a figure to be revered," Councilwoman Kuch responded once she had regained her composure.

"If you're willing, I would love to hear the events from your perspective," Gidyon told her, abating the discomfort he had caused with a masterful ease.

Her composure recovered, the Councilwoman smiled. "Perhaps if we get the opportunity," she replied.

Picking up on her comment, the Councilman interjected before anybody else could speak. "However, other more urgent matters require our attention."

They were a good pair, despite, or perhaps because of, their unpolished diplomacy, Elen-ai thought.

"Ah yes. The issue of the Fourth Country." The Queen spoke, having watched the exchange between her son and the female dignitary in silence. Elen-ai wondered if she detected a note of pride in the Queen's voice. The Prince certainly had kept a certain mastery of the conversation.

"Your Highness, I'm not sure what your merchant friends might have told you, but in recent years the instability in the Fourth Country has caused concern to both our nations."

The Councilwoman's slight jibe did not seem to affect the Prince. Perhaps because he knew that it said that he had shaken her earlier. "From what I understand, the Lord Protector's interest in keeping the peace amongst her own people is limited. While it has historically been a country of changing powers, its more wealthy members taking control from each other as often as some of us might change clothes, recent instability has meant that some of the Fourth Country's regions are almost autonomous. Most of the time that means that those who maintain control of the areas are not particularly interested in maintaining order for the people who inhabit them, merely in maintaining their own position," he said evenly.

Councilman Hart leaned forward to address the Prince. "That's more or less correct. Recently, parties of raiders have crossed the borders of the Third Country in increasingly violent attacks. Something that used to happen occasionally is now occurring far more frequently. Given that both our countries share a border with the Fourth Country, it is only a matter of time before the one or two raids that your own provinces have seen become increasingly common. The need for a common approach is one that both the lovely Queen and our own Council agree is reasonably urgent."

While Elen-ai was aware of the situation within the Fourth Country, she hadn't realised that things were quite that dire in terms of the lawlessness which plagued the oft-invaded lands. It was a piece of information she filed away to share with one of the Family's Mothers or Fathers when the opportunity arose.

Her attention began to wander as the discussion became one of strategy and mutually agreeable outcomes. Such discussions were not of particular interest to her; the only thing that she was ever sought was finalities and truths, not negotiations that could dissolve as quickly as the blink of an eye. Eventually, the light all but waned and it was time for dinner. The little party moved into the dining room, Elen-ai following them a few paces behind. Her presence had been seemingly forgotten, and that suited her. She had no desire whatsoever to partake in any of the pleasant conversations that seemed to be standard for this sort of exchange.

The Queen's brothers joined them for dinner and the discussion turned to more trivial matters such as music and the best ways to travel a long distance. Elen-ai sat and ate in silence, her own thoughts enough company for her. She watched the Queen, trying to discern what she was hiding from the world, but the monarch gave no indication that she was harbouring any secret. If Elen-ai hadn't witnessed the exchange between Latana and her brother the previous evening, she would never have even been aware that there was something to know.

Finally, the day was over and Elen-ai followed the Prince back to his rooms. He read for some time while Elen-ai meditated on the other side of the room, then he went to bed.

He did not speak a word to her as he climbed into the small mountain that was his bed, nor did she say anything to him. Inwardly she sighed. She did not like the royal life one bit.

FIVE

Rain cloaked Herran, the capital of the Second Country. Elen-ai awoke to hear its soft sound outside the Prince's window. She scowled. Rain was at once a blessing and a curse for any assassin, offering concealment while also giving them away with the droplets that they could not help but leave as a marker of their passage. In the crowded marketplace, anyone could easily sneak close to Gidyon under the guise of a passer-by trying to stay dry.

Despite her hope that the rain would abate, by the time the Prince was to leave the Palace if anything, it had become heavier.

"How far away are you going to stay from everybody?" Elen-ai asked the Prince as they stood in the Palace's main courtyard. He demonstrated the distance, stepping slightly away from her.

She nodded. "Make sure you keep it that way," she instructed him, making no effort to be polite. She already regretted her decision of the previous day to help him get to the market.

The Prince and his assassin set out from the Palace, escorted by five royal guards. The area of Herran closest to the Palace housed the city residences of the Second Country's seven great families. For the most part, the families lived on their estates, but one or two lesser members of the family generally resided in the capital to keep an eye on political developments and report back via either messenger bird or runners. There was no more trustworthy set of eyes than a member of one's own family. The houses were beautiful structures, often several stories high, made from dark timbers – large, beautiful planks from the Harete forest - or stone. Each one was a subtle attempt by the Family who built it to assert their importance and authority. It was obvious in a tower here or an architectural flourish there. However, all of the houses were dwarfed by the Palace both in height and beauty, their darkened forms a mere smudge against the Palace's pale high walls.

In this part of the city the streets were wide, leaving more than enough room for carts to approach or depart the Palace. As they moved closer to the wharves where the market was situated, the streets narrowed as did the buildings. The magnificent, elegant architecture became more cramped, less well maintained. Shops for all manner of things began to appear. The symbols for people offering medical assistance, rare herbs, financial services, or various artefacts appeared in the windows of buildings that they passed. One store even promised genuine Katan plates inside, although Elen-ai doubted how authentic they were. Katan plates were just as rare as fine jewels. The rain kept people inside with the doors firmly closed. On a more pleasant day, a passer-by might be able to sneak a glimpse into the various stores, seeing rows of bottles, wares, or the eyes of a crafty dealer, depending on the store they passed.

They reached the market. Elen-ai was impressed with the pace that the Prince had set. He headed straight for one of the fishmongers and immediately was greeted with an effusive warmth. "Master Gidyon, how d'you fare?" the plump woman behind the stall holding a vicious-looking knife greeted him.

"Mar-ai, it's good to see you." The Prince's warmth was palpable, his smile genuine and open. Suddenly the Prince had become a boy talking with his favourite stall keeper rather than the entitled brat with whom Elen-ai dealt. He didn't even seem to mind the malodorous reek of the fish market.

"How's your lessons going, m'young man?" she demanded, returning to gutting a fish as she chatted with him.

"Always harder, Mar-ai," he told her.

"You must study m'love, it's important. Here - try this," she ordered him, putting down her knife and picking up another piece of fish. "It's best t'eat uncooked." She waggled the piece at him when he hesitated.

Elen-ai sighed as she watched him step forward and take the fish from the fishmonger's outstretched hand, far closer than the distance that she had mandated. Her eyes were on the knife the woman had been using as she waited for it to whip up and be plunged into the Prince's chest. Instead, all that happened was that she pinched his cheek as he chewed and made noises of appreciation.

"You're a good boy t'come out in t'rain young Gidyon." She smiled fondly at him.

"You're too kind, Mar-ai," he told her.

As they kept chatting, Elen-ai only relaxed when he retreated to the distance that she deemed safe. Something about the exchange was niggled at her. Then she realised what it was. The people here did not know that he had been named heir. There was none of the deference – or hostility – that should accompany the knowledge that this boy was going to break hundreds of years of tradition. She wondered how Mar-ai would behave once she knew the truth. Suddenly the knife seemed once again an object of concern.

A slight presence at her side had her tensing, but she relaxed when she recognised the touch on her arm. "My daughter."

It was one of the Fathers of the Family. She wondered how he had found her. She had not sent word to the Family of this outing.

"Father," she greeted him, keeping her eyes on the Prince.

"You took the contract."

"Yes."

The Prince moved on, and Elen-ai followed a slight distance behind. Her Father kept step with her. "And?"

"The Family has been contracted to protect the heir to the throne," she replied.

"I was unaware that there was an heir, Elen-ai."

"You're looking at him," she said, amused to hear his surprised intake of breath.

"Surely not," he murmured. It was unclear whether he was outraged at the decision, as she had been. He sounded more reflective than anything else.

"The Queen is quite determined that her only child will succeed her," Elen-ai informed him.

"And she fears for his life as a result of this decision," the Father deduced. "Not an unreasonable concern. So you are to protect him?"

"More like mind him. Father, I was not trained to mind children." Elen-ai turned to look at her Father, chancing the risk of taking her eyes off the Prince for a moment.

The Father with whom she was speaking was one she had not had much to do with during her childhood; he chose not to partake in the training of the Family's children. Elen-ai had seen him more as she aged, often discussing the finer points of a particular assassination method, comparing preferred poisons or knife designs, but she still did not know him as she did some of the other Mothers and Fathers.

"Daughter, you accepted the contract and you must see it through." His voice was firm.

She returned her gaze to the Prince. He was currently sharing a joke with a fruit seller. "I am an assassin, not a bodyguard," she told her Father, a petulant edge to her voice.

"Elen-ai, you accepted a contract. You must ensure it is completed." There was a note of chastisement in his voice.

"But it is not the work of an assassin to babysit some Prince," she objected.

"You said it yourself, child. We are assassins. The position we hold in this society is safe only because we keep our word. You gave your word to none other than the Queen that you would protect her son. If you break that promise, you bring the Family into disrepute." He spoke calmly but with a firmness that told her she was being chastised.

"And what if I am to stay by the side of this Princeling for years?" she challenged.

"Then you shall stay protecting him for years. You chose to accept the contract, Elen-ai," he repeated before she could say anything else.

"But I never chose to be a member of the Family," she fumed, sweeping her gaze along the marketplace to ensure that no menace lurked waiting for Gidyon. To have him killed here in front of her Father would be quite humiliating.

She felt her Father's eyes on her, flat and dispassionate. "You may choose to leave the Family any time you wish. Nobody will ever stop you," he reminded her.

"You make the choice sound so simple." She gave an angry laugh.

"You are so young, Elen-ai. I wish you could see how loved you are and how all we ever try to do is guide you to be happy." He sighed a little sadly.

"Don't speak down to me, Father." She bristled at his demeanour.

"Do you know who make the best assassins?" he asked. Elen-ai did not reply. Rhetorical questions were a favoured teaching method of the Mothers and Fathers of the Family. "The oldest among us. Not because they are the strongest or the quickest, but because they have the patience to be willing to wait and find the best way to carry out the task. They are willing to take the time to see everything of worth. It is a thought I would counsel you to consider." His words mingled with the cacophony of the market. "If you truly believe that it was a mistake to accept the Queen's contract, then it is a mistake from which you must learn."

Elen-ai began to protest but felt his departure from her side before she could say anything.

It was with irritation that she followed the Prince from the shadows of the market, her eyes everywhere in search of a possible attack. She observed sourly that the Prince appeared willing to be charming and amiable with everybody he encountered provided they were not her. She wondered if these people would view him with the same adulation when the Queen announced that he was not simply destined to be advisor to the next Queen but instead, that he would be their ruler one day. People were very attached to tradition, and she could well imagine that they would be very angry with Gidyon for being the individual who broke a centuries-old custom even if it was not at his instigation.

Gidyon made several purchases, arranging for them to be delivered to the Palace kitchens. It was clear that these transactions were regular occurrences. Yet again, the Prince surprised Elen-ai. She would not have thought him so involved, so invested in the lives of Herran's lowborn.

Finally, the Prince was ready to depart, and they travelled back through the city to the safety of the Palace walls.

Almost as soon as they had returned the summons came for Elen-ai from the Queen. With a shrug, she departed the Prince's side and followed the servant to the Queen. She hoped that Gidyon would not get himself killed during her absence from him. She would doubtless be blamed if he were. Another lecture from a Mother or Father would be tedious.

Today the Queen met her in the blue sitting room wearing black trousers and a simple white blouse. The plainness of the clothes somehow made her seem all the more authoritative. Here was a woman who did not need to establish her command with ornate finery. Elen-ai had taken the lives of many who had. As always, the gold cuffs glinted at the Queen's throat and wrists.

"Did anything happen at the market?" The Queen asked without preamble.

The dark wood of the furniture enriched the blue of the walls. With the gloominess of the day, it made Elen-ai feel as though she were underwater.

"Aside from the fact that it rained, nothing of note. Except of course that nobody knew they were speaking with the Prince." Elen-ai looked steadily at the Queen's face, ignoring the slight pool of water her sodden clothes were creating on the floor.

The Queen sighed, her face giving nothing away of her thoughts.

"Why have you not announced your decision?" Elen-ai asked. The Queen may have told her that she would announce appointing Gidyon as her heir at the Summer Council when the heads of the seven families would be present, but Elen-ai couldn't see any reason to delay the declaration.

The Queen regarded Elen-ai for a moment, pursing her lips as she thought. Eventually, she answered.

"Because I am afraid for Gidyon. He does not understand how his life will change once the world knows he is my heir," the Queen admitted. Elen-ai wondered if this was the truth, or simply a reason that the Queen was giving her.

"You must tell your people," Elen-ai implored her.

"You need not tell me that," the Queen responded some-what frostily. "In fact, I plan to send out the proclamation within a few days, rather than at the Summer Council as I initially told you. I think it will be better if the heads of the families have some time to become accustomed to the idea before I find myself in a room with them discussing the state of the country. That is what I called you here to discuss."

"Oh?" Elen-ai knew her familiarity with the Queen may see her rebuked, but she suspected the Queen was too focused on her son's safety to take issue with Elen-ai's demeanour.

"I do not want Gidyon in the capital when I announce my decision." By the brusqueness of the Queen's tone, it seemed Latana had indeed noticed and taken issue with Elen-ai's informal manner after all.

"He'll be no safer outside it," Elen-ai pointed out.

"This is not to do with an attempt on his life. I fear that there will be much anger from the people in the street. You saw how he was in the market. While I have never accompanied him, I have heard enough to know that he has a special fondness for many of the sellers there. I cannot be sure that their affection for him will outweigh their anger at his new title. I...I would like to shield him from that for as long as possible. Once the people have time to reflect on the change, they may be less vitriolic in the expression of their anger. I wish to protect him from whatever hurt I can, and I think sending him to the country estate is the easiest way to do this."

Elen-ai was silent for a moment. The Queen's desire to protect Gidyon from the near-certain anger of the people was understandable. But there was something else behind the Queen's reasoning that she hadn't been told. "And you still think that someone may try to kill him?" she asked.

The Queen nodded, slipping her hands into the pockets of her trousers. Elen-ai wondered if it was to hide any agitation.

"Can you be any more specific about these threats?"

"No." The Queen replied curtly, making it quite clear she knew something that she was declining to share. While Elen-ai had seen nothing to suggest Gidyon's life was in danger, Elen-ai was certain that the Queen had some other piece of information which suggested the threat was real.

"Your Majesty, if you want me to protect your son, I need to know everything," Elen-ai said, trying not to sound impatient.

The Queen's face remained calm. "I enlisted the services of the Family because you are the best. That means you can protect him from anything that may occur."

"And you can trust me to keep your secrets. You yourself spoke of the Family's discretion," Elen-ai pointed out.

"That is an added convenience," the Queen noted coolly.

Elen-ai looked at the Queen - her Queen. She did not appreciate whatever secret the Queen was keeping from her, but she had absolutely no power to compel her ruler to divulge what it was. "Your Majesty is wise. I'm sure you have your reasons," Elen-ai said eventually. After all, she could hardly expect the Queen to suddenly share something she hid from her closest brother.

"I will send the Councillors from the Third Country with you. It will be a good opportunity to show them our lands." The Queen picked up a piece of paper from the table in front of her and began to scan it, her method of dismissal a clear signal that she was irked with Elen-ai.

Unperturbed by the monarch's anger, Elen-ai left the Queen to find her charge.

For the first time, the Prince initiated a conversation with Elen-ai when they were in his rooms later that evening. "Who was that man you spoke with in the market?"

She paused midway through the task of repairing a seam for one of her pockets which held a blade and turned to look at him. She wasn't even aware that he had been looking at her when she and her Father had spoken. "He is my Father," she told him.

"Your Father?" He sounded surprised.

Realising his mistake, she corrected him. "All the older members of the Family are Mothers and Fathers to us. As those members close in age to me are my brothers and sisters."

"Does that get confusing?" he asked.

"No more than not having anyone to call father," she replied.

She saw the shock and hurt cross his face. He hadn't expected her to be unkind. For a moment she felt bad, but that guilt was overtaken by a chastisement that she let her personal dislike of the Prince lead to an emotional response.

"That was uncalled for," the Prince said softly.

"My apologies." She didn't often apologise. It felt strange doing so to the Prince.

"Are one of the Mothers and Fathers your actual parents?" Gidyon's curiosity clearly was stronger than his impulse to sulk.

"No," she said shortly. When he continued to regard her, she elaborated. "Family members are not permitted to have children. If they want to they must leave."

"So how did you join the Family? I hear you are all trained from a young age." Gidyon stepped forward and came to sit on the chair opposite her.

Elen-ai did not feel entirely comfortable discussing the ways of the Family, but she felt she owed the Prince something following her jibe. "I was sold to the Family when I was very young."

"What!"

"The Family will give people who have an unwanted child money in exchange for that child," Elen-ai said.

"Why would anybody do that?" The Prince seemed genuinely aghast at the prospect.

"Mostly because they don't have the money to care for the child," Elen-ai explained.

"I still don't understand why you would give your child away." Gidyon shook his head to punctuate the comment.

"Members of the seven families are willing to do that all the time," Elen-ai pointed out, trying to be as delicate as possible about the Prince's paternity.

He inclined his head, acknowledging her point. "Do you remember your parents?" he asked.

She shook her head. "The Family only accepts very young children - less than a year old. The only life I've ever known is with the Family."

"Does that bother you?"

She looked at him in incomprehension. "Why would it?"

"Because you never had a choice about being an assassin." He made it sound perfectly obvious.

"Did you have a choice about being the next ruler?" Elen-ai asked, ignoring the fact that she had made a similar comment in irritation to her Father earlier that day.

"No, but that's different," he retorted.

"Why?"

"Because I don't kill people," he told her.

Elen-ai laughed one short bark. "Princeling, your mother will have ordered the deaths of people in her years on the throne. Any ruler does. They just get someone else to do the job for them. When you take the throne, you'll have just as much blood on your hands as me. Probably more."

Gidyon stared at her for a moment before getting up and stalking back into his bedroom. Elen-ai listened for a moment to make sure that no assailant had jumped out from a hiding spot, then went back to her sewing.

SIX

A few days later, Elen-ai, the Prince, and the two Councillors from the Third Country waited in the main courtyard of the Palace, ready to depart for the Royal country estate. The Queen stood before them, her hair in an ornate plait. She wore a dress the colour of new grass and an expression of concern.

"Be careful, Gidyon," she told her son, taking his hands in her own. Her head bowed to him in quiet conference between mother and son.

"I promise I'll be safe," he said. "I have Elen-ai to take care of me."

Elen-ai pursed her lips at the comment. In the days that had passed, he had not spoken a single word to Elen-ai. Given that the Queen had also barely spoken to Elen-ai whenever they had happened to encounter each other, it had made for a certain surrealness to her time in the Palace. Clearly, mother and son shared the ability to hold a grudge.

"I love you my darling," the Queen told him, unabashed at giving her son an effusive hug.

"You be safe too, Mother. You'll be all alone in the Palace." Gidyon's brow crinkled with concern at the prospect.

"I have your uncles to watch over me," she chided him gently.

"Sil is the only one I trust to actually watch out for you," he said, causing her to laugh.

"I won't tell them that." She giggled as she embraced him again quickly.

The exchange was conducted in undertones that only Elen-ai was able to hear thanks to her sharp ears. Despite her irritation with both of the Royals, there was something heart-warming about the tender relationship between them.

The Queen walked with her son to the waiting carriage. The hearat pulling it stood patiently. Now that Elen-ai had seen the kittanae, the poor hearat seemed particularly lumbering, clumsy beasts in comparison to the felines who had a sleek elegance even in sleep.

"I am sorry that I am unable to come with you," she said to the Councillors, "but I trust that Gidyon will be a good host in my stead. Please enjoy yourselves." She smiled with her usual grace and charm at the two foreigners.

"We look forward to seeing more of your country, your Majesty. I'm sure we'll have many stories to recount to you upon our return." Councilman Hart returned her smile with that earnest charm.

With a final nod to Elen-ai from the Queen, the party climbed into the carriage and set off, surrounded by an escort of ten guards. Elen-ai took one final look at the Queen as they pulled away. Whatever secret lay within the monarch's heart, Elen-ai hadn't discovered it yet. She promised herself that somehow, she would.

The carriage itself was a luxurious affair, easily wide enough for four people to sit inside it in comfort. Cushions abounded, as did curtains on the windows that provided both privacy and a shield from the sun. It would take five days of travel on the great road that ran through the heart of the Queendom to reach the royal estate, due to the luxurious pace of the carriage. Elen-ai did not relish the prospect of such a great amount of time in close confines with the Prince, especially given his surly attitude toward her. She told herself that she could always ride outside if things truly became unbearable, but that thought was little comfort.

As the carriage rattled through the streets of Herran, the Councilman fixed her with his gaze. Elen-ai couldn't help but notice how vivid the green of his eyes was. It was almost as captivating as the blue of Gidyon's eyes. "Lady Elen-ai, I still am not certain of what role you play at court." There was something about his voice that made it sound as though he was perpetually amused by some secret joke. If he wasn't so charming it would be quite obnoxious.

Elen-ai shrugged. "I'm not sure that there is that much to say."

"What is it exactly is it that you do? Freya and I can't quite work it out," he pressed.

"Elen-ai kills people, Councilman. It so happens that she is currently engaged to kill people who are trying to kill me." The Prince spoke with his usual charisma, even though his comment was designed to shock. Unfortunately for him, neither Councillor seemed particularly perturbed by the statement. Elen-ai wanted to hit him for his casual revelation about her, especially after the Queen had expressed her desire to keep Elen-ai's trade unknown. She kept that impulse in check – barely.

"Does that mean you're a member of the Family that I've heard so much about?" The Councilwoman leaned forward, her eyes bright with intelligent curiosity.

Elen-ai did not say anything, merely nodding an uncomfortable affirmation and wishing there was some way that she could hurt the Prince for this uncharacteristic lack of discretion. It seemed pettiness had made him reckless.

"Have you travelled much beyond the Second Country?" Councilwoman Kuch asked, not seeming at all concerned by who Elen-ai was or what she did.

"A little. I've been into the Fourth Country a few times, although not recently," she admitted.

"You must know then about the situation there," the Councilman noted.

Memories of the curious land flashed through her mind, the manner in which the men were made to cover themselves, the unusual customs, the excessive choler of the people that was considered ordinary to them. "Somewhat. The Lord Protector seems to arbitrate on the cruelty of her people invading one another as though it were some game, although now that her authority may be threatened, it seems she is willing to be quite cruel in asserting her position. A whole group of landowners do not care about whatever suffering their exchange of lands may inflict on others, simply holding lavish parties for one another while other parts of the country starve. Many people have sought the services of the Family in the hope of changing power favourably." She divulged the information after a moment of consideration, deciding that nothing she said violated the Family's preference for secrecy. Any merchant could have given the same information, and now she may receive information in return for free.

Despite his resentment of Elen-ai, the Prince's curiosity had been aroused and he had listened intently to Elen-ai. "That's so sad," he murmured.

"People struggling for power always ends with innocent people being hurt," the Councilwoman said softly.

"Is that why you participated in the rebellion?" The Prince looked at her, clearly intrigued.

"Yes," the Councilwoman answered, her tone clear that she did not want to say any more on the matter.

Gidyon evidently noticed and did not pursue the issue.

The inside of the carriage lapsed into silence, the Councilwoman resting her head on Councilman Hart's shoulder as she looked out the window. He absentmindedly took her hand in his as he too watched the land pass by. They sat like that in contented silence, comfortably resting against each other, unabashed by the display of intimacy. The Prince read while Elen-ai modified the seam she had been mending a few days earlier. In the many hours of silence when she had been with Gidyon, she had decided that there was a better way in which the pocket could be constructed.

After a few hours, the carriage stopped so that they could have lunch. The Palace kitchens had prepared a picnic for the travellers which they ate by the side of the road. To their left, the mountains that were the domain of the Bertak family were just visible. Within those mountains were the precious metals that enriched clan Bertak. Likely the gold that the Queen always wore at her wrists and throat came from those mountains, although the items themselves would have been made in Herran. The Bertak family did not cultivate artisans to fashion delicate jewellery from the metal they mined in the way that the Katan family employed an array of skilled clayworkers to make the delicate pieces that were so highly prized across the Second Country. It was why the Bertak family were not as wealthy or powerful as they could have been. That was a source of great bitterness for them.

Elen-ai decided to ride outside the pampered comfort of the carriage when they set off again, claiming she could better see the surrounds from there. She was tired of the Prince's clear resentment of her presence and was desperate to be as far away from it as possible. The Councilwoman cheerfully said that she would accompany Elen-ai, to get a better view of the countryside. Elen-ai had no option but to accept the unwanted company.

Contrary to her fears though, the Councilwoman made no attempt to engage her in any meaningless conversation, appearing instead to have a genuine interest in the land as it passed by them. Thus it was Elen-ai who spoke first.

"You and the Councilman - you are married?" she asked.

The Councilwoman looked at her in confusion. "Ashtyn and I are bound if that's what you are asking," she replied.

"Bound?" Elen-ai frowned at the unfamiliar term.

"Our lives are intertwined in union," she explained. "Is that the same thing?"

Elen-ai considered for a moment. "It can be. Not all marriages are for love, though."

The Councilwoman nodded. "That would be a joining."

"Do you differentiate between a marriage of love and politics?" Elen-ai asked.

The Councilwoman shook her head. "No. In the Third Country it is simply that the Kade join and the Pious are bound."

"And the Kade are?" She feigned more ignorance than was strictly true of the goings-on within Third Country, interested to hear how the Councilwoman described her home.

"The Kade follow their gods and the Pious follow the Goddess," the Councilwoman explained.

"So you are Pious," Elen-ai surmised.

The Councilwoman nodded.

"It seems strange to have to different religions existing so peacefully side by side, especially if their customs are so different," Elen-ai commented. Indeed, few in the Queendom knew the Family followed a different god to the Divine One.

The Councilwoman laughed. "Not so different. But there was a time when the Kade ruled and forced the Pious to live as they do."

"What happened?" Elen-ai looked at the Councilwoman. She was looking away from Elen-ai at the gently undulating hills that currently were on either side of the road. Elen-ai wasn't certain that the Councilwoman had the delicate beauty of the Queen, but she was certainly striking in her own way, and deeply compelling. "We rebelled," she said softly.

"And now you can support your own god?" Elen-ai asked.

"Yes." For a moment, the Councilwoman was silent. "What gods do the people of the Second Country follow?" she asked.

"Mostly the people of the Queendom do not pay much attention to gods," Elen-ai replied slowly. "They believe in the Divine One, but do not think overly of its existence. The here and now are the more important concerns."

"Foolish to ignore the Gods. But you don't," the Councilwoman noted.

"No. I pray to the Shadow God." Elen-ai wondered how the Councilwoman had known that she was devout in her faith. Her surprise made her frank.

"Is that the god of the Family?" the other woman asked.

"Yes," Elen-ai said, not elaborating any further. For someone who was not a skilled diplomat, she had certainly found out much that Elen-ai would have told few others. Perhaps sensing she had pushed as far as she could go, the Councilwoman did not ask further questions, lapsing into an easy silence.

Elen-ai had always enjoyed this part of the Queendom. Especially now that it was almost the beginning of summer, the lush green coaxed into the landscape by the spring rains had not yet faded, while the weather was pleasant without being too warm or too cold. The only downside to the time of year was occasional days of rain such as they had experienced when the Prince had gone to the market, but so far the sky was a tender blue that bore no inkling of rain. Elen-ai was grateful for that. It meant that she didn't have to ride in the cabin with the Prince.

That night they set up camp rather than detour off the road into the land of one of the seven families. It was easier to set up a makeshift shelter than travel several days out of their way to impose themselves onto the hospitality of any of the families, as would be required if they were to cross into non-sovereign land.

After checking that no assailants lurked in the nearby area, Elen-ai took herself a little to the side of the camp so that she could pray to the Shadow God. Her talk with the Council-woman had made her realise that it had been too many days since she had paid her due to the patron deity of the Family. The Family's devotion to the Shadow God had endured while others forgot their gods. One of Elen-ai's earliest memories was the silent prayer of the Mothers and Fathers, seeing them in the home's courtyard one winter morning when the mist still skulked across the ground. The quiet depth of the Family's faith offered in return many gifts, one of them the ability to slip unseen where others would be clearly visible. She prayed kneeling, her focus locked totally on the prayer and the quiet serenity that prayer and her god gave her. Once her worship was complete, she stood, brushing the dirt off her knees.

"What were you doing?" The Prince's voice made her jump. It was an unforgivable oversight that she had not real-ised he was nearby.

"I was praying," she told him stiffly.

"To what?" As she had learned was the case when he was curious, he had dropped the unpleasant manner with which he normally addressed her. She wasn't certain if she was glad for the reprieve or resentful that he was nice because he wanted something from her.

"The god of shadows," she replied curtly. She figured the easiest way to deal with him was to give him what he wanted.

"Not the Divine One?" he asked.

"No. I didn't think most inhabitants of the Queendom ac-tually gave much thought to truly worshipping the Divine One," Elen-ai added as an afterthought.

"I certainly think there's something else out there aside from this." Gidyon swept his arms wide in a gesture around him. "As apparently do you," he noted.

"Is it a problem that I worship?" Elen-ai snapped.

"No actually. It's just...unexpected," Gidyon replied.

Elen-ai paused for a moment, trying to come up with a response, but inspiration did not strike in a timely fashion.

"You should get back to the main camp," she told him. "It's safer there."

Despite her expectation that a snark-infused quip would come her way, nothing eventuated. Gidyon merely accompanied her back to the camp, a thoughtful expression on his face.

The Councillors sat hand in hand by the makeshift fire that the guards had built. Elen-ai looked at them for a moment, fascinated by their perfect unity. They seemed so content with each other, so completed by the other's presence. She had always believed such love a mere myth. However here before her, she saw that she was wrong. Fleetingly, she wondered if she would ever find such completion in another person. The thought that her very personhood would be so tied up in the existence of another was terrifying. She dismissed the notion quickly. To have such a relationship would mean leaving the Family, and she would never leave the Family.

The Prince conversed with the two Councillors over the meal while Elen-ai sat contentedly in her own silence. Eventually, the meal was finished and the conversation petered out. The Councillors and Prince went to sleep while the royal guards kept watch in shifts. Elen-ai dozed lightly, unable to shake the sense that something uncertain loomed on the edge of her awareness. However despite her unease, when she awoke in the morning, no harm had come to any member of the party.

It was as they were breaking camp, when everybody's arms were full of one thing or another, that the attack occurred.

SEVEN

Elen-ai was not by the Prince's side when she saw the first of the mercenaries come seemingly out of nowhere and charge at him, blade drawn. Her yell prompted the Prince to turn and catch sight of his attacker while several paces still separated them. He threw the bundle he was carrying at the approaching assailant, but given he had been tasked with carrying blankets, it was an ineffective defence. Elen-ai dropped what she was carrying and released one of her blades in a motion faster than the eye could see, sending it flying past the Prince's head and deep into the eye of Gidyon's would-be killer.

Before she could get to the Prince's side however, she found herself dodging the scything blow of another attacker. She freed another blade and ducked under his wild swing. She twisted around him, calling upon the skills of the Family to shimmer out of his sight. Confused, he swung wildly rather than stopping as she had hoped he would. His blade nicked her arm, the pain flashing up along her shoulder before she shut it away as a problem to resolve later. Her retribution for the injury was swift. She used the speed built up over many years of training to flank him, drawing another knife and pushing it into his back between his ribs. Even with only a half-second to look, she had picked the correct spot and the knife had found his heart. He fell and she yanked the blade free, throwing it at another man trying to get to Gidyon.

Out of the corner of her eye, she saw three men approaching the Councillors drop in quick succession. She didn't have time to be concerned with the foreigners. Her first priority was the Prince. To let him die, especially at the hands of these untrained ruffians, would be mortifying, especially as she had not noticed their approach.

The sound of their guards fighting off the attackers rang in her ears as she ran over to the Prince's side, the pain in her arm forgotten, his safety her only thought. A third attacker made for him, knocking over the guard who had placed herself in front of Gidyon. Elen-ai cut him down by sliding forward and putting her knife in the softness of his belly. She didn't want to waste any time trying to break through the bone of his chest. Easier to leave him in agonising pain on the ground.

One more person tried to take the life of the heir to the throne, but Elen-ai intercepted her, driving a knife into the woman's arm, twirling around her and then breaking her neck in a sharp, brutal motion.

The sound of fighting stopped, replaced by the ragged intake of breath. There was something quite jarring about the sudden quiet.

Elen-ai turned to the Prince. "Gidyon, are you hurt?" she demanded.

The Prince, arms coiled across his abdomen, did not respond. Elen-ai grabbed him, concern making her rough. She pulled his arms free and gasped when she saw the blood from the slash, similar to the one she had given one of his attackers.

"I need bandages," Elen-ai called out, taking the Prince's weight and helping him to the ground. She couldn't see the cut, but judging by how much blood there was, it was deep enough to be fatal.

"Bandages! Now!" she yelled, pressing her hands to Gidyon's wound. His face was a sickly yellow colour. The smell of gore came to her nose.

Gentle hands pulled Elen-ai back. She struggled against them but whoever had gripped her was far stronger than she had expected and she did not immediately break free. "Let

Freya help him, lady Elen-ai. She is a healer of great skill," the Councilman told her.

She stopped struggling and he let her go. Every muscle tense, she watched as the Councilwoman knelt by the Prince who now was going pale, blood oozing sickeningly from his stomach. When Councilwoman Kuch made no attempt to touch him, Elen-ai started forward again, but she was arrested by the Councilman's arm shooting out. "Just watch," he advised.

"But she isn't even touching him," Elen-ai protested, readying a knife to strike him.

"Just watch," he repeated.

Elen-ai kept her eyes on the Prince. Sure enough, he did appear to look a little less like he was on the verge of death. The blood remained on his clothes and pooled on the ground around him, but it did not appear to be increasing in volume as it should be from such a severe wound.

"Oh," Elen-ai realised suddenly, turning to regard the Councilman. "She's-"

"A healer," he replied firmly.

Elen-ai knew that the skills of the Family were not unique, but there were precious few in the Queendom who had any knowledge of the gifts of faith. However, it seemed that the foreigners before her were well acquainted with the gifts of their gods and used them with as much skill as the Family. Perhaps there was more to the legends surrounding these two than she had initially thought. She went to her knees by the Prince's side, her fingers finding the pulse on his throat. It beat strong, if not a little fast. The Councilwoman was sitting back on her heels, a slight smile on her face.

"He should be fine. He just needs rest now," she told Elen-ai. She frowned slightly. "Wait. Ah, it's you. Stay still," she commanded.

Elen-ai looked in puzzlement at the Councilwoman who was staring intently at Elen-ai. "Your arm," she explained after a few moments had passed, the look of intense focus wiped from her face.

Elen-ai glanced at the arm that had been pierced earlier. Her sleeve was bloodied but the injury was healed completely. "I've never met a healer as powerful as you," she told the Councilwoman as she returned to her inspection of the Prince. He was gazing around in a daze but seemed to be otherwise completely fine.

"You aren't afraid of me?" The Councilwoman seemed unconcerned by that possibility, merely curious.

Elen-ai shrugged. "You have been given the gifts of faith. Why is that something to fear?"

The Councilwoman smiled at Elen-ai then turned to her companion. "Are you alright, Ashtyn?"

He came to her side then, helping her up and putting an arm gently around her. "I'm fine, Freya. I didn't even get a chance to be touched. You took care of that before they even came close to us."

Elen-ai looked back to the attackers she had seen drop as she made her way over to the Prince. At the time she hadn't given them any thought, but now that she considered it, she hadn't seen any weapon touch them. It seemed that the Councilwoman's ability to heal could also be used to inflict damage. Tactfully, she said nothing. A few of the royal guards had survived and such a conversation was best conducted away from the ears of those who didn't understand what it meant to be kissed by a god's power. She turned her attention back to her charge.

"Your Highness, can you hear me?" she asked him.

The glazed look in his eye cleared slightly. "We were attacked," he mumbled.

"Quite right."

"I thought I was hurt." He struggled to sit up further, looking down at his stomach.

"You were, but the Councilwoman fixed you," Elen-ai said, her voice imbued with a cheerfulness to deter him from asking too many questions. "Come on, let's get you into the carriage. You need some rest." She heaved the Prince to his feet, giving him some dignity by not draping him across her shoulders, but instead putting her arm around his waist and allowing him to lean on her as she guided him toward the carriage.

"Who were the attackers?" he asked her as they walked. He appeared to be rapidly recovering his wits.

"Not sure. I'll have a look at them once you're inside the carriage," she replied.

"Will it be safe in there?" He sounded concerned, probably afraid at the prospect of facing an actual fight again. No practice sparring could prepare anyone for the unpredictability or fear that accompanied a fight for one's life. Not that the Prince had done much fighting.

"Don't worry, I'll make certain it's safe," Elen-ai assured him.

They reached the carriage and he climbed inside, settling himself among the cushions and looking like a frightened child which, in fairness, was exactly what he was.

Elen-ai clambered to the carriage roof and crouched there, listening for sounds that didn't fit with the aftermath of the fight. She heard moans, the sound of someone weeping softly, and quiet conversation, but nothing that could be even remotely mistaken for someone lying in wait to attack. She climbed back down, giving the Prince a businesslike nod.

"How many do we have left?" she asked the guard standing by the carriage once she had firmly closed the door. The guard seemed to be in a state of shock, standing in the one spot and staring about him. His weapon was held loosely in his hands, but Elen-ai did not think that he was aware of it. She repeated her question, causing him to start.

"Uh, I don't know," he admitted.

"Well go and find out," she suggested, going over to the body of one of the attackers. She heard his footsteps as he plodded away and the murmur as he spoke with one of the other guards and the sharp sob, but those were things she paid no heed. Her attention was focused on the still-warm body.

Some may have felt squeamish about handing a dead person, but Elen-ai was well acquainted with death. There was nothing threatening about a corpse. A corpse couldn't try to kill you. Her search revealed no information of any value. The man's clothes were nondescript and there was nothing on his person that might give some indication of who he was or who had sent him. She conducted the same investigation on the other five assailants just to be sure, but her searches yielded similar results.

Elen-ai straightened up from the final body. She hadn't expected to find anything. These were the kind of brutal, amoral thugs who could be found anywhere and would perform any task without questions provided the right amount of money was placed in front of them. They were completely anonymous, possibly foreigners, the kind of people who had racked up some large debt in an unpleasant place and were willing to do anything to repay it quickly. Elen-ai was nevertheless frustrated. She had hoped someone would have been careless.

The smell of gore and death lingered over the area. It didn't much bother Elen-ai. When she was nine, she had been sent to work in a slaughter yard. Her first task had been poultry, plucking birds from one side, detaching their heads with a swift movement, then tossing the decapitated corpses onto a pile on her other side. From there, she had been given more and more messy tasks. The larger animals were far less pleasant to deal with. After four months in the slaughter yard, she never found the smell of blood or gore overly troubling again.

She walked over to the Councillors who were conferring quietly together, their heads close, arms loosely about each other. They appeared to reach some kind of consensus.

"Did you find anything?" the Councilwoman asked as Elen-ai approached.

She shook her head. "Nothing. The attackers were the sort of brute that's easy to hire and won't care what the task is so long as they're paid – even killing a Queen's son. If I had to guess, though, they would have tried to make it look like a robbery."

"It wasn't?" Despite the question, it was clear that the Councilwoman knew very well that there was more than simple greed behind the attack. Elen-ai saw no point in pretending otherwise.

"I doubt that very much," she replied.

"That's a problem," the Councilwoman said, her expression wry.

Elen-ai quirked an eyebrow, stifling a laugh. Perhaps she was more shocked by the attack than she had first thought. This was not the time for laughter. "I think I should go and consult with the Prince," she said.

"Certainly," the Councilwoman agreed. "We'll do whatever you decide," she added. She seemed completely unperturbed by the events of the day. Whatever she had seen in that rebellion, it must have been quite awful for her to be so unconcerned by the sudden attack, or the near-death of the Prince.

Elen-ai returned to the carriage. The Prince was starting to regain his colour although he still looked very fragile.

"I think we should head back to the capital," she told him. When the Prince didn't respond, Elen-ai continued. "We only have a few guards left, and it seems someone does actually want you dead. There was even a halfway decent attempt to make it look as though they were simply robbers. Not convincing enough, but still, not bad. I recommend we go back to the capital. Hopefully, the guards we have left will be enough to fend off another attack if it occurs."

"No." He said it softly, but with the obstinate tone that she had come to know well.

"No?" she repeated back, incredulous.

"We should go to the Veertak estate. We're only a few hours from Atak." He named the Veertak capital, a town populated almost exclusively by scholars.

"Why?"

"The Veertak are loyal to my mother. It is in their interests to be so. They should agree to loan us some of their guards if we request. That would be safer than just going back." The acrimony toward her seemed to have dissipated in the face of the more pressing issue that someone had tried to kill him.

"Gidyon, all it takes is one member of the Veertak to want you to dead," Elen-ai protested.

"How many guards do we have left?" he asked.

"Five."

"That won't be enough." The Prince's tone may have been firm, but Elen-ai could see the fear on his face. And as much as she wouldn't say to him, he did have a point. All it would take would be for her to be distracted for one second and the Prince could be killed by another assailant. It was good fortune that the Councilwoman and her skills had been there to save him this time, but no healing gift could revive him if he were killed by a lucky blow. She thought for a moment longer, evaluating the benefit of simply returning to Herran straight away or of making their way across to Atak. Her preference was to return to the capital as fast as possible and lock Gidyon safely in the Palace surrounded by the Royal Guards. But she wasn't certain that the Prince would manage. He was clearly terrified despite the veneer of calm he had somehow mustered. That fact alone in the wrong situation could be just as dangerous as a blade. Besides, a former member of the Family lived in Atak. She was sure that she could approach Sam-et for help.

"Atak it is," she sighed.

The carriage with its ornate decorations was far too conspicuous for Elen-ai's liking but there was no alternative. She rode on top of the carriage with the remaining guards riding alongside it. Everyone was tense as they made their way across the countryside, waiting for another attack. She wondered how they felt at the deaths of the other guards, or the fact that the bodies of those who had died had been left by the side of the road out of brutal necessity. Her musing went so far as to be impressed by the fact that those who had survived were so focused on the task at hand. Then again, grief and shock would often dissipate in the face of necessity. Likely, when they got to the Veertak home they would all seek the solace of a big mug of ale.

The Councilwoman sat beside her, having elected again to not ride in the carriage. Had it been anyone else, Elen-ai would have worried that another attack could put them in danger, but after she had seen what the woman could do, she was not concerned in the slightest.

"Thank you. For your help back there," she said after some time had passed. She liked that about the foreign woman, that she did not feel the need to incessantly chatter. People who were not members of the Family often filled silence with empty words. It was tiresome.

Councilwoman Kuch looked slightly bemused. "Why would I not help?"

"To reveal what you can do in a country where that sort of knowledge has been largely lost could be dangerous. More dangerous than being attacked by a band of second-rate hired killers," Elen-ai replied.

"It was once a secret in the Third Country, too," the Councilwoman replied.

"What changed?" Elen-ai asked.

"I was put in a position where I had to reveal my abilities in front of a great many people."

"Why?"

The other woman hesitated. "It's complicated. Anyway, once people had seen what happened, there was no trying to pretend it hadn't. People knew what faith could bestow. There was great concern that it would lead to total chaos. But faith isn't as simple as believing in order to attain abilities. Which you would know, of course."

Elen-ai ducked her head in a non-response. There were members of the Family who did not manage to find that true belief in the god of shadows. They were not cast out, but their role within the Family was limited. Many of them chose to leave.

"May I ask you a question?" the Councilwoman said after a moment of silence had passed.

"Certainly, Councilwoman."

"Please, call me Freya, I have never quite gotten used to the title of Councilwoman." The other woman smiled.

"If you insist...Freya." Elen-ai was never one to stand on ceremony. "Your question?"   "I was just wondering why anyone would want to kill Prince Gidyon," she said thoughtfully.

Elen-ai shrugged. "I mean, we've never had a man on the throne before. The mere thought is deeply unsettling. The Queen certainly felt that he would be in danger as a result of her decision to name him her heir. But there are many motivations behind why someone may want him dead. People want another person dead for the oddest of reasons."

"To order someone killed seems very," Freya hesitated for a moment, "personal," she finished.

Elen-ai shrugged again. "Sometimes people come to the Family wanting to eliminate someone in the way of their business interests. Seems pretty impersonal to me." She scanned the area as she spoke. Fortunately, they were travelling on flat land that offered few places for an individual to hide, let alone a large group. The verdant green of the grass that covered the land on either side of the road was almost overwhelming.

"Even then," Freya countered, sounding quite content, despite the brutal events of the day, not to mention the macabre nature of their discussion. She did not say anything else.

She didn't need to. There was a certain truth to the fact that wanting someone else dead was quite personal. In some cases, wanting the certainty of someone's death at the hands of another person spoke to a certain coldly intense rage.

"Thank you for your help with Gidyon," Elen-ai said hesitantly. She felt awkward. Members of the Family traditionally only relied on one another. She was enormously in the debt of this woman next to her. It was a new feeling.

"I am a healer first and foremost. It is my duty to heal when I can. But you are welcome," Freya replied, a smile on her face.

Very few words were exchanged between members of the party for the remainder of the journey. There was a certain comfort in the silence that existed between Elen-ai and Freya. Something in what the foreign dignitary had revealed about herself made Elen-ai feel more at ease around her, even while others might have been put off. They had only been travelling for a few hours when they reached the outskirts of the large township Atak. Held by the Veertak and located on the shore of one of the Queendom's seven huge lakes, it was a quaint and peaceful area populated by people whose interest mostly lay more in books than people. Unlike the varying designs and styles of the buildings in the capital, most of the buildings in Atak were low-lying timber structures. The exception was the Veertak's family home and the great library within it. The house was a compound of several stories made of stone to minimise the risk of fire.

The carriage made its way through the streets, drawing barely any glances. Elen-ai was inwardly amused, knowing well the way of scholars and their interest in the outside world. Unless of course, a rival scholar threatened to steal some important discovery. Scholars were some of the Family's best customers, willing to kill for the credit - or suppression - of some discovery. For the most part though, their willingness to kill was limited purely to the world of academia. Nevertheless, that unexpected savagery could have been directed at Gidyon, Elen-ai reminded herself.

Because of the scholars' patronage of the Family, Elen-ai was well acquainted with Atak. She was quite fond of the town, having thought to herself that if she ever had to leave the Family, this would be where she would go. Tranquillity reigned there, for the most part. That tranquillity was uncharacteristically disrupted as the carriage entered the gates of the Veertak home. An elderly man came rushing out to meet the carriage. Elen-ai knew him by sight as the patriarch of the Veertak family, custodian of their knowledge alongside his somewhat fierce, if not adored, wife. Elen-ai raised her eyebrows at his speed, wondering if he would topple over from his forward momentum. For him, a fall would surely lead to an egregious break, although perhaps Freya could be prevailed upon to heal such an injury if it occurred.

Prince Gidyon cautiously opened the door to the carriage and stuck his head out. "My lord Veertak, is everything alright?" He greeted the old man, his voice carrying a note of uncertainty at the unceremonious appearance of the aged man.

"Master Gidyon. I might ask the same of you," the old man gasped, coming to a perilously hasty stop before the carriage. Elen-ai feared that he may crash into the carriage and break several of his fragile old bones.

"How could you possibly know?" Gidyon asked, his face creasing into a frown of puzzlement.

"Why Master Gidyon, your mother. The attack. Have you not heard?" the old man wheezed.

EIGHT

The Prince's face grew quite pale. He tumbled out of the carriage to the old man's side. "Varl what happened?" he asked urgently, formality totally forgotten.

"Word reached us this morning by messenger bird of an attempt on her life that took place last night."

The merit of keeping people in city residences seemed to have proved itself yet again even as the speed with which such information spread across the country seemed almost indecent.

"What happened?" Gidyon all but reached out and grabbed the octogenarian by the shoulders to shake him. Elen-ai worried that such an action may very well snap the Veertak patriarch in half.

"That I do not know," the old man responded gravely. "Don't worry, she's not harmed badly," he added, seeing the stricken look on Gidyon's face.

"Who was behind it?" Gidyon demanded. Elen-ai, watching his face, could see fear for his mother giving way to anger.

"As yet, nobody knows. I'm sorry." Varl Veertak looked with great compassion at the Prince whose composure had utterly deserted him.

Gidyon was silent for several moments, his stare vacant. Then he took a deep breath and with evident effort looked at the old man. "Obviously it's not your fault. May we come inside? An attack was made on my own life this morning. I somehow doubt that they're unrelated." Elen-ai was impressed at the self-discipline it would have taken him to pull himself to-gether like that.

"Divine one! Are you hurt? Of course, come inside at once." Like a clucking mother, Varl ushered the Prince and his retinue inside, greeting the Councillors quickly and with flus-tered warmth. He looked curiously at Elen-ai whose name was given with no other explanation, but given the tumultuous cir-cumstances of the Prince's arrival, there was no time for him to ask any questions about her place in the party.

"Let us go to the library," he suggested. "We can discuss this at greater length there. We will make up rooms for our for-eign friends where they can relax after what I'm sure would have been a most awful ordeal." He truly did bustle, giving dis-tracted orders to servants who were clearly accustomed to vague directives from him.

Elen-ai followed the Prince along the mansion's corridors, every sense on alert. She expected a trap of some sort, the Prince having been lured into the Veertak estate seeking refuge after the events of the morning, in case the first attempt did not succeed. Such complex plans were not unheard of. Certain-ly, it was what she would have arranged had she been attempt-ing to take the life of the Prince. While she doubted that the Veertak family were interested in killing Gidyon, the surprising ruthlessness of scholars should never be underestimated. Until she had seen more, she could not eliminate them as suspects.

As they reached the library, a servant with a tray of drinks and food met them, placing it on the large reading table in the middle of the room before exiting.

"Oh." Gidyon glanced down at his stained shirt. The blood which had dried on it flaked off as he moved, falling onto the expensive rug on the floor.

"Never mind that," Varl reassured him.

Gidyon took a seat, his eyes hungrily on the plate of smoked meats and fruit. Elen-ai made a motion for him to wait, taking a mug of the slightly warmed fruit juice - a specialty of the Veertak region - and a piece of the meat, and sampling them. When the tell-tale tingle of poison did not reach her tongue she nodded to him and he helped himself. The whole exchange was conducted in a few seconds, but she realised that the head of the Veertak family had been watching with a keen interest.

"Lady Elen-ai, I'm terribly sorry but I didn't quite catch where you were from." He addressed her with the courtesy he would afford someone of the seven families, despite the fact that her name gave away that she was not of such lineage. The suffix -ai or -am for women and -et or -en for men was adopted by all but those who were members of the families of power.

"That's because the information wasn't volunteered," she replied before the Prince could speak.

"Perhaps you can tell me what you know of what happened," Gidyon interjected, either picking up on her reluctance to divulge anything about her identity or simply preoccupied with the news of his mother's attack.

Nodding in deference to the Prince's point, Varl sat down. He opened his mouth to speak but was interrupted by the entrance of an austere-looking woman. VArlena Veertak, the matriarch of the family and renowned scholar held herself with the poise of a woman decades her junior. Unlike her husband's wispy white hair that looked as though it had not seen a comb since his sixth decade of life, her hair was tightly plaited to ensure that not one stray strand escaped. She looked every part the authority figure that he did not. The only thing that was similar about their appearance was their eyes. Both had sharp bright eyes that spoke of a keen intellect and spelled trouble for anyone foolish enough to forget it.

"My lady Varlena." Gidyon stood and bowed to her, courtesy emerging despite the shocking circumstances of the day.

"Master Gidyon," she replied, her deep voice without any hint of the quaver that often accompanied age.

"Gidyon had not heard of the attack on his mother. He came following an attack on his own life to us to seek shelter." The manner in which her husband efficiently gave her crucial information spoke to decades of practice and partnership.

"Surely the same hand is behind each effort," she replied, outwardly not shocked by the news, logic her primary response. It gave much away about who she was.

"It seems the logical conclusion," Varl agreed.

Understanding flashed between them on an unspoken level, a communication refined over a lifetime together. It reminded Elen-ai of the dynamic that existed between the two Councillors from the Third Country.

"My Lord Gidyon, I do not believe I have met your companion before," the matriarch said abruptly, her gaze turning to Elen-ai.

"My apologies lady VArlena," Gidyon had remained standing, his own lifetime of manners at work. "This is lady Elen-ai. She-"

"-is a member of the Family," VArlena concluded for him, fixing Elen-ai with an intense stare. Unlike many who looked at her knowing who she was, it was not a look that held judgment, merely evaluation, and perhaps a little consideration of what the presence a member of the Family at the side of the Queen's son might suggest. Beside her, Varl murmured "oh of course," more to himself than anyone else.

The door was flung open once again before anything more could be said. Elen-ai's concern over the Veertaks' knowledge of her identity was pushed aside by the man who walked in. It would be conservative to say he was the most handsome man Elen-ai had ever seen.

"Did I hear-" He stopped and looked at Gidyon, staring with eyes that were a captivating shade of blue. "It seems I heard correctly," he answered himself, not taking his eyes from the Prince. There was something unnerving about the unblinking intensity of his stare.

"Master Gidyon, lady Elen-ai, Erek of the Rasatan family. He is visiting us to conduct research on boat design," Varl said calmly.

"Erek is often in Herran on business. We actually meet quite often when he pays his respects to my mother. Erek, it's good to see you again," Gidyon said, his words soothing the possible awkwardness of Erek's unannounced intrusion into the room.

The man's eyes slid over Elen-ai ever so briefly then returned to scrutinise the Prince. "Master Gidyon, I am so sorry about your mother. I am sure you share our deep relief to learn she survived such a heinous attack." Sincerity imbued his melodious voice as he advanced, still looking at the Prince. He noticed the dried blood on Gidyon's clothes. "What happened!" he exclaimed.

"It would seem my mother was not the only target," Gidyon explained. "The blood is not mine," he added.

"Thank the Divine One. I can only hope that justice was swiftly delivered to whoever would seek to harm you or your wonderful mother," the man said, putting a hand to his chest to emphasise the point.

"That's very kind of you to say, Erek," Gidyon replied, sitting back down and taking a sip of the warmed juice. "But I still don't know what exactly happened to my mother," he added, a pointed edge to his tone.

VArlena took a seat next to her husband, picking up a mug of her own. "Please, join us, Erek. We were just about to tell Master Gidyon what we had heard," she said smoothly.

After a moment's hesitation, Erek accepted the invitation, sitting down in one of the room's other luxurious chairs. He leaned forward, adopting the pose of an intent listener.

"What we know is only from a message sent by one of our own within Herran. From what she could gather, a delivery of food brought several individuals into the Palace yesterday late afternoon. They killed their way through the kitchens and managed to actually find the Queen. She was hurt, but the guards intervened before she could be gravely wounded," VArlena said.

"Surely the guards would have checked to ensure that the delivery was safe." Erek sounded shocked at the laxity of the royal guards. Elen-ai was not. They may have been well trained, even skilled with weapons, but carelessness was nestled within most people who did the same thing day in, day out. She would know, she had used that to her advantage many times.

"No. Today the delivery will have been what I order from the market on my weekly walk there." Gidyon glanced at Elen-ai. "It seems you were correct about not being able to trust them," he told her, sounding terribly sad. Elen-ai felt sorry for him to be so crushed by the truth of the world.

"We can't fathom why anyone would want to kill your mother, Gidyon. She has been nothing but a fair and just ruler, even if she is currently without an heir." Varl turned to his wife as he spoke. She nodded once to signal her approval of his comment.

"Actually, she isn't," Gidyon said.

Three pairs of eyes snapped to look at the Prince. Elen-ai's own eyes flicked between each face.

"Is there something we don't know?" VArlena enquired politely.

"I believe my mother was going to announce it today, but it seems she was," Gidyon hesitated, "distracted by other matters. She has decided that I am to be her heir."

Total silence descended on the room. Elen-ai saw little shock on the faces of the three people opposite her, but she did see the reflexive disapproval against the complete rupture from tradition.

"We heard rumours," Varl admitted. "Although nobody was certain if they were true or not."

An uncomfortable silence followed his words. Eventually, Gidyon spoke. "What my mother wishes is unprecedented, but in studying of our country's laws I have found nothing written which forbids it. I know that it is a change, but you yourself said, Lord Veertak, my mother has been a fair and just Queen. I would ask you to trust her judgment once more."

At some point in Gidyon's life, someone had done a spectacular job of training him to muster himself under stressful circumstances, Elen-ai thought. How he could be so eloquent after such a day, she had no idea.

"You know why there has never been a man on the throne. It could lead to great political turmoil," Varl said gently.

"I've thought about this ever since my mother told me what she wanted to do. Every Queen...consorts with a number of members of the seven families to ensure that any child born is of unclear parentage. This means that no favour can be bestowed upon a particular family as a result of this link. What if I pledged to marry someone of common birth, with no ties to any of the seven families? That way any child I bore would be similarly without any attachment to a particular family. As I am now." Gidyon leaned forward slightly as he waited for the consideration of his proposal to be completed.

"You would marry someone of low birth?" Erek spoke, not bothering to hide his disdain at the prospect.

"Erek, if we only married from within the seven families, we'd be so inbred it would be quite terrible," VArlena said to him, her polite delivery lessening the bite of her dismissiveness.

"The idea now, though? You're only what - sixteen years? Something you promise to do now you may not wish to do when the time comes," Varl cautioned him, leaning forward in his chair.

"I'm committing to taking the throne, aren't I?" Gidyon answered, a slight smile on his face.

Varl chuckled in response. He looked at his wife who gave him a slight nod.

"Gidyon, you have the support of the Veertak family," VArlena told him.

A slight relaxing of the muscles in Gidyon's throat gave away his fear that the Veertaks would reject his claim. "I'm glad to hear that," he said evenly, his voice not giving away his relief at all.

Erek, who had been watching the exchange spoke then. "Well Gidyon, I can tell you that I personally support your claim to the throne, but I am not sure the rest of my family will. The best that I can do is promise to try and talk them around."

"It is all I could ask of you, and I cannot tell you how much I appreciate it. From all three of you," Gidyon responded, gratitude clearly on his face as he looked at the three adults.

Erek moved first. "If you'll excuse me, I must get back to that research. The faster I finish it, the faster I can get back home and start trying to convince my family that you will be the wonderful ruler I know you can be." Erek stood, gave a little nod of parting and left the room.

Once he had left, VArlena snorted. "Don't expect much from Erek's honeyed promises. He has no idea what he just undertook to do. Thinks he can talk his father around? Divine One, he'd have better luck talking a tree out of being timber. His father won't be charmed by Erek's good looks, stubborn, stupid man, and his wife wouldn't say anything even if she did think otherwise, she's so timid," she told Gidyon, making absolutely no effort to disguise her scorn for the head of the Rasatan family. Given that the Veertaks shared a border with the Rasatan lands, it seemed a dangerous move for her to so openly express the derisive opinion. Not that anything she said wasn't commonly held wisdom. Wenden Rasatan was considered a domineering and dogmatic man whose petty tyranny was given free reign by the timidity of his wife, Keela. Some whispers even suggested that there was madness somewhere in the family.

"What will change his family's mind?" Gidyon asked.

"The promise of greater power," VArlena answered immediately, putting her juice aside and folding her hands in her lap.

It was true; the Rasatan family was one of the three minor families within the Queendom alongside the Veertak and Bertak families. While the Veertak had never displayed meaningful interest in gaining a greater political position, the desire of the Rasatan and Bertak families for ever-greater riches and importance was renowned. That being said, all of the seven families vied for greater power and importance in some way or another. That ambition was why the tradition of the Queen remaining unmarried and bearing children of unknown paternity had been implemented - to always keep them at arm's length from the throne.

"That's why someone tried to kill my mother and me, isn't it?" Gidyon asked suddenly.

Elen-ai tensed, worried that he had just indirectly accused the heads of the Veertak family of the attack on him and his mother.

"It wouldn't surprise me," Varl shrugged, making no effort to hide his disdain for such behaviour.

"I know this has all happened very quickly, and there is much to consider. Perhaps it may be worth bathing and resting for a little?" VArlena suggested kindly.

"I would appreciate that greatly." Gidyon seized upon the suggestion. "I cannot tell you how much your support and hospitality means to me," he told the wizened couple, letting his mask of composure slip just a fraction and exposing the afraid young man beneath.

"I remember when you were very young, and you came to visit us here with your mother. You displayed a desire to learn and a humility regarding the limits of your knowledge even then. Perhaps you don't remember," VArlena told him.

"Of course I remember. You brought me into the library - this room, wasn't it? And you helped me understand how I could find books that I wanted." The Prince smiled at the memory.

"You made quite the impression on me then. At the time I thought that you would make a superb advisor to the sister who would follow you. It seems I will have to amend that impression to think you will make a good King," she said gently. Gidyon blushed at the compliment, perhaps the first that he had received in relation to his new position.

"If I could offer you a piece of counsel, though. Perhaps you should not advertise the identity of your companion," VArlena added.

"How did you know?" Elen-ai asked. It was the first time she had spoken.

"I have lived a very long time, young lady, and I have seen a great many things. Your kind has a distinctiveness that one learns to recognise," the old woman responded. "But if you are at Gidyon's side perhaps there is more at work here than even I first thought. Do not worry, neither of us will speak of this to anybody else."

The ambiguity of her comment had Elen-ai frowning. Perhaps the old woman knew something in relation to the Queen's secret, but Varl chimed in, moving Elen-ai's thoughts and the conversation, elsewhere before she could ask any questions of VArlena. "Our servants should have prepared rooms for you and lady Elen-ai. They should be ready by now. Your Highness," he added, testing out the word.

"Please, call me Gidyon." The Prince smiled at the old man, his whole face lighting up.

Elen-ai remained alert as Gidyon bathed. The grand family home of the Veertaks was made from a grey stone that left the interior of the building somewhat dim. Attempts had been made to counter this through large windows and large fireplaces. This, combined with the crammed bookshelves in nearly every room, gave the grand mansion a deceptively cosy and intimate feel. Elen-ai could hear the tread of people coming and going through the entire house as various scholars came in search of one text or another. The Veertak family guarded the source of its power just as fiercely as the other six families within the Queendom guarded theirs, keeping the knowledge of which they were the guardians inside their very house. While Elen-ai was inclined to believe that Varl and VArlena had every intention to support the Prince and his claim to the throne, the constant comings and goings of scholars in search of an obscure text or a consultation with one of their learned colleagues meant that the security of the building was woeful. Anybody could come in and try to finish the job that had been left incomplete that morning.

Gidyon emerged from the bathing room, his hair wet. Something about the washing left him looking his age, his face round with youth. The very adult worries of politics and power games had temporarily departed from his shoulders, sloughed off with the dirt and blood from the road.

He threw himself down into a chair and finally let the fear that he had been containing show on his face.

"Are you alright?" Elen-ai asked.

He took several deep breaths. "I think so," he replied. "It is odd to realise that you are one of the few people I can truly trust," he added. "Normally loyalty can't be bought," he concluded, a sardonic smile twisting his mouth.

Elen-ai didn't know if that was a barb or simply the Prince's struggle to come to terms with the unfaithfulness of the world.

"It seems I am in a predicament," Gidyon continued. "Some member of the seven families wants my mother and me dead."

"Are you sure that it's a member of the seven families?" Elen-ai challenged.

He tilted his head to look at her. "Who else would have the resources and the knowledge to effect such attacks?" he asked.

She couldn't disagree with his point. "You would be much safer in Herran," she said instead, restating her earlier claim.

"But surely they may try again."

Taking her silence as an affirmative, he went on. "But it is not just question of safety. I want whoever is behind this brought to justice. I need to prove to all who doubt me that I can control my people. That I am worthy of the throne. How can I do that if an attack on my mother's and my lives is an unsolved mystery?"

"An admirable objective, but how exactly do you propose to bring whoever ordered this attack to justice?" Elen-ai asked.

"I am going to find out who was behind this," he said, determination making him sit a little straighter in his chair.

"How exactly will you do that?"

She didn't mean it as a challenge, but perhaps it came out that way in her tone. His eyes focusing as he outlined his plan to her. "The only way to do it is to meet with each of the families and request their approval for my claim. It is a reasonable thing to do, especially given my...situation. Support from enough of the families will make the announcement acceptable to the rest of the Second Country. In the course of meeting the families, I'm bound to see something that will give me some indication of who was behind this. That, or someone will try again to end my life – hopefully we can catch them in the act rather than after I am killed."

Elen-ai sighed. How he expected clues to simply manifest themselves, she had no idea. Nevertheless, he had a point in that simply returning to Herran would not necessarily make him safer. And if he was not safe, then her contract was not fulfilled, and she could not go home. "I will follow you wherever you choose to go," she told him. "Aren't you worried about your mother, though?"

"I am," he admitted, hesitating slightly before going on. "If it were simple, I would go back to Herran now and see for myself that she's alright. But this is more important. It's about the stability of the Second Country, not just what I want. That has to come first. I will send her a message explaining what I intend to do. She will understand."

"Just tell me where we go." Elen-ai shrugged.

He nodded. "Thank you for your efforts this morning," he added. "I know that I would have likely died were it not for you."

"Just doing my job," she told the Prince, mentally crediting Freya's help to ensuring that outcome.

Despite it being against her every instinct, she left the Prince for a short while, venturing into the township around which the Veertak mansion was built. The Family believed knowledge was the key to almost everything, and information was sorely lacking in relation to who may have tried to kill the Queen and her son. So she had to see if she could redress this problem. She made her way to the door of a well-constructed little house near the lakeside part of the town and knocked. It was flung open by Sam-et who gave her a beaming welcome and ushered her into the house, showing no surprise at her unannounced appearance. "Elen-ai. What a wonderful surprise," he enthused.

Elen-ai smiled. Sam-et had been one of her brothers, only a few years older than her. They had always gotten along, even on occasion sharing a contract that required more than one person to complete. However, he had fallen in love with a girl that he had encountered on one of his contracts within the Veertak family's region. Because members of the Family were not permitted to be married, he had left to pursue a life with her. Elen-ai watched as he crossed the room, the training of the Family still obvious in the smooth silence of his stride. He picked up an infant from a crib.

"This is Am-ai," he said proudly, presenting the child to Elen-ai for inspection.

Unaware of how she was supposed to hold or respond to the child, Elen-ai leaned forward and gave an approving nod. "She's very...clean," she said lamely.

Sam-et roared with laughter. "Still very much a member of the Family, I see," he said, cradling his daughter close and giving her a loud kiss on the forehead. There was something fundamentally absentminded about his kiss that made it particularly profound. Elen-ai stared, amazed at the transformation of someone who had once taken life without flinching into this doting father.

"I can only assume you're in the region on a contract, Elen-ai?" he asked.

She nodded. "Of sorts. I've been engaged to protect the Prince."

He frowned in confusion. "Prince?"

"The Queen will name her son Gidyon her heir," she explained.

Instead of the outrage that Elen-ai had felt upon learning of the Queen's decision, a thoughtful look crossed Sam-et's face. "To place such a burden on him. Poor lad. So someone's trying to kill him?" Sam-et had always been quick. His departure had been a loss to the Family.

She nodded. "Have you heard anything that might help me know who it is?"

The child started to cry. Sam-et began to sway lightly from side to side to shush her. "Whispers. Nothing certain. I did once hear a rumour that the Queen had a lover, but it could simply be the product of an idle tongue."

"Rumour is rarely based on nothing," Elen-ai mused, watching as her former brother calmed his daughter.

He shrugged as much as he was able to with an armful of infant. "I'll keep an ear out for you, let you know if I hear anything."

"Thank you. I'm in your debt," she told him.

"You're leaving already? Stay, Len-am should be back soon. She'd love to meet you."

Elen-ai privately doubted that his wife would, in fact, be pleased to meet her. "I should get back to the Prince. Make sure he hasn't tripped over his own feet." She rolled her eyes.

She gave him a rough embrace around the child as he accompanied her to the door. "You're different," she added.

"Oh?" He tickled the baby under the chin, eliciting a giggle. Or perhaps a gurgle. Elen-ai had no idea.

"More...content," she said.

"I used to think there was no life outside the Family. There is, you know," he told her. "Be safe, Elen-ai."

She found the Prince in the Veertak library, a stack of books beside him. All the titles related to the gods or supernatural skills. "So you saw," she said.

He nodded. "There was a rip in my shirt, blood everywhere, and no wound. I would have to be pretty thick to not realise. Besides, I've heard the stories about the Councilwoman – her strange magic. I just thought it was made up to exaggerate her feats, but it seems I was wrong."

She wandered over to the books and picked one up. It was old, made by hand as was the case with all books, but with a cover made from some sort of timber. She suspected that it came from one of the other countries, judging by the design on the front. "What have you discovered?"

"Nothing substantial. I would need a lot more time in here to put anything meaningful together, but as far as I can tell, those whose faith is particularly strong have a variety of unusual skills. How that works, I cannot say."

"Is it that important to understand?" Elen-ai asked. She went over to the window. It looked out over the township to the calm, grey waters of lake Veertak beyond.

"To me, yes," he answered, closing the book he had been reading. "But this is not the most pressing matter. I have spoken with the Councillors. They will return to Herran and watch over my mother. You and I leave tomorrow."

"With guards?"

"No. A large party would draw too much attention, and possibly be off-putting to whoever tried to have me and mother killed," he said definitely. "I will say if anyone asks that this is a discreet visit, a personal journey. And if they ask, you are my aide."

She could agree with the wisdom in that approach. In fact, she likely would have proposed something similar herself. A large number of bodies to place in front of an oncoming blade were good and well, but she was too accustomed to stealth, to being able to slip along back roads and shadows. That could not be achieved when being accompanied by a retinue of guards. Besides, the Prince was right, better to lure out his would-be killer with the suggestion that he was vulnerable and naïve.

The Veertak's unexpected guests left early the next morning. The Prince had been treated to a very pleasant dinner the evening before – a Tak low had been slaughtered for the occasion - during which two of Varl and VArlena's children were present. While both were older than Gidyon's mother, they deferred to him with a politeness that was not feigned. Try as she might, Elen-ai could not see the Veertak family as a threat to the throne in any way. As she observed the courteous and genuinely respectful treatment of Gidyon, she crossed the Veertak family off her mental list of suspects.

It had been decided that the two Councillors were to return to Herran in the royal carriage. Elen-ai crossed the small courtyard to farewell them, surprised to find that she was sad to part ways with them.

"Thank you again for your help," she said to Freya.

The older woman took Elen-ai's hand in one of her own and pressed her thumb into the palm. "We do it happily." She smiled. "Ashtyn and I haven't had an adventure for a while, so it is enjoyable to do something to help a good cause."

"You are so perfect together," Elen-ai told Freya, shaking her head.

The older woman laughed. "It was not always so," she responded, her eyes crinkling with the emotion of whatever memory the comment elicited. "Good luck," she added, briefly reaching out a hand to touch Elen-ai's shoulder and squeezing it in a gesture of friendship.

"Thank you," Elen-ai replied. "I think we'll need it."

NINE

It seemed the Prince realised he could either speak with Elen-ai, or sit in silence for the entirety of their travel.

"Where did you go yesterday?" he asked after they had been on the road for a little over an hour. The Veertaks had generously loaned Gidyon a small carriage. Two of his original five trunks came with them, taking up nearly all of the space in the tiny vehicle, the rest had been back sent to the Palace with the Councillors. Gidyon sat on the driver's seat with Elen-ai while she drove, holding the reins of the two hearat drawing the carriage. She had been dismayed when he had decided not to squeeze in with the trunks – she had been looking forward to the serenity of solitude.

"I went to see a former member of the Family," she answered, her eyes on the road. Rather than traversing the main road that ran through sovereign land, Elen-ai had elected to take them on a less frequented route running through the Veertak and Tak lands. Gidyon had deferred to her judgment without comment or question.

"Why?"

"Mostly the people who leave the Family tend to see quite a lot of what goes on wherever they end up. It's a habit drilled in to all of us from a young age, noticing things."

"I thought that if you left the Family all ties were cut." The Prince looked confused.

Elen-ai twisted her mouth as she thought of how to explain it. "It's technically true. I think the point is more that leaving the Family requires you to build a life from the very beginning. To whatever extent you still see former brothers and sisters, it is infrequent, and never for very long."

Gidyon looked down, thinking. Then he nodded. "That makes sense. It's similar with my uncles."

"Oh?" Elen-ai casually adjusted the reins to bring the hearat under closer control as they entered a poorly maintained section of the road.

"If they want to marry that's perfectly fine, but they must give up any connection to the royal family, even their name. They have to take a common name."

"I suppose I haven't ever heard of a Queen's advisor with a family," Elen-ai said thoughtfully, manoeuvring the carriage around a particularly large pothole.

The rattle of the carriage as it negotiated the road claimed the silence that fell between them. The road wound along the shore of lake Veertak, the clear day reflected in the water's surface, rippled only by a slight breeze. At one stage, they passed the mill which manufactured the paper that the Veertak family supplied to the rest of the Queendom. Of course, the cloth scraps that were made into the pages came from all over the country in the same way that the animal skins which made the vellum - used for particularly important documents - came from the Tak family's animals. The interconnectedness of the Second Country was woven across the landscape if you cared to look for it.

Despite the fact that she preferred the bustle and activity of the city, Elen-ai had always held a particular fascination for the manner in which the countryside could be deceptively silent. It was filled with uncounted unseen animals going about their business, or the wind through the trees. She appreciated the fact that such noises masked the footsteps of someone coming up behind you just as effectively as the sound of the city, provided you knew what you were doing.

A few people came from the opposite direction, but once they passed the mill, they encountered barely any travellers. It meant that they entered the Tak territory almost completely unnoticed. Elen-ai felt far safer than she had the previous day. This was what she knew, not travelling along in a gilded monstrosity screaming out their presence to anyone even remotely within eyesight.

The landscape flattened out even further as they crossed into the Tak lands. Herds of livestock became visible, watched over by lazy youths and individuals whose age gave them a relaxed competence. Elen-ai pointed as the shimmering blue waters of the Tak lake came into view many hours after they had left lake Veertak behind.

"Can you teach me to defend myself?" Gidyon asked abruptly.

Elen-ai glanced at him in surprise. "What?"

"You had me on the ground instantly when we fought. And when we were attacked yesterday, the only thing I did was get stabbed." He ran a hand over his abdomen despite there being no trace there of the injury he had sustained.

"I started learning how to fight as soon as I could hold a weapon," Elen-ai told him.

"Does that mean I can't learn anything?" he challenged.

She shrugged in thought. He waited for her to respond with no outward sign of impatience.

"I can try. But I can't promise that it will stop you from getting stabbed," she said after she had considered it.

"Isn't that what you're supposed to do?" he asked.

"Well I didn't exactly succeed, did I?" she muttered.

To her surprise, he laughed. "I survived," he reassured her.

So that evening when they stopped, she did her full set of exercises. Lasting almost an hour, Elen-ai rigorously tested and used every muscle in her body, practising kicks, punches, and a series of tumbles and rolls to work her agility, strength, and focus. The Prince spent most of the time watching her, fascinated by the display of physical prowess. It left her some-what self-conscious, the way in which this young man seemed to observe her with such complete focus.

Elen-ai finished off her practice with a series of held pos-es, stretching out the muscles she was reasonably certain would ache in the morning. She had let herself become lax dur-ing her days with the Prince and she had paid the price when the hired thugs had tried to take his life. It was her good for-tune that Freya had been on hand to heal him. But Freya was gone now. Elen-ai could not afford to be in any condition other than her peak.

"Come here," she ordered Gidyon.

He scrambled awkwardly to his feet at her instruction.

"Let me guess. When you were taught to use a sword you were taught that people adhere to certain conventions of swordcraft?"

He nodded.

Elen-ai chuckled. "That's a polite lie told to people who are never going to have to actually fight for their life. When you're in a proper fight, you do anything it takes to win. Don't simply think about the conventions of swordcraft. Think about how you can kick, punch, bite, to win. Can you pull their hair?" To emphasise her point, she circled around him and quickly stepped forward, grabbing a handful of his hair in her fist and giving it a slight tug. "But let's look at other things first," she continued.

As the light faded, Elen-ai made Gidyon practice punching and kicking. He uttered no word of protest, merely doing as she bade with the same obedience that he showed his tutors in the Palace. When she saw that he was growing weary, she called a halt to the lesson and set about making a small fire. Despite the onset of Spring, it was still cool at night. Elen-ai may have been content to simply be a little cold, but she wasn't certain that the Prince's delicate sensibilities would be able to cope.

"You'll hurt in the morning," she cautioned him as they ate the food that had been given to them by the Veertaks.

He shrugged. "I should know how to do this," he said. "Thank you for teaching me," he added.

"Any time." Elen-ai found his genuine gratitude strangely touching.

"Is it safe to sleep?" Gidyon asked as they laid out bedrolls and blankets once dinner was finished. Despite the life of luxury he lived in the Palace, he had raised no objection to the prospect of sleeping in such basic conditions. He probably wouldn't even have said anything about being too cold had she not lit a fire, either.

"I'll keep watch, don't worry," Elen-ai reassured him.

"Don't you need to sleep?"

She shook her head. "Members of the Family are trained to require very little sleep."

"You should still sleep," he insisted.

"I promise I'll be fine."

"I want to take a watch," he said stubbornly.

It was going to be easier to give in than argue. "Fine, I'll wake you to take a few hours' watch just before dawn," she promised.

Satisfied, the Prince obediently went to sleep.

Elen-ai lay down on her bedroll so she was comfortable and closed her eyes, listening to the noises of the night. Insects moved, night animals shuffled. In the peace, she sorted through the cluttered collection of facts about the attempt on the life of both the Queen and her heir in an attempt to start trying to discover who was behind it.

The Prince dozed the next day as the carriage followed the shoreline of lake Tak. The lows from which the Tak family earned their significant fortune remained scattered across the land as far as the eye could see. Elen-ai had allowed Gidyon to take a few hours of watch but clearly, that had been more than the Prince was accustomed to missing of his regular night's sleep. She didn't mind. In fact, she preferred the absence of his questions which had become disconcertingly regular. She had almost preferred when he could barely stand to talk to her.

It took them the better part of the morning to reach the Tak family home. Having driven since it became light, they had been on the road for several hours already. Elen-ai drove up to the gates and nudged Gidyon awake. He blinked sleepily at her then straightened into wakefulness when he saw where they were.

"Gidyon, son of the Queen, here to visit the Tak family," Gidyon said to the guard outside with as much authority as he could muster, given the single-carriage retinue.

The guard dubiously eyed Gidyon, trying to decide whether or not he was serious. When too much time had elapsed the Prince snapped.

"Are you going to leave me waiting all day?"

At this, the guard moved, directing another guard to go and deliver the message to. In the time that they waited for news of their arrival to reach whoever was inside the house, Elen-ai looked around the yard. The carriage waiting in the corner told her that someone else was visiting. The meagre presence of the guards as more a formality than out of genuine concern spoke of the fact that the Tak family was secure in both their fortunes and political position. Neither piece of information was a great surprise. The Tak and the Aadran families – the two most powerful families in the Queendom - were closely aligned. It made sense from a practical point of view: the Aadran family held lands on which grain practically overflowed. Much of their harvest went to feed the Tak animals in winter. In turn, the two families would often combine their produce to leverage better prices for their wares in various markets. That closeness had been formalised through regular inter-family marriages. Their combined wealth rivalled the Queen's. Nobody really wanted to challenge them if it could be helped. It wouldn't end well. That knowledge lent both families a certain security.

The Tak family home as placed on top of a hill overlooking lake Tak. It was a low, sprawling affair constructed of thick timber that could only be from the Harete family's forest. Unlike the Veertak estate, there was no settlement built around the building. Most of the people who lived in the Tak province were scattered, living in homes - or shacks - where they watched herds of lows for the Tak family. The closest to a settlement was the great collection of mustering pens half a day's ride away where the lows designated for sale were driven before they fetched an outrageously high price for those wealthy enough to afford them.

No trees grew near the Tak house, giving it and the immediate area a curiously barren feel. The warm sun beat down on the two waiting visitors in the yard. Elen-ai pondered how the house stayed cool in the deepest summer days.

A man emerged from the main door, his broad shoulders and sun-browned skin speaking of many years' hard work. He seemed almost a different species to the Veertaks whose pale complexions and narrow frames were the legacy of a life devoted to poring over books indoors.

"Master Gidyon," the man boomed.

Gidyon alighted from the carriage, crossing the space to meet the man and clasp his hand in greeting. Next to him, the Prince who had looked so broad-shouldered and tall for his age in the Palace, seemed a thin boy.

"Serek." If Gidyon was aware of the difference in stature between himself and this man, he did not seem it. Instead, the charming diplomat had appeared, infusing the single word with warmth and familiarity.

"Word reached us of the attempt on your mother's life. It's a terrible thing for anyone to even consider." The man continued to speak in a loud tone. It gave the impression of simplicity on his part, but given he was a member of the seven families, that impression was unlikely to be an accurate one. Gidyon's hair shone like spun gold in the sunlight, a stark contrast against the bleached white of Serek's.

"Please come inside," Serek said. "Is this ah," he peered at Elen-ai and their unmarked, modest carriage, "all there is of your entourage?"

"Yes," Gidyon said, as though there were nothing unusual with someone of his position travelling in such a modest manner.

"Ah, well of course. I'll get our people to unpack your trunks. I'll show you and your ah...companion inside." Serek waved to two waiting servants. They immediately approached the carriage and began to unload the Prince's trunks.

Taking her cue, Elen-ai alighted and came to Gidyon's side.

"Elen-ai, this is Serek, head of the Tak family alongside his lovely wife Karan. Serek, may I present to you lady Elen-ai," Gidyon said.

A light smile touched Serek's mouth. "It's a pleasure to meet you," he told her with a sincerity that she did not quite believe.

As they followed him into the mansion, Elen-ai leaned in close to the Prince. "He thinks I'm your lover," she whispered in his ear, barely managing to keep the amusement from her tone.

Despite the proximity of their host preventing Gidyon from saying anything in reply, his expression of horrified surprise was reward enough.

"You've come in the midst of lunch - Arlena and her son Zekken are here on a business matter. If you're content to forgo a bathe, you would both be welcome to join us at the table," Serek offered.

"Zekken! I know him well." The Prince's voice contained genuine warmth. "I must confess, I would love a proper meal."

Gidyon increased his pace so that he was walking along-side Serek rather than behind him. Elen-ai remained trailing by a few steps. Serek paused and looked back at her in confusion. It was amusing to watch him try to understand the dynamic between the Prince and the woman he presumed to be Gidyon's lover. Elen-ai made no move to offer any form of clarification. It was far too funny to see her charge put in that awkward position.

They passed through the broad, open spaces of the house. Windows lined many of the walls, providing clear views of the land surrounding the house. It was quite pleasant, although Elen-ai wondered how lovely the vista would be in summer when the heat had scorched the grass to a pale yellow. Her personal preference was always for somewhere with shade and shadows.

Serek led them into the dining room, another wide, open affair that offered beautiful views of the surrounding country-side, in this instance, out onto lake Tak. The water glimmered blue in the sunlight, reflecting the brightness of the day into the room. The Tak family home was smaller than the Veertaks' but as equally grand in its own way, if not more suffused with understated yet confident wealth.

The scent of cooked meat met Elen-ai's nose. There was something particularly delicious about the smell. She presumed that it was meat from an animal butchered on that very day. Most of the produce in the markets of Herran was fish caught off the coast on which the capital was located. Keeping the meat of animals fresh for more than one or two days was near-ly impossible. Most of the meat Elen-ai had eaten over the course of her life had been outside the city in taverns where it was possible to bring a beast from the surrounding countryside near to the building and kill it there. Since the beginning of her time with the Prince, she had almost eaten more meat than over the course of her entire life.

"Gidyon!" The affectionate cry arose from the man seated at the table who Elen-ai presumed was Zekken. The second eldest child of the Aadran family, roughly of an age with Serek, he had a reputation for his plain face and lovely temperament.

"Zekken." Gidyon returned the warmth, going immediately to embrace the man, who stood to embrace the Prince. Zekken was known to frequently travel into Herran on business for his family. He had dined at the Palace on many of those visits as a guest of the Queen and representative of his family. That, Elen-ai assumed, was how he had come to be on such good terms with the Prince. She presumed his mother would be pleased that a member of her family had the ear of the future ruler. Perhaps Gidyon would find a supporter in the Aadran family.

"Gidyon, you've met Karan before," Serek said.

Gidyon turned to his hostess and offered her one of his charming smiles. "How could I forget? I often think on our discussion about the poetry of Ulate. It made me go back and re-read her earlier work."

Karan Tak was a woman who did not pay particular heed to the preference of being extremely thin, as did some women of wealth. While by no means fat, her curves attested to an appreciation of food as well as other fine things in life, such as poetry and music. This stature made her a somewhat imposing presence. However, under Gidyon's charm, she simply returned the smile, the corners of her eyes crinkling with genuine appreciation for the young man in front of her. "You must sit next to me. I'm very interested to hear what you have to say," she told him firmly.

"I'm so glad you said that," Gidyon responded, keeping a friendly hand Zekken's arm as he leaned forward to speak with Karan.

"And have you met Arlena Aadran?" Karan indicated the woman sitting opposite from her.

"Only once, several years ago when I was very young. But your reputation precedes you, lady Aadran." At this, Gidyon did leave Zekken's side and move around the table to take the proffered hand of the Aadran matriarch.

Her reputation certainly did precede her. The early death of her husband due to an unexpected illness had devastated Arlena, who had adored him. Despite being young enough to re-marry, she never had, managing the family estate with a formidable competence and Zekken as her trusted deputy.

"I've heard much about who you have grown into, young man." She took his hand and held it, scrutinising his face. She nodded once in a definite motion and released his hand. He went over to the seat which had been swiftly set for him with fine Katan plates and glass wine and water cups next to Karan Tak. The Tak family had begun to pay their servants more generously in the last few years. Perhaps someone had made them aware of the perils of a disgruntled employee. The movements of the servants were efficient and unobtrusive.

"Aren't you going to introduce us to your companion?" Karan asked innocently.

Gidyon's eyes widened with minute shock. The manner of their entrance meant that there was no point at which Elen-ai could have been mistaken as a servant, and for him not to introduce her was a terrible breach of etiquette. "Elen-ai, please forgive me. May I present to you lady Karan Tak and lady Arlena Aadran, lord Serek Tak and of course, lord Zekken Aadran. This is Elen-ai, my companion." Only Elen-ai would have caught the slight hesitation before he settled upon describing her as his companion. She suppressed a chuckle. She would enjoy that thought properly at a later time. As it was, she fixed her face into a smile and bowed in what she hoped was the appropriate manner.

"Please, join us Elen-ai," Karan invited her, indicating the space on the other side of her which a judicious servant was already setting with competent speed.

Karan and Serek had an amicable marriage that had produced two children who were a few years older than Gidyon and
lived in different parts of the estate, minding their own herds.
Karan was the eldest of four other children, one of whom Elen-
ai had been responsible for killing – her first kill, in fact. The
realisation was not uncomfortable but instead unusual as Elen-
ai sat down and looked at the woman's polite smile.

Serek and Zekken resumed their seats and the meal continued. Plates of lightly seared meat were put down in front of
Elen-ai and Gidyon, completing the illusion that they had always been present at the lunch.

"I'm sure Serek has already said this, but let me express
our relief to learn that your mother was not harmed in that awful attack on her life," Karan said. Perhaps Elen-ai was overly
suspicious, but she wondered if Karan's expression of sympa-
thy concealed some darker thought, or darker purpose. Certainly, she was a woman who would be willing to get her hands
dirty in pursuit of a goal.

"It's very kind of you to say lady Tak. It was a terrible
shock to hear," Gidyon responded, putting down a forkful of
his food to address her. He appeared to have no such suspicion.

"Do you have any idea why someone may seek to do such
an awful thing?" Zekken asked. There was a note of outrage in
his tone. His mother threw him a look that Elen-ai saw but he
did not due to the fact that he was focusing intently on Gidyon.
She frowned slightly to herself, wondering what was behind
such an expression of warning.

"Perhaps this is not the best topic for the table," Serek
suggested. Evidently, he had seen Arlena's unimpressed expression.

"Quite right," Arlena added. She was several years older
than the Taks which gave her words a certain authority. "How
about we move on to more pleasant things. Elen-ai, was it?
From where do you come?"

All attention turned to Elen-ai. The Prince opened his mouth, but Elen-ai quickly spoke before he got the chance.

"I come from a merchant family. Cloth, mostly. I met Gidyon in the marketplace one day," she said.

"And how is it you two came to be travelling alone in such a nondescript carriage?" Karan's smirk suggested that she thought she knew exactly how this had come to occur. If she was curious as to why they had decided to stop at the Tak family's residence, she did not ask - yet.

"Well actually we were on the way to the Royal country estate when we were attacked," Gidyon responded.

"Surely not! Are you alright?" Karan exclaimed. Her surprise certainly seemed genuine enough.

"Yes, fortunately. But we thought it best to travel in a less conspicuous manner," he said.

"For a member of the royal family to be attacked on the road. It's outrageous," Arlena added, that outrage clear in her stiffened posture. Her son's contribution and silent agreement was to turn white with shock. Elen-ai, watching the reactions of everybody at the table certainly thought she saw genuine surprise on all faces, but appearances could be deceptive as she – the person who had killed Karan's brother – knew all too well.

"Why would anyone be so audacious as to do such a thing?" Serek's demand was aimed at nobody in particular.

The Prince answered him nevertheless. "It was a deliberate attempt on my life, I'm afraid."

"But this is madness. First the Queen, now you. Why?" Karan interjected.

"Well lady Tak, I can not be completely sure, but I'm reasonably certain that it is because my mother has named me her heir," Gidyon said calmly.

The silence that followed was broken by Serek dropping his glass wine cup.

TEN

The Taks and Aadrans sat at the table for several silent moments, simply staring at Gidyon. He did not seem particularly perturbed by their shock or indeed, that aware of it. He had calmly returned to the meat in front of him as though he hadn't announced something so monumental.

"Are you quite serious?" Karan leaned forward, her mouth a grim slash in a face which had been so pleasant only a few moments before.

"Of course he is. We've all heard the speculation for weeks now." Arlena spoke before Gidyon could respond, her own face far from the visage of someone delirious with joy.

Gidyon sat and ate his meal in silence, letting the quiet argument that took place across the table ebb and flow over him. Elen-ai watched with curiosity, wondering how he was going to respond to the clear dissatisfaction that had met his announcement. Eventually, he put down his cutlery and spoke. "Would you mind if I ask what your objections are?"

"Gidyon, it's not even a question of objecting to *you*, my dear. It's that no man can hold the throne," Karan explained in a somewhat patronising manner.

"So you're concerned about the change this would bring, then?" Gidyon asked, apparently unoffended by Karan's tone.

He waited a beat for everybody to register the uncomfortable tenor to the silence, then spoke again. "Change has always been resisted. My great-great grandmother's reforms on education were met with much resistance. Or her grandmother's

111

decision to allow men to lead families and hold land? She almost faced down a revolt for that. Yet surely the Second Country is better off for those changes."

Gidyon was certainly persuasive. Elen-ai's own lingering resistance to the prospect of him taking the throne was weakened in the face of his argument.

"This is a matter of maintaining –" Karan began to say, but Gidyon cut her off patiently.

"Serek controls the Tak family estate along with you. And he's not even Tak by birth."

"That's different. We're talking about the Royal family," Arlena interjected before Karan could respond. Unlike the younger woman, she did not speak down to the Prince but rather in the cool, direct tone of business.

"What exactly is the concern with a male holding a throne? If it is to maintain stability, I have pledged to marry outside the seven families. Any child of mine will be as apolitical as I am." Gidyon calmly took another bite of his meal after he finished speaking.

"Gidyon, are you certain about that?" Zekken spoke for the first time since Gidyon had made his announcement. He was the only person in the room who looked as though he was actually concerned for Gidyon rather than about the change him being named heir would bring. For someone who was so involved in the maintenance of his family's position, he certainly did not seem to have the heart for the power games of the Queendom.

Gidyon turned to face Zekken. "I have thought long and hard over it, Zek. And it is the best solution. It is my duty to make certain that stability and the prosperity of the Queendom remains. This is the way to do it. And I ask the support of both of your families to my claim." Gidyon turned back to address his later comments to the rest of the room.

"Well I for one have no doubt about your ability to be a good ruler," Zekken said warmly.

"Unfortunately you do not speak for our family, Zekken. I do. Gidyon, might I have some time before I give you an answer?" Arlena's question was not really question. She did not look at her son as she addressed Gidyon, but Elen-ai could sense her displeasure with his rush to offer support that was not his to give. However, unlike Erek Rasatan, who had spoken in open disagreement with the stance of his family, Zekken, despite looking as though he wanted to defy his mother, remained silent.

"Lady Aadran, I would expect nothing less. You would not enter into a business agreement without due consideration. This is not that different. I presume you would also like some time, Karan and Serek?"

"If you please," Serek answered before his wife could.

"Certainly. Perhaps I may take you up on that offer of a bathe, then." Gidyon put down his cutlery and dabbed at his mouth before standing. Elen-ai followed his lead, feeling far less comfortable and confident than the Prince looked.

"Before you go. Lady Elen-ai, may I ask what you think of all this?" Karan's question arrested Elen-ai's escape, much to her dismay.

She faced the table of people whose scrutiny was now turned to her. Being so noticed made her feel profoundly uncomfortable. This room full of people awaiting to hear her opinion on a political matter was a far cry from her preferred place within the shadows. She opened her mouth, then thought for a moment, reflecting that she must look quite stupid with her mouth hanging open.

"I think that Gidyon will make a fine ruler. I've never seen someone with more charm, intelligence, or dedication to his role," she said honestly. "And I've been given a perspective that means that my opinion is an informed one."

"Such admiration," Arlena commented. Elen-ai could not tell whether or not it was meant as an insult, a compliment, or something else entirely.

"I'll have someone show you to quarters," Serek said after a moment, a servant scurrying forward at his words, to usher them out of the room.

Elen-ai and Gidyon followed the servant to rooms which had been prepared for them. To one side was an alcove that housed a large tub. The water in it drained down underneath the house and presumably, down the hill. It was a far less sophisticated system than the complicated pipes that ran through the Palace but a clever one nevertheless.

The high ceilings of the Tak household gave the room a very airy, light quality that most would have found pleasant. However, the tension that had bloomed in Elen-ai at the politics around the table left her unable to appreciate her surroundings. She longed for the silence and shadow of the Family's home in Herran with an acute ache. There was something about the way everybody spoke with double meanings and careful consideration of their own interests that left a bad taste in her mouth, and a lingering uncertainty of what was true or false.

"Do you really think that of me?" Gidyon asked once the servant had left.

Elen-ai finished her inspection of the room and turned to face him. "I do."

Indeed, it was true. The fact that she had no great personal affection for him did not detract from her conclusion that he would make a fine ruler one day. Somewhere between Herran and the Tak estate, she had arrived at a sort of peace with the prospect of a male on the throne, provided that male was Gidyon.

"That's...very kind," the Prince said, an odd look on his face.

Elen-ai didn't bother trying to decipher it. "Either you bathe or I will," was all she said, looking to dispel the emotion of the moment. She still wasn't entirely certain that she actually liked the Prince, but she didn't have to like him to think he would be a good ruler.

Gidyon quickly stripped off his outer clothes, laying them to one side so that a servant could take them and clean them. Elen-ai turned away to afford him some modesty.

"How long will we stay here?" she asked, trying to make the fact that he was naked only a few steps away from her less awkward.

A splash signalled that he had gotten into the bath. "I'm not sure. Perhaps a few days," he called to her.

"Do you think they'll support you?" She idly stretched out her arms. Her muscles, sore from the punishing exercise that she had put herself through the previous evening, complained.

"I would be surprised if they chose to actively not support me," he responded over the slosh of water.

"But that's not the same as actively support," Elen-ai noted.

"Quite right. If I had to guess, I think that they will remain neutral, make no public declaration either way until I have secured a claim by myself, or lost the ability to make a claim."

"How would you lose the ability to make a claim?" Elen-ai turned, forgetting that he was in the bath. She quickly turned back, hoping that Gidyon hadn't realised – not that she had seen anything of note.

"Someone would likely procure an alternate heir from somewhere." The sound of water being displaced told Elen-ai that Gidyon had gotten out of the bath.

"Do you trust the Taks and Aadrans?" Elen-ai asked, still studying the wall with a concerted interest.

"I do not distrust them," he replied. "You should bathe too," he added.

"I'm fine, thank you," she said automatically, noticing the absence of any significant declaration of trust.

"You are supposed to be my lover, aren't you?" He sounded faintly accusatory. "You can turn around, by the way," he added.

She did as he bade, finding that he had just finished pulling on a pair of trousers and was buttoning them up. "It will be safer if people think you're travelling with a lover rather than a bodyguard," she pointed out. Perhaps she could have posed as a servant, but the discomfort the Prince felt at people thinking she was sharing his bed gave her a sense of juvenile glee.

Again, a look of faint pain crossed the Prince's face. "I do not even disagree. It's just..."

"Not a pleasant thought to think of us as lovers?" Elen-ai suggested when he did not complete his sentence.

"It's an odd thought," he corrected. "Anyway. My lover should be clean," he returned to his original point.

Muttering in discontent, Elen-ai checked to ensure that he wasn't watching, then swiftly removed her clothes and climbed into the tepid water. Grabbing the animal fat bar of soap, she scrubbed quickly then heaved herself from the bath, grabbing for a towel just in case the Prince wasn't quite as respectful of her modesty as she was of his. She wasn't certain why she was so uncomfortable with the prospect of them seeing each other naked – children of the Family often saw each other in various states of undress – but she was. It seemed that her concern was unfounded, though. Gidyon was absorbed in the pages of a book he had pulled from one of the trunks.

Elen-ai went to pull the clothes she had been wearing back on but then reconsidered. Gidyon did have a point about her appearance. If she was to pretend to be his lover, putting back on clothes that were covered in dust from their travels was not going to be acceptable. Holding the towel tightly around herself, she went to the trunk with her clothes in it and rifled around, searching for something to wear.

Gidyon turned to look at her, arching an eyebrow. "Are you alright?"

Elen-ai looked up at him, clutching the towel to her chest. "I'm trying to look the part," she snapped, grabbing the first things that she could find.

"Well you certainly don't look it right now," he commented in a haughty tone.

"Obviously not!" she snarled, slamming the lid of the trunk closed and moving a little distance away from him to pull on the clothes she had found. Fortunately, the black trousers and burgundy tunic that she had grabbed at random seemed to be an acceptable outfit, so there was no need for her to change in front of Gidyon again.

"I wonder what exactly they're discussing," Gidyon said thoughtfully, putting his finger to mark the place on the page as he looked up in thought.

"I could always find out for you," Elen-ai offered as she began to transfer her blades from one set of clothes to the other.

"How?" He looked at her, keeping his finger firmly on the page.

"I could get in unnoticed." Elen-ai shrugged offhandedly, her fingers deftly concealing the blades.

She could tell by the way his eyes took on a faraway look for a moment that Gidyon seriously considered it, but then he shook his head. "I think I'd prefer you by my side."

"Just thought I'd offer."

He threw an amused look at her before returning his attention to his book.

Approximately an hour later a servant came to take them to hear the Taks and Aadrans' decision. In that time, Gidyon had read while Elen-ai had taken the opportunity to pray, sitting in a chair cross-legged and closing her eyes. Despite the unpleasantness of suspense, a curious serenity had descended on the bedroom, perhaps indicative that she and the Prince might finally be getting along.

The Taks and Aadrans had moved from the dining room into a parlour room which contained several stringed instruments on various stands. Elen-ai recalled that Karan was a skilled musician, although she felt there would be no opportunity to verify this today. Perhaps she would be able to learn something else, though, if she watched carefully enough.

The late afternoon sun came through a window, sending a gentle glow onto the walls.

"My apologies for keeping you waiting so long," Arlena said. Given the frequent Tak and Aadran marriages, they were effectively one extended family. As the oldest person in the room, her seniority meant that she was the voice for them all.

"It's no trouble," Gidyon answered easily. He showed no sign of unease or concern, even though the support of these people before him could secure his claim to the throne if they pledged their support to him then and there.

"We have discussed at length the matter at hand. While there is no question about your competence, that is not the only issue at play. Ultimately, we will not speak against you, but Gidyon, we cannot declare our support for you. In this, we remain decidedly neutral." Arlena spoke with a directness that gave no ambiguity or room for argument.

"I appreciate your honesty Arlena. I must say, it is what I would do in your position." Gidyon smiled faintly, ambling over to a spare seat. Elen-ai followed his lead, reclining in an armchair of her own.

"You are very gracious in accepting this news," Arlena noted. "May I offer you a piece of advice?"

"Given the long battle I face with the other families, I welcome your wisdom, Arlena."

It did not escape Elen-ai's notice that Gidyon was calling the matriarch of one of the country's most powerful families by her first name. She was sure Arlena had also noticed it.

"I would be wary of the Katan family. I cannot expect that they would support you."

Gidyon's smile was thin. "I would be a fool to expect they would. Especially given they are the most likely to be able to challenge my claim."

"I researched it this afternoon. My mother had one sister. She married Enges, one of the Katan sons. They have a twelve-year-old daughter, Serenah. My cousin. She would fit a claim if it came to it. Although her father is known, which may weigh against her."

The mystery of what Gidyon had been intently reading while they waited revealed, Elen-ai watched in fascination as he tossed the knowledge of his cousin's possible claim out into the room with a nonchalance she was sure he did not feel.

"Rest assured, Gidyon. If such a claim were to be made public, we would not speak to it, either," Serek noted.

Gidyon's smile was icy. "And in so doing, earn the frustration from both of us."

"Likely," Karan replied with a little laugh. Elen-ai glanced over to Zekken. He stood with his back to the room, staring out the window at the dying light, hands in his pockets. If she was any judge – and she was – his stiff shoulders and clenched jaw suggested he had argued that the Taks and Aadrans should support Gidyon's right to succeed his mother. She wondered why he would have so vehemently supported a male ascending to the throne. Perhaps his anger was a show devised to misdirect attention away from the possibility that the Taks and Aadrans had attempted to kill the Queen and her son in some play for greater power. After all, it seemed everyone was aware of the Queen's supposedly secret decision to name Gidyon her heir. Somehow though, Elen-ai couldn't quite believe Zekken was so superb an actor.

"May I ask your honest opinions?" Gidyon leaned forward, the picture of earnestness.

"Certainly," Arlena responded.

"How likely do you think is it that the Katan family is behind the attempt on my and my mother's lives?"

Voicing such a question left a silence in the room. Zekken actually turned back from his scrutiny of the sunset and looked at his mother, Serek, and Karan. The fact that he said nothing made Elen-ai wonder if he had been directed to not speak at all. She wondered what he had said. She should have argued harder with Gidyon to eavesdrop on the conversation.

It seemed nobody wanted to be the first person to speak. Eventually, Arlena once again spoke for the room. "Nothing is outside the realm of possibility. But I would be very surprised if they were behind those attacks, Gidyon. If it were to be discovered, their credibility, along with any hope of Serenah claiming the throne, would be lost."

Gidyon thought for a moment, then nodded in curt agreement. It seemed then that the matter was settled, and would not be discussed any further.

Dinner was a modest affair; a selection of food brought into the sitting room. Elen-ai made herself unnoticed, sinking into her chair while she watched everybody else. Gidyon appeared to harbour no ill will toward his hosts or Arlena for their decision, conducting an animated conversation with Karan about the works of the poet Ulate. Arlena and Serek spoke in quiet tones about business deals without mentioning anything particularly specific, while Zekken ate in what looked like a moody silence. At one point he came to sit in the vacant armchair next to Elen-ai.

"Take good care of Gidyon, please," he said to her, his face earnest.

It took Elen-ai a moment to realise that he didn't actually know of her place as a member of the Family, but was asking in a more emotional sense. Her fleeting suspicion that he might have been merely pretending to support Gidyon's claim to the throne seemed ever more flimsy.

"I plan to," she replied, her reply somewhat stilted by her initial concern that he may know of her true role at Gidyon's side.

"I can only assume that whatever this is between you two is relatively new," he continued.

"What makes you think this?" she asked.

"I feel he would have told me about something like this. I come to Herran every few weeks on business for mother. I try always to speak with Gidyon when I am there. He is a good young man." Tenderness infused his voice as he spoke of the Prince.

Zekken's unmarried state was the subject of much speculation. Elen-ai's favourite explanation was that he had a particular fondness for the lows of the Tak family. More widely accepted as an explanation though, was that his mother had never authorised a marriage for him because she did not wish to lose her deputy to marriage. It was certainly what Elen-ai had always assumed. Perhaps the fact that he had never gotten the opportunity to be a father himself meant that he had a certain paternal sentiment toward Gidyon. But Elen-ai still found it odd.

"What are you to the Prince, exactly?" she asked Zekken so softly that nobody aside from him could hear it.

Like Serek, Zekken's simple demeanour was a useful tool. The simplicity that Zekken donned remained completely unchanged but for the most negligible tilt of his head as he placed her under a greater scrutiny than had originally been conducted.

"I am his friend, I hope," Zekken answered, his voice just as soft as hers. "I have known him his whole life, and I watched him as he grew up."

"How did Queen Latana let you see him from such a young age?" Elen-ai wondered aloud.

Zekken may have had control over his face, but Elen-ai was not watching his face. She was paying attention to the vein in his throat which jumped at the mention of the Queen's name. "The Queen's reasons are her own," he said in careful reply.

Musing on what she may have just learned, Elen-ai felt it was time to act the devoted lover. "Tell me a story of Gidyon when he was young," she enthused.

Either accepting the diversion or genuinely distracted by the question, Zekken launched into a retelling of Gidyon being only six or seven years old, demanding to play hide and seek and somehow hiding for several hours in plain sight under- neath a chair. It was a pointless story that only someone with genuine affection for the child could truly find interesting, but Elen-ai nevertheless played along, laughing where it was ap- propriate and demanding another such tale when it was fin- ished. As he told her these stories, Elen-ai saw that his face, which she like the rest of the world had initially thought plain, lit up with a certain appeal when he laughed or smiled. There was something peculiarly charming about such reserve in showing such animation and light.

Only many hours later when she lay on the very opposite side of the bed to Gidyon – both of them had refused to allow the other to sleep on the small divan in the room – did she re- turn to the thoughts raised by her conversation with Zekken.

Gidyon was still awake, she could tell by his breathing.

"May I ask something?" she said into the space between them.

His reply was immediate. "Certainly."

"What if a Queen falls in love?"

"The duty of the Queen is not to love one of her subjects more than the others, but to love them equally and well." From the cadence, Elen-ai could tell that he was reciting something he had learned long ago.

"And if she does love one more than the rest?"

"Then she must try to forget it. Why are you asking?"

"I just wondered," she said vaguely.

Gidyon seemed satisfied with her response, lapsing back into silence temporarily.

"Have you ever been in love, Elen-ai?" There was a soft intimacy to his question brought out by the darkness.

She didn't even need to think about it. There was no place in her heart to love anyone other than a member of the Family. "No."

"Alright then, goodnight," Gidyon said comfortably, turning over with a rustle and sigh.

Elen-ai lay in the darkness, thinking about love. The closest she had ever come to something like love was with a tavern keeper in Herran two years previously. He hadn't been her first lover, but he had been the first that had made her want to return to him, which was something. Tavern keepers were treasures to the Family. They saw much and were often unnoticed in their own observance. They often knew the comings and goings of an area's inhabitants more so than many of those individuals' own lovers. Elen-ai had come into Tim-en's bar one evening seeking information about the habits of a particular merchant. He had given her the answers she sought than boldly suggested she remain with him for the evening. While he had known she was a member of the Family, unlike many others might have, he had shown no fear of her. He treated her with an offhand callousness, tender only in the throes of passion.

Elen-ai wasn't even certain if she had liked him that much, yet something about him compelled her to return to his bed again and again. She lost count of the number of times that she had slipped into his room in the latest hours of the night after she had completed some business of her own. No matter how or when she entered the room, he had never looked at her with surprise. He had simply drawn her to him, his body ready for hers, his mouth soft and hungry against her skin. Somewhere between desire and love she had found herself unable to stay away from him until the day he had died in a tavern brawl. She had tracked down his killer and exacted a swift retribution, more out of respect for Tim-en's memory than her own need for some vengeful farewell. Often in the intervening time, she had wondered how much more difficult his death would have been had actually loved him.

That night she dreamed of love and betrayal.

ELEVEN

Gidyon and Elen-ai stayed three more days in the Tak family home. Any animosity that their hosts may have felt toward Gidyon due to the Queen's decision to break with history and make her heir a male was not reflected in their hospitality. He was offered every comfort, shown the greatest courtesy, and even taken on several tours of the Tak estate. Wherever he went, Elen-ai followed, observing their hosts to see if someone slipped, if someone gave away an indication that they may have been involved in the attacks on Gidyon and Latana's lives. She saw nothing conclusive.

One day, they even ventured into the Aadran lands with Zekken, riding kittanae generously loaned to them by the Tak family. The graceful beasts were magnificent to ride on. Elen-ai found the barely-tamed power of the large cat intoxicating, requiring skill and concentration to maintain control of the animal as they sped across the countryside. She could see why they were such a symbol of wealth and power.

It was harvest time, just before the onset of summer. Gidyon seemed mesmerised by the undulating lake of golden-ripe crops. Standing on the crest of a small hill, the trio observed the grain being cut and bundled. There was something profoundly sad about the beautiful ripping sea being thoughtlessly hacked at and taken away piece by piece. Zekken explained that two harvests occurred each year, with every third half-year devoted to keeping the field fallow. Gidyon listened, even nodding at various points, but his eyes were on the dismantling of that magnificent sight.

Over those three days, the temperature suddenly became warmer, as though the land had decided that it was summer time. The twilight lengthened into an extended show of light, and each evening Gidyon would sit and watch it with whoever within the Tak home happened to be idle at that time. Elen-ai seemed to have been accepted as his silent companion, more comfortable to simply observe than speak. Or perhaps her aptitude for slipping into the shadows meant that she was mostly unnoticed.

On midmorning of the second day, Gidyon received a response to the message he had sent his mother from the Veertak estate. The servant brought it into the parlour room where Gidyon and Elen-ai were sitting with Serek and Arlena.

"Pardon me, but a messenger has just arrived from the Palace," the servant said, nervously looking at Gidyon. Word of Gidyon's position as heir to the throne had spread through the house. The servants looked at him with awe, discomfort, or a combination of the two. The Prince either didn't notice or pretended not to notice. Elen-ai was certain it was the latter.

Gidyon took the leather envelope held out to him, offering the servant a smile. "Thank you." He turned to Serek and Arlena. "I may read this in our room, if you would excuse me."

Upon receiving an absentminded nod from Arlena, he turned on his heel and walked out of the room. Elen-ai slid out of her chair and joined him, his constant silent shadow.

Once inside the room that they had become accustomed to sharing, he unbound the leather. Elen-ai took a quick glance at it to determine that it had not been opened before, but the wax sealing the envelope shut was untouched. There were several thick pages. Gidyon read through them quickly, then once more at a slower pace. Elen-ai watched his face closely. She saw flashes of anger, confusion, and perhaps even upset as he read different sections. After several minutes had passed he put down the message.

"My uncle, Silius wants me to come home."

"Is that what your mother said?" Elen-ai asked.

"No. It's what he said. He wrote to me."

"Not your mother?"

"He said she is unable to write following the attack – her hand was injured. So she asked him to write down what she dictated. Which he did. Adding his own comments along the way." Gidyon's mouth was a thin line.

"What does your mother think?"

"According to what Sil wrote, she says that my plan is a good one, but to be careful."

"Does Silius normally contradict the Queen?" Elen-ai wondered.

Gidyon shrugged. "Not in public. If he disagrees with something she wants to do though, he will tell her in private."

Elen-ai thought back to the conversation she had witnessed between the Queen and her brother. For the briefest of moments, she entertained the possibility that Silius may have ordered the attempt on the lives of the Queen and Gidyon. Frustration over the Queen's decision and perhaps even rage over the fact that Latana was appointing a man to succeed her when he himself had been denied that right despite being the first born would certainly be a strong motivation. But she could not dismiss the expression she had seen on his face when talking with his sister. It was a look of profound love, and that meant she could not quite bring herself to find him a truly viable suspect of such a crime.

It was on the third night that she and Zekken spoke alone again. The Prince was engrossed in a game of fa'thong with Karan, Serek, and Arlena. Elen-ai had curled herself into a chair and was reading a book of stories that she had chanced upon. Zekken sat beside her, staring into a glass of liquor. He suddenly looked up at her and spoke, drawing her out of a story about a princess who had lost her memory.

"It seems you prefer to observe than be observed, lady Elen-ai."

Echoing the gesture of Gidyon a few days ago, Elen-ai put her finger to the page to keep her place. "It is difficult to learn when one is at the centre of things, Zekken," she replied, casting a glance over at the adults and Gidyon who were enthralled by the game of strategy and chance.

"What have you learned then?" Zekken asked.

Elen-ai shifted her gaze to him, trying to gauge how intoxicated he may be. Thinking quickly back over what she had seen, she decided that the answer was not very. "That Karan and Serek do not love each other, but are comfortably amicable, which sometimes can be better than love. That your mother has worked hard to ensure that she is not solely dependent upon the Tak lows for coin, and that you are the Queen's lover."

Zekken's hand jerked involuntarily at her final comment, although his expression did not change. The liquor jumped out of his glass and landed on his shirt.

"I beg your pardon?" He did not pay any heed to the strong-smelling stain spreading across his shirt.

Elen-ai looked down at the page quickly to note the number and closed the book, smoothing her hands over the cover. "Don't worry, your secret is safe."

"What makes you think this?" Zekken leaned forward, the picture of amused interest, albeit a little bit too interested to be truly convincing.

Elen-ai met his gaze and tilted her head. "Why else would you think that he's your son?"

Zekken leaned forward and dropped his voice further. "Even if I thought that, it's a large leap of logic to claim I'm Queen Latana's lover."

"There's no other reason that she would make certain that you were able to see Gidyon from the time he was born," Elen-ai challenged, her voice just as quiet. It wouldn't have mattered, the other four were totally engrossed in the game on the other side of the room.

"This is preposterous," Zekken told her.

"Then why are you still talking to me?" she asked. The suspicion that had germinated and bloomed in her mind seemed to be completely correct. A tight smugness coiled around her chest at the knowledge that she had discovered what the Queen had kept from everyone, even as some part of her wished she did not know to what foolish depths her Queen had sunk.

"Who are you?" Zekken asked, his eyes narrowing as he looked at her.

"A friend," she said quietly. "My interest is in protecting Gidyon."

Zekken thought for a moment, the grey of his eyes dark in the low light. "Tana did say she would make sure he was taken care of," he admitted finally.

"I think you had better tell me everything," Elen-ai suggested.

Zekken threw a cautious glance at the other side of the room. "Perhaps a stroll outside?" he offered.

The night was not quite as warm as it would be in a few weeks' time, but the chill of even a few days earlier was no longer present. The sound of insects infused the evening air, making it a beautiful night. Elen-ai paid it very little heed, more intent on what Zekken would reveal to her.

"What can I say?" Zekken asked once they had put a reasonable distance between themselves and the walls of the house.

"I think it would be easier if you start at the beginning," Elen-ai suggested.

He took a breath. "If you breathe a word of this to the wrong person, the consequences you invite..."

"I have no interest in gossiping," Elen-ai cut him off, her tone flat.

"Alright then. I suppose I don't have a choice in telling you this, do I?"

"Not really."

"Well, it started at one of the first seasons - when the men of the seven families come to the Queen and -"

"I know what the seasons are," Elen-ai interrupted.

"Of course. Sorry. Well, the seasons are useful for more than just the creation of an heir. It's an opportunity for the families to use their eligible men as informal emissaries. Mother had sent me to speak with Latana about trading directly across the border we hold with the Third Country. At the time, Tana was the heir. She took the throne two years later when her own mother passed. So I went to try and secure the goodwill of a future Queen." He paused and took a breath. "That first night when I saw her she had just turned sixteen. She was a girl. I was just a boy myself. Her hair was down, flowing around her shoulders, and I fell into her eyes. I've never seen eyes quite like hers, you know. I was too afraid to even approach her," he admitted with a little laugh.

Elen-ai suspected Zekken had never told anyone this. Perhaps there was a certain sense of liberation to be felt in telling a secret kept hidden for so long. She said nothing, letting him tell the story at his own pace.

"She took someone else to her bed that first night. But on the second night, I made sure that I spoke with her. Mother had asked me to complete a task and I had to at least try. Quite quickly we stopped talking about trade and started talking about all manner of things. Her beauty was nothing compared to...do you know what an incredible woman she is, Elen-ai?" He paused mid-stride and turned to face Elen-ai, almost entreating her to agree with him.

"She certainly is a formidable woman," Elen-ai said.

"Her mind is the true jewel. And the most remarkable thing happened. She found me worth her time. She took me to her bed that night and has never been with anyone else since."

"Wouldn't that raise suspicion?" Elen-ai asked.

"How could that be proved? Who would want to admit that they had not been chosen by the Queen?"

Elen-ai nodded slowly and resumed pacing down the hill toward the shore of lake Tak. Zekken followed her. "So Gidyon was conceived in that first year?" she verified.

"Yes. And I have been as much of a father to him as I can over the years."

"I assume you were aware of the Queen's plan to put him on the throne," Elen-ai commented instead of asking outright.

She could easily see his face in the dark as he nodded.

"You two have played a dangerous game," Elen-ai said, feeling anger stir within her. "And the outcome might be disastrous for the whole Queendom." The small part of her that had initially regretted that she had discovered the Queen's secret was now screaming. It was far worse than she could possibly have imagined. It seemed almost profane to know of this sort of foolishness in her ruler.

"We cannot help how we feel about each other," Zekken protested.

"But you can help what you do about it," she hissed, anger stoked by his reply. "You and the Queen playing at being a family when, if discovered, it could tear apart the whole country. It makes everything so much harder for Gidyon than it already was."

He looked at her, his face defiant. "People have done worse things for worse reasons."

Elen-ai threw her arms up, the anger sparking into flame. "They say nobody is quite so self-righteous and unwilling to listen to reason as a person in love. I now see what is meant by such a claim." Disgusted, she turned away from him to look out at the expanse of the lake. It stretched away from sight, serene and massive in the calm evening. The white of the moon glistened on the tips of the tiny ripples stirred by the slight breeze.

"Will you still keep him safe?" Zekken pleaded.

Elen-ai sighed heavily, more for show than anything else. "For him. Not for either of you. And if this results in disorder or chaos, it's on both of your selfish heads."

"Will you find out who tried to kill both of them?" Zekken asked, his tone subdued. Probably it was in response to her anger rather than because he truly believed he had done anything wrong.

"That's what I'm trying to do," Elen-ai snarled. She turned and stalked back toward the lights of the house. Halfway there, she paused and returned to Zekken, who was following her at a more leisurely pace. "What does your mother know of this?" she asked, as an uncomfortable thought occurred to her.

"Not exactly everything. She knows of my feelings for Tana, but not that they are returned. Nor does she know the exact nature of my relationship to Gidyon."

Elen-ai breathed out through her nose, willing herself to be calm. Anger was not encouraged by the Family. It did not lead to a well made or well executed plan. "This keeps getting better and better," she muttered to herself.

Without another word, she turned on her heel and stalked back up the hill, taking a running leap as she reached one of the house's walls. She scaled it easily and alighted on the roof, making no sound in her landing or as she moved along the tiles, using the skills of the Family to remove her silhouette from the sight of anyone who may be outside and glancing up. She didn't care if Zekken had seen her climb the wall or what he may have thought. As far as she was concerned, his opinion was irrelevant.

She traversed the extensive length of the house, fragments of conversation floating up to her. She paid them no heed, instead working to make herself as light as possible so that even she could not hear her own footfalls. The roof of the house was peaked, answering her question of where the heat would go on hot summer days. To run along the very apex required quite a degree of concentration. Once she had run back and forth a few times, she had calmed down at least enough to go back inside.

Everybody was still in the parlour room when she finally returned. The game had evidently finished and a discussion on where to find the best tailors had taken its place. Elen-ai was bored with the stifling confines of polite society, yet even her walk with Zekken had been an absence from the Prince's side that she should not have taken, especially given that the revelation of Zekken and Latana's relationship gave yet more motivation for why someone might want to kill the Prince due to the political imbalance he represented. So she returned to her chair and picked up her book once more.

"Did you enjoy your walk?" Serek asked her from across the room.

Inwardly sighing, Elen-ai again put her finger on the page to mark her progress. "The lake is quite lovely in the moonlight," she answered, mustering a smile.

"It's a shame you won't be here in a few weeks, the middle of summer is particularly beautiful. Especially when the flowers on the lake's shore bloom," Karan said.

"I've heard tales of the summer flowers of Lake Tak," Gidyon enthused. "I am sorry that we won't be able to see them."

"Perhaps another time," Serek suggested. The offer certainly did seem genuine.

"I'd like that," Gidyon replied happily.

Elen-ai looked around the room, her eye resting on Arlena. The dowager sat quietly, her head slightly bowed. The restful pose was deceptive. Arlena was clearly deep in thought. The possibility that had entered Elen-ai's mind earlier, that Arlena could be behind the attacks on Gidyon and his mother, returned as she regarded the formidable woman. It was entirely likely that she knew far more about her son's relationship with the Queen than Zekken thought she did. If the truth about Zekken's connection to either Gidyon or Latana were to be revealed, the Aadran family would be disgraced. Regardless of their wealth, power, and the land they held, the other families – even the Taks – would turn on them. It wasn't even outside the realm of possibility that the Aadran family's lands would be forcibly taken from them if her son's affair with the Queen were discovered. The people who lived and worked on them might welcome the forces of another family, one whose members did not seek to break the sacred neutrality that was supposed to be maintained in relation to Royal family. Elen-ai did not doubt that Arlena would take the necessary steps to protect her family. Whether she was ruthless enough to attempt to kill the Queen and the Queen's son – her grandson – was the question. She had seen worse things done by better people. It certainly was a theory that Elen-ai could not dismiss out of hand.

That was a theory to which Elen-ai returned later that evening as she and the Prince lay on their respective sides of the bed.

"Where did you and Zek go tonight?" Gidyon asked.

"Down to the shores of the lake," Elen-ai replied.

"Why did he come back before you?"

Elen-ai paused, trying to decide how much she should tell Gidyon. "I wanted a bit of time to myself," she decided upon.

"Why?"

"He does not agree with his mother's decision on supporting you," she said cautiously.

"Is it because he's my father?" Gidyon asked quietly.

Elen-ai sighed. There was nothing else she could say. "Yes."

Silence came from the other side of the bed. Elen-ai sat up, looking at Gidyon's face. With the Family's skills, she could easily see him in the dark. However, whatever his thoughts were, she could not discern them. "Are you alright?"

He was silent a moment longer. "Yes. It's just odd to know for sure."

"Did you suspect?"

"Not until you asked me about what happens if a Queen falls in love. It made me think about the way Zek is always so nice to me, and then the fact that mother is always just happier somehow whenever he is in Herran. I've never seen anything odd when they have been together, but there is something about her that just seems more vibrant, somehow. I had never thought about it before, but it makes sense, I suppose." He sat up himself. "Is that why someone is trying to kill her and me?"

Elen-ai shrugged, the movement rustling the covers. "I don't know. This evening I wondered..." she cut herself off, unwilling to upset Gidyon with her suspicions about Arlena.

"Tell me." He leaned forward. "Please."

Relenting, Elen-ai went on. "I wondered if Arlena may be behind the attacks in an attempt to safeguard the Aadran family's reputation."

Gidyon considered the proposition, then shook his head slightly. "It's possible, but I don't think likely."

"Why?"

"If Arlena were to organise such an attack, she'd make sure that it would be done properly. She's never seemed to me to be the sort of person who sets up something that may not succeed." He paused for a moment. "Has she ever employed the Family?"

"I can't tell you," Elen-ai responded almost before he had finished asking the question; a knee-jerk protection of the Family's secrets.

"Why not?" Gidyon's eyes flashed in the slight light let in by the gap in the curtain.

"The Family does not speak of its contracts to anyone but its members," Elen-ai told him.

"But if she is behind the attack on me and my mother, knowing whether or not she has had people killed before might help me know it," Gidyon protested.

"I cannot, Gidyon, I'm sorry," Elen-ai was firm. On this, she would not be moved.

He didn't respond but instead lay back down, turning away from her.

Elen-ai stared at his back for a moment longer. Perhaps she should have told him what she knew of the matriarch's business with the Family. But to do so would have unacceptably violated the Family's rules. Regardless, she did not think that his sudden silence was solely due to anger with her. The revelation of his parentage and the possibility of Arlena's involvement in the attempt on his life was confronting simply for her to think about. He probably needed some time to consider everything that Elen-ai had learned in his own way. So she let the issue drop, lying back down herself and remaining in the dark with her thoughts, as she so often was.

TWELVE

They left the Tak estate in the early hours of the next morning. Their hosts farewelled them in the yard as the sun was just rising, its pale yellow rays touching the Tak house's rooftop. Elen-ai could understand why the Taks had chosen to build their house on the top of the hill. It offered the perfect vantage to watch colour seep into or out of the landscape below. It was quite a magnificent sight.

Elen-ai farewelled Karan and Serek, who offered her a polite goodbye. She did actually like them despite the stance of neutrality that they had decided to take on the matter of Gidyon's legitimacy. They were an interesting couple. Not two people who felt a passionate love for each other, but who had been bound by a shared understanding of the importance of family and by the common purpose of keeping that family protected at all costs. It gave them a certain unity. It was also something Elen-ai understood and respected.

Arlena stood with her usual reserve, her son by her side. She nodded formally to Elen-ai, as did Zekken. However, while his mother met Elen-ai's eyes, he did not, staring studiously at her left ear. She wanted to glower at him, her anger and shock at the extent of his transgression against tradition still burning, but to do so would have been noticeably odd, so her face remained politely neutral.

Elen-ai watched as Zekken embraced Gidyon, enfolding the boy in a tight embrace. Gidyon returned the hug, although with less enthusiasm.

He mounted the carriage with no word to Elen-ai and gave one final wave to the assembled people in the yard before they set off.

Only when their little carriage had made its way out of the gates of the Tak home did either of them speak.

"Are you alright?" Elen-ai asked.

He looked down at his lap. "It's strange to think that he has been my father all this time," he said softly, his words competing to be heard against the rattle of the carriage wheels.

"Strange in a bad way?"

He shrugged, a motion that was curiously bird-like. Despite the width of his shoulders, the Prince was still narrow of frame. Some things could only come with age.

"Does it bother you?" she pursued.

Gidyon bit his lip as he considered. "I can't be too angry. I do want to succeed mother. So I can't exactly pick and choose what bothers me, given the unusualness of the circumstances in which I find myself." He took a breath. "But it does bother me. They've kept it a secret from everyone, even me. Having a bond with one of the Families is the one things a Queen is never supposed to do," he added.

"What about naming her son heir?" Elen-ai squinted slightly at the road ahead in the glare of the sun.

Gidyon inclined his head. "See what I mean?" His mouth twisted into a slightly sardonic smile.

Elen-ai nodded. He had a point.

"I just don't understand how they can be so reckless," Gidyon continued after a moment longer, raising his hands slightly to emphasise his confusion. "Just because they are in love or whatever does not mean that they should give in to it."

Elen-ai made a non-committal sound. It seemed some things truly did only come with age. Like understanding the insidiousness of the way a person could get under your skin, lingering there, leaving you aching for their touch, driving you to distraction, to the edge of reason.

"You've read Ulate's poetry, haven't you?" she asked.

Gidyon nodded.

"Have you read her collection of love poems?"

Gidyon threw a look at her. "I didn't know you were familiar with poetry," he said.

"Because you think that members of the Family are only taught how to kill?" she asked, more amused than anything else.

"Well, yes," he admitted.

Elen-ai uttered a short bark of laughter. "Even if that were true, words can be deadly in their own way," she told him. "We are encouraged to know about the world around us. That includes reading works of high literature, or knowing about art." She did not add that such familiarity allowed the Family's members to blend into the circles of people for whom such knowledge was assumed and slip unnoticed to the side of a particular target. After all, that did not detract from the fact that such knowledge in itself could be enjoyable to know and learn.

"Oh," was all he said, causing Elen-ai to laugh again.

"Anyway," she continued. "Those love poems. There is only one collection of them, and they speak of great love, or loss. And of the infatuation with one person that is like an itch, burning you from the inside out, right?"

"You are the flame in the dark, the rain in the heat, the food given to me as I starve. Without you, my anchor, I am lost, cannot find my way," Gidyon quoted.

"Mm, that one's one of my favourites, actually," Elen-ai said.

"You have a favourite love poem?" Gidyon was incredulous.

"That's really not the point," Elen-ai said patiently.

"Even so," Gidyon protested.

"Can we please not become distracted?"

"Sorry. You were talking about the contents of these poems." Gidyon collected himself with not a little visible effort.

"Exactly. I think that the love poems are among Ulate's most powerful, but also in some ways the least refined, of her work. And she didn't write them when she was young. Her younger work was about landscape, or family. So such lack of technical skill can't be put down to a lack of refinement in her writing. No, that rawness is her trying to put into words a consuming passion for another person. Consider what emotion caused a poet who is renowned for her measure and refinement to write not one, but a series of poems that deviate so completely from that precision," Elen-ai said.

"I cannot believe I am having this discussion with you," Gidyon muttered.

"Do you mind!" Elen-ai exclaimed. "I'm trying to make a point."

"Sorry, sorry. I agree. But she's a poet. The job of writers is to consider what it is to be human and explore that through their work," he replied.

"Well that's a different discussion in and of itself on the job of writers," Elen-ai said.

"I still can't believe that you and I are discussing this." Gidyon shook his head in disbelief.

"You know what? Fine. I give up." Elen-ai pursed her lips in irritation.

"You have to admit that this is not something one would expect to discuss with an assassin," Gidyon pointed out.

"How would you know what people normally discuss with an assassin?" Elen-ai snapped, feeling decidedly petulant.

"I'm sorry, Elen-ai. I have misjudged you," Gidyon said, still sounding amused.

In a display of immaturity, she turned her head away from him so that he could only see her profile. That was the final straw for him. He burst into laughter.

They stopped for lunch in the middle of the day. Elen-ai slid moodily from the carriage's seat and pulled out their food, handing it wordlessly to him. Her frustration with his unwillingness to take her seriously had yet to abate. For all his unusually adept capacity to charm various individuals, he had yet again failed to use that charm and insight when speaking with her.

"Elen-ai, I'm sorry about before." He approached her with his food in hand, as though it were an offering of some sort.

She deliberated whether or not she should remain annoyed with him but decided that it was ultimately pointless to do so. Relaxing her shoulders slightly, she made a wordless gesture that indicated she had accepted his apology.

"It was an enjoyable moment of levity, given everything that is going on. Now that I know about mother and Zekken, it makes me feel even more pressured to get the support of the other families and to find out who wants me and my mother dead so badly. If I cannot know I have sufficient support, I cannot be safe. It was already a hard task, but it just seems even more...urgent," he finished somewhat lamely, an unusually inelegant phrasing for him.

"How do you plan to deal with the Katan family?" she asked, feeling a squeeze of pity for him. The dangerous relationship between Zekken and the Queen was yet another concern for Gidyon to navigate in the course of trying to charm or bribe the families into supporting him. It lent a certain sense of precariousness to securing their support, too, lest this be found out and used against him.

He rubbed a finger along the bridge of his nose, a slight scowl on his face. "I know we were initially planning to go to them, but perhaps it may be better to bypass them entirely and just go as far as the Harete estate."

To reach the Katan family residence would require at least three weeks' journey. They resided in one of the most remote parts of the Queendom. The town where ceramics artisans all gathered was practically on the border of the Second Country and the Fourth Country. To traverse the vast plains which housed the clay off which the Katan fortune was spun required the navigation of several ill-maintained roads. Such isolation was the Katan family's preferred method of maintaining a haughty distance from the rest of the Queendom. Their belief that they did not need to frequently come to Herran to pay homage to the Queen due to the substantial wealth that they held was always hidden behind the excuse of their remoteness, although everybody knew that it was a remoteness that they themselves chose to maintain. The marriage of the Queen's younger sister to the Katan family had been an effort to engender some sort of loyalty from them while also conveniently keeping the girl as far away as possible from the Capital so that she could never lay claim to the throne.

"Are you sure that's wise?" Elen-ai asked. As much as she would rather not traverse through the territory of someone known to not have Gidyon's best interests at heart for several weeks, if Gidyon did visit the rest of the families, such a snub would at the very least be unwise, offering them the political grudge that would legitimise a move against him.

"I know, I know," he muttered. "I'll think about it on the way." The weight he had placed on himself to find his attackers and bring them to justice as well as to secure support for his claim to the throne was obvious in the frown that creased his forehead.

She shrugged, biting into a slice of bread. "I'll go wherever you decide," she said around the mouthful.

"Can you show me that move again, Elen-ai?" The question was a sudden change in subject.

"You'll have to be a bit more specific, my Prince," she responded, wondering why he had so abruptly changed topics.

"The kick, you know, to the side." To demonstrate, he awkwardly lifted one of his legs. Unfortunately for him, with his hands still full of food and his balance already poor, he toppled straight onto the ground.

Elen-ai stared at him, eyes wide and mouth paused mid-chew, at this display of complete incoordination.

The Prince looked up at her in surprise, then started to laugh. "You should see your face," he said in between giggles. Breathless with laughter, his blue eyes were vibrant in the sunlight. She saw a small chip in one of his teeth that she hadn't noticed before, and the slight dusting of freckles across the top of his cheeks. Amid the grass he didn't look in the slightest bit regal, he looked like a boy who was carefree and happy. She couldn't help herself. She laughed too, coming to sit beside him, looking up at the sky with the sun shining down upon them. As much of a prat as he could be, and as much as sometimes this Princeling was too haughty for his own good, she could not deny that sometime in the past few days, she had come to like him, and he was no longer simply a contract, but someone by whom she wanted to do right.

After two more days of travel, they crossed back into the sovereign land. The territory encompassed the main road of the Queendom that intersected with the border of the Fourth and Third Countries, off which smaller roads and tracks led into the lands of the seven families. Elen-ai guided the carriage toward a roadside inn that she frequented when she travelled this way. Both she and Gidyon had grown tired of the fruits, smoked meat, and increasingly stale loaves of bread that had been given to them by the Tak kitchens. While Elen-ai had survived on a lot less, she still preferred the luxury of a meal with at least more than two ingredients, if it could be helped.

"Are you certain it will be safe there?" Gidyon worried, asking the question for perhaps the tenth time that day.

Elen-ai looked at him, shaking her head slightly. Gidyon may have known many things, but in other ways he was completely ignorant. "Inns are very safe, provided you don't do anything stupid," she reassured him.

"What if I'm recognised?" he asked.

Elen-ai snorted the mouthful of water she had just sipped out of her nose as she laughed. "You're not that well known, Gidyon," she replied once she had finished cleaning herself up.

"That was disgusting," he informed her.

Elen-ai shrugged and attempted another sip, this time succeeding in swallowing it. "Anyway, we've been practising those kicks and throws. You can always put that to good use if it comes to it." She smirked.

"Thank you for the suggestion. The seat's still wet," he complained, shuffling further away from the drops of water in question.

"Have you thought about how to deal with the Katan family yet?" she asked, diverting the subject away from her hygiene practices.

Gidyon nodded. "I thought I'd invite them to court as honoured guests. That way it seems I'm giving them preference that they cannot refuse, rather than snubbing them by not visiting."

She considered his solution. It wasn't bad. "In the Palace we can keep a closer eye on them, too."

"And we can also prove that their would-be heir is far too unaccustomed to the world of the Court to be a good ruler," Gidyon added as the inn came in to view.

It was a good plan, and Elen-ai was not disappointed to hear that they would see the Katans in the Royal Palace. There was a certain irrationality to her impulse to lock the Prince away, after all, the Queen had been attacked inside the Palace, but she felt as though danger lurked along this journey in many forms, not all of them holding a knife. And she was not skilled enough in the politics and intrigue of the court to detect and deflect that kind of threat.

There seemed to be some unwritten law that all inns required to have a certain universality. They were populated generally by a mix of people who were hard workers looking for a little respite, or a little trouble, or perhaps a little of both, and a great many patrons who were fiercely loyal to whichever inn they frequented the most. While the level of cleanliness varied from inn to inn, they were staffed by the same sort of individual; highly competent and very much able to hold their own in a fight.

The sun had started its descent towards the horizon and both Elen-ai and Gidyon were quite hungry. As soon as they entered the tavern area, Elen-ai's gaze was instantly drawn to the door leading into the kitchen. An appetising smell was emanating from it that didn't necessarily promise meat, but certainly promised an actual meal rather than the sparse supplies that they had been eating over the last few days.

The innkeeper was an elderly woman who was clearing a table. Elen-ai knew her by sight from the previous times she had been at the inn. People sat at various tables either quietly talking amongst themselves or looking with an idle fascination at whatever was in front of them. Most of them were the usual assemblage of people who could be found at an inn that was in the middle of the way to somewhere but not quite anywhere in particular: a bookkeeper, a messenger, several travellers, and perhaps one or two individuals who would give a lonely soul human comfort in exchange for financial comfort. Elen-ai was almost certain that the slender young man with the sensuous mouth was for sale, although she was less certain about the woman who sat next to him who was looking at Elen-ai and Gidyon in cool appraisal. Several such individuals lived within inns for as long as they chose to keep their business there. It wasn't how Elen-ai would want to earn a living, but it certainly could be very profitable, especially if the inn was a good one.

"Can I help you?" The woman who was clearing the tables approached the Prince and Elen-ai, looking them up and down with professional boredom.

"We're after some food. And lodgings for the night," Elen-ai said.

Her only response a nod. The woman turned and marched into the kitchen, easily balancing the crockery piled high in each hand. Elen-ai led Gidyon to a table and sat down, sighing with pleasure at being able to actually stretch out her legs.

"We left our trunks in the carriage," Gidyon leaned forward and said to her in an undertone.

"And?" Elen-ai looked at him blankly.

"What if they're stolen, or gone through?" He glanced about himself nervously.

"Then I will be very irritated," Elen-ai replied, leaning back in her chair comfortably. "I thought you liked to be among the lowborn people, Gidyon." She smirked.

"There's a difference between the marketplace and a tavern in the middle of nowhere," Gidyon said, his unease palpable.

"What exactly are you worried is going to happen?" She linked her hands behind her head.

"I don't know," Gidyon muttered.

The woman came out from the kitchen with two wooden bowls filled to the brim with stew and put them down on the table. "And two ales, please," Elen-ai added.

The woman nodded and returned presently with two large tankards. "Thank you. By the by, that messenger over in the corner, is she reliable?" Elen-ai asked.

The woman gave a noncommittal shrug. "Not the worst messenger we've ever had here. Anything else?"

Elen-ai shook her head, making a gesture of thanks with her hand as she picked up the wooden spoon – a far cry from the delicate metal cutlery that graced the tables of the seven families and the Palace – and leaned forward to start eating.

Throughout the exchange, Gidyon had been staring at the tankard as though mesmerised.

"You're meant to drink it, not admire it," Elen-ai advised.

He obediently lifted the mug to his lips and took a sip which immediately set him coughing. Elen-ai roared with laughter. Even though she had anticipated that Gidyon had never drunk the rough ale that most of the country enjoyed, it was nevertheless hilarious to see his eyes water as the potency of the drink hit him.

"You should have warned me," he said reproachfully.

"Where's the fun in that?" She grinned and took a sip from her own mug. She stifled a small cough of her own – it was very strong. "Don't stay angry with me," she implored as she ate, chucking at the memory of his reaction.

He pulled a face and took another sip. "Divine One around us! This stuff is vile. How can people drink it?"

"Mostly it's all people know. Your fancy spirits and distilled drinks are things that most people can't even pronounce properly, let alone afford." Elen-ai spoke between mouthfuls. Whatever other flaws this tavern may have had, its food was good and always had been.

"Mother never let me have luxuries like that," Gidyon protested. "I only was allowed them on special occasions."

"Look around you, Princeling. You have always lived in luxury, regardless of what you may think. But remember that the decisions of your mother, and certain others close to her, affect people here."

"I know that," Gidyon protested.

"Maybe up here," Elen-ai pointed to his head. "But it's different to actually knowing it."

Gidyon threw his hands up. "Sometimes you are so annoying!" he told her, although there was no real fire in his voice. Both of them knew she had a point.

Elen-ai inclined her head as she sipped her ale. "Oh, just give it to me," she snapped, grabbing his mug from him.

"No," he insisted, reaching across the table and pulling it back. "I want to finish it."

"You'll die," Elen-ai said, completely serious.

"Then it'll be your fault," he replied, before drinking long and deep from the tankard that looked much taller than Elen-ai first thought.

The ale took a while to hit the Prince, but soon his speech began to slur and his movements became exaggerated. All things considered, he held his ale surprisingly well. Elen-ai feared he would pass out in the middle of the tavern. When he began to slump in his chair, she paid for a room, asked their cases to be brought to it, and helped the staggering Prince up the stairs to the second level on which the tavern's small rooms were situated. She set Gidyon down onto the simple bed of stuffed straw and a mostly clean blanket. Once he was flat on his back, he immediately started to lightly snore.

He remained asleep for the rest of the afternoon, slumbering off the worst of the ale. Elen-ai passed the time by writing messages to be sent to the Family, using the small area of the room to do some stretches, and praying. All in all, the pace of the afternoon, punctuated by Gidyon's snores, was pleasantly peaceful.

The light had faded almost completely when she could no longer deny the call of nature. She glanced at Gidyon. From time to time, he mumbled something in his sleep, but he appeared to be soundly unconscious. It seemed safe to leave him for the briefest of moments. The day when she could be away from another person's side for more than the shortest time possible would be one of great delight, she reflected as she dashed down the corridor to the privy.

She came back to find Gidyon gone. Fighting the impulse to panic, she made her way back downstairs and toward the sound of a scuffle. As she came into the lower level of the tavern, she was greeted by the sight Gidyon against a wall with three knives to his throat.

THIRTEEN

Elen-ai had never been the fastest member of the Family, but she couldn't imagine that anybody had ever moved as quickly as she did. In perhaps two or three breaths, she had disarmed the three individuals who had looked very much as though they wanted to inflict considerable damage on the Prince, and even put one of them on his back. Their knives now in her hands, she pushed the Prince aside and put herself where he had been only an instant previously.

The two would-be assailants who were still standing looked in surprise at the woman who had appeared to come out of nowhere and taken their knives.

"Gidyon, what happened?" Elen-ai asked, her tone sharp and hard as she held the knives up, ready to attack.

"I woke up and you weren't there, so I came down here." The Prince's mumbled speech suggested he was still feeling the effects of the ale.

"And what, these three people decided they didn't like your face so they tried to stab you?"

"I..."

"Explain yourselves," Elen-ai cut Gidyon off and addressed her question to the people whose knives she now held.

"What's all this about?" Before they could answer, the woman who served them came up to them, hands on hips and a furious expression on her face.

"He upset our game," the person to Elen-ai's left said, glaring at Gidyon.

"Wait, what?" Elen-ai lowered the knives slightly, throwing a brief look of confusion at the Prince.

"I wasn't watching what I was doing, and I stumbled into him." Gidyon waved to the man on the ground. "His cards fell out of his hand, and then..." The Prince trailed off, a delicate blush spreading across his cheeks.

"There was a lot of money on the table for that hand," the woman on Elen-ai's right snarled.

"And what do you expect to achieve by stabbing him?" Elen-ai demanded.

The blank looks that met her question suggested that they had not considered what they were going to do subsequent to taking out their ire on Gidyon with the pointed end of their knives.

"I'll have no fighting of any kind in here," the innkeeper interjected, causing everyone to look at her. "A boy bumps 'nto your game, 'ts an accident, you treat t'as such. Who draws a blade 't such a thing? Honestly!" She swatted at the air to prove a point, her gnarled fingers curving as though she wanted to grab someone by the ear and haul them around the room to teach them a lesson. "And you." She turned her gaze to Elen-ai, the thickness of her speech making her surprisingly intimidating. "I've seen you in'ere before. What's about coming in and causing a ruckus? Who raised you t'mean t'you think fighting's where all things start?"

Elen-ai dropped her gaze, chastened by this woman's anger. "I'm sorry." She offered the weapons back to their owners.

" 'Nd you young man. Watch your walking. You never know who you may't upset if yaren't careful. T' world's full o'fools." She threw a pointed look at the three ruffians who looked quite shamefaced under the might of her wrath.

Apologies were mumbled and the two small parties went their own ways. The commotion had attracted the attention of the tavern's various inhabitants, whose number had grown since earlier in the day. Heads gradually began to turn back to their business and Elen-ai felt herself relaxing once more. This at least was the sort of threat to Gidyon's life that she could protect him from, provided he didn't go stumbling into any more tavern gamblers without her.

"Sorry," Gidyon mumbled beside her.

"It's alright. Like the old lady said, though. You should be careful where you step." Elen-ai slid into a chair, signalling for some food. "You may have been practising those kicks but you're no match for someone with a knife. You do know I was just joking earlier when I said you could try them out tonight, right?"

He didn't respond, merely putting a hand to his head as the innkeeper brought over a plate of something that looked suspiciously similar to lunch with one or two alterations. Elen-ai tucked into the food, simply glad that it wasn't more stale bread. After a moment of hesitation, Gidyon followed her lead.

"We should send those messages tonight," Elen-ai said after she had eaten a few mouthfuls.

"Mm," Gidyon answered.

"Will you write to your mother?" she asked.

The expression on his face was reply enough.

"I take it you're not particularly pleased with her?"

Gidyon looked out across the rest of the tavern as he spoke. "I don't want to talk about it."

Elen-ai scrutinised Gidyon's face. His eyes were completely blue. Some people who had blue eyes also had other colours in their iris; flecks of yellow or green. But Gidyon's eyes were pure blue. When he properly looked at someone, it was quite unnerving. The molten gold of his mother's eyes made anyone looking at them feel as though they were falling into them. The Prince's eyes made one feel as though he could see right through them. It was why his unwillingness to meet Elen-ai's gaze unnerved her so much. She hadn't realised how much she took his competence and control for granted. Sometimes she forgot that he was still a boy on the cusp of manhood rather than a man. Then again, her first kill had been when she was a full year younger than Gidyon was now. A death that had been exacted upon a member of the family whose hospitality she had just enjoyed for several days. But Gidyon's childhood had been different from her own. He had learned to choose his words carefully, and she had learned to choose her blades carefully.

Leaving him to his mood, Elen-ai ate in a contented silence, occasionally raising her eyes to survey the rest of the room and ensure that there was no potential assailant lurking in wait. A man hurled the door open with great abandon, causing her to momentarily tense in readiness, but amicable cries of familiarity greeted him.

"Al-et, haven't seen you for quite a'time." The old woman who had so competently broken up the earlier altercation greeted the newcomer, giving him a quick kiss of greeting on the cheek.

"That damned magistrate ruled 'gainst me a'few weeks back s'I had t'go t'Herran and appeal." The anger with which the man spoke was understandable, although it caused his skipped lowborn to become even more exaggerated. Local magistrates decided on legal disputes, but they weren't always competent or fair. The decision could be appealed, arbitrated normally by a member of the family from the relevant estate. However, in rare instances, a case may need to be appealed directly to a judge in Herran, or even the Queen herself. Mostly that didn't happen, though. To submit an appeal, the individual had to forfeit days, sometimes weeks, of work in order to make the trek to Herran and wait for the appeal to be heard. Likely, the man, Al-et, had lost a significant amount of money in pursuit of his appeal.

"How did't go?" the woman asked.

The man made a disgusted sound. "The judge ruled f'me, but t'trip took far longer than I expected. I t'was waiting in

Herran f'five days, t's not cheap t'stay there. I should'a stayed here a'worked."

The woman guided him to a seat and placed a large tankard in front of him. "T'one's on me," she said, earning a gruff word of appreciation before the man lost himself in the depths of his drink.

"Is there a mirror in the washroom?" Gidyon suddenly asked, seemingly oblivious to the exchange that had just occurred.

Elen-ai looked at him in confusion. "What?"

"Somewhere I can see my reflection," he explained patiently.

"Yes, there was. Why?"

"I should shave before we get on our way," he said.

Elen-ai nearly choked on the mouthful of ale she had just sipped. "You shave?" She made no effort to hide her incredulity.

He looked mildly offended. "Of course I do."

"What do you shave?" She asked. When he simply stared at her, his eyes widening slightly, she went on. "No, seriously. What is there to shave?"

He put a hand to his cheek self-consciously. "I shave my face," he protested.

It took a great deal of self-control for Elen-ai to swallow the ale rather than spit it out all over the table in a gale of laughter. In a voice constrained by that withheld laughter she spoke. "I see. How does that go for you?"

Looking decidedly upset now, he leaned away from her. "It goes fine, thank you."

The muscles of her face fighting to allow the laughter free, she managed to get one final question out. "And uh, are you certain you shave or do you just comb your fluff?"

"I'm going back to bed," he snapped, pushing his food away and standing up.

It was too much. There was something about the wounded pride of an adolescent's masculinity that was universally hilarious, regardless of what position they held. Elen-ai broke down into a howl of laughter, putting her forehead down on the top of the table as the laugh took on a life of its own. She glanced up at Gidyon, whose unimpressed look sent her into further spasms.

Without another word, he set off up the stairs. Elen-ai hastily drained the rest of her ale and spooned up another mouthful of the rejuvenated lunch before following him up the stairs.

Gidyon had stalked into their room and was rummaging around in a trunk. "I'm not talking to you," he informed her as she walked in.

Chuckling to herself, Elen-ai took out several of her knives and began to clean them, putting each one down carefully once she had ensured the blades were free from any spots.

After a time, Gidyon sidled over to stand near her, watching her with his customary curiosity. Certainly, the array of knives would be impressive to someone who had never seen them before. Elen-ai put down the blade she had just finished cleaning. It was the thickness of a few strands of hair and one of her favourites.

"Why do you need so many blades? I thought the Family made the deaths of their contracts look..." he trailed off, clearly uncertain of how to delicately phrase it.

"Not suspicious?" she finished the sentence for him.

"Well, yes." He leaned forward so he could examine the line of wickedly sharp weapons more closely.

"We do. But it's not that simple."

He looked at her, clearly waiting for her to elaborate.

"An unsuspicious death is very different to a death that isn't violent. A brawl can just as easily kill someone as a seemingly-unfortunate fall. If the circumstances look reasonable, people tend not to examine a body too closely for a killing blow delivered by a very skilled hand. But I don't just stay armed to kill one target. Sometimes a member of the Family may find themselves in a tricky situation. After all, most people don't want to die. We have been known to encounter hostility, as surprising as that may sound. Being well armed and ready is important."

Gidyon considered the explanation, then nodded, apparently satisfied.

"Are you still upset with me?" Elen-ai enquired, unable to contain her smirk.

"Yes," he told her, raising his chin slightly and turning back to whatever his own purpose had been.

He did end up shaving that evening, although Elen-ai was not certain that she could see any discernible difference when he emerged from the washroom. She decided that it would not be particularly tactful to say as much, though.

They left the inn the next morning, Gidyon having forgiven Elen-ai's wound to his pride and returning to his normal self. The inn was on the edge of the Harete estate, which itself was composed of a large, sprawling forest. Lake Harete was nestled in the very heart of the forest. While Elen-ai had never seen it – and would not on this occasion either, it was reportedly often so still that it provided a perfect reflection of the forest that came right to the water's edge.

The trees closed in over the track, slightly dampening the noise of the day. The light that came down was filtered through that canopy, a softer yellow than the open brightness that had beaten down on their heads as they crossed the flat Tak plains. Something about the forest reminded Elen-ai of the Family's home. The dense growth of the trees made her somehow think that the quiet forest was full of secrets. She felt more at ease here than she had over the past weeks when being in the homes of those whose political schemes and plans in search of the fulfilment of their own lofty ambition left her feeling a little grubby.

"You seem more comfortable here." Gidyon's comment interrupted her reverie, seeming to read her thoughts.

"I suppose that's because I am," she replied.

"I don't think I've really thanked you for coming with me. I could not have done this without you," he said hesitantly after she said no more.

"You'd have been fine. You'd probably have needed a few more guards, but you'd have been fine," she said.

"No, I didn't mean safe. I meant that you've been by my side. I can talk to you, I can trust you. It, it means a great deal." He reached between them and placed a hand on her arm to emphasise the point.

Touched, Elen-ai found herself lost for words.

"How old are you, Elen-ai?"

His question was a departure from the sentimentality of the moment, but Elen-ai appreciated it. She had never been one for excessive displays of emotion. "At my next birthday, I'll be twenty-two," she said.

"What?" The sound of his exclamation was loud in the muted greenery of the forest.

"You heard me."

"But you're only a few years older than me," he protested.

Elen-ai shifted in her seat. "I am aware. What's your point?"

"I suppose I didn't expect you to be so young. You seem to be so..." He caught himself, biting off the rest of his sentence.

"So what, Gidyon?" She turned to look at him, raising her eyebrows into an anticipatory expression.

"So competent," he finished somewhat lamely.

"That was definitely not what you were initially going to say," Elen-ai accused.

"I don't know what you're talking about." His feigned pomposity made her smile.

She had come to love these moments on the road with Gidyon. Away from the politics and schemes, he was someone else entirely, a boy on the precipice of adulthood who she caught herself thinking of more and more not as her contract, but as her friend.

That night they camped in the forest. The dense growth of the trees meant it was impossible to see the sky clearly, but the glimpses of the night sky in the gaps between the trees made it somehow even more beautiful.

"I must discuss something important with you," Gidyon said once they had finished eating their dinner.

"Mm?" Elen-ai leaned forward to see his face a little better. They hadn't lit a fire that night. It was warm enough for them to go without.

"You know that I have pledged to marry a common woman?"

"I do recall," Elen-ai responded. She hoped he wasn't going to ask her to help him choose a bride. Nothing could be more tedious to her mind.

"Elen-ai." He reached out to touch her hand. "I think it's time that we stop denying what's between us."

Her eyes went wide. "What?"

"I know I'm not the only one who feels it. Elen-ai, marry me." He moved so that he could take both of her hands in his.

"Uh..." She could see his face and the earnest set of his jaw clearly. She didn't move, paralysed by the horror she felt.

He waited for a full minute of awkward tension before he broke, bursting into uncontrollable laughter.

"That wasn't funny!" she protested, yanking her hands from his.

"I beg to differ," he gasped, surrendering to a relapse of laughter.

Elen-ai looked at the Prince's shaking form. "It really wasn't funny."

"It was hilarious," he repudiated as he returned to where he had been sitting before. Every few moments, he would erupt into giggles that he would unsuccessfully try to stifle.

"And what if I would have said yes?" she challenged.

"Would you really have?" That prospect made him dissolve into laughter again.

"Of course not. I would never leave the Family."

"See? Oh, Divine One, that was spectacular." He brought his hands together, making a soft clap.

Declining to reply, Elen-ai shook her head, smiling despite herself. He really had gotten her. She resolved to exact revenge the next evening when he practised kicks and punches under her tuition. It was a petty response to be sure, but that didn't mean it wouldn't be satisfying.

They arrived at the Harete home two days later. On their travel through the massive forest, they had only encountered carts full of the cut timbers that the Harete estate produced. It had been a peaceful bliss for Elen-ai.

Nestled in a cleared valley, the high timber house seemed almost to blend into the backdrop of trees. Elen-ai had never travelled to this part of the country. No contract had ever required the visit of her deadly skills upon people who were connected with the Harete estate. Of course, that did not mean that the Family's presence had not been known here. There was no part of the land where the services of the Family were not sought. From their vantage point, the house looked far less auspicious than the Veertak or Tak family homes. It was smaller, more cosy. It did not announce the excessive wealth that the Harete family possessed, although perhaps that in itself was a testament to their vast fortunes.

The ribbon of the path wound down the valley to lead the small carriage neatly to the house's front courtyard. A girl, perhaps Gidyon's age or slightly younger, ran out to greet them, her long hair streaming untied down her back. She was barefoot and wearing a simple skirt and shirt that hugged close to emphasise a femininity that Elen-ai noticed drew Gidyon's gaze.

"Master Gidyon, we saw your carriage descending."

Elen-ai did not like the breathless excitement with which this girl spoke. It seemed unnecessarily airy.

"I'm sorry, I don't believe we've been introduced," Gidyon leaned down to address the girl, a particularly charming smile on his face.

"I am Rania." She contrived to summon a slight flush that enhanced her delicate prettiness.

"Second-born to Timet and Janyce?"

"The very same," she announced, smiling apparently at the fact that he knew who she was.

"It's a pleasure to meet you. This is Elen-ai, my companion." He gestured quickly, almost dismissively, to Elen-ai.

"Lovely to meet you." Rania barely spared a glance at Elen-ai, her attention was so focused on the Prince. "Please, come inside, both of you."

A servant came forward to take the reins of the carriage from Elen-ai. She handed them over and joined Gidyon in following Rania into the home, a sense of unease at this pretty girl and the Prince's interest in her growing with every step.

FOURTEEN

The Harete family was unusual in that the eldest members who would otherwise lead had given their authority to their eldest son and his wife, Rania's parents. This was because the former patriarch, Lindel, had succumbed to a deterioration of the mind, and his wife, Lilea, had no interest in leading unless it was by the side of her husband. The genuine bond of affection that existed between them did not appear to be present in Rania's parents, a fact which Elen-ai observed as she sat in their parlour room on the lowest level of the house, a drink in her hand and Gidyon to her right. Gentle green light came in through the wide open window that looked onto a small, neatly organised garden which was a world of imposed order against the haphazard wilderness of the rest of the forest.

The two old people warbled at each other quietly in the way that older people tend to do. Lilea's hand was resting on top of her husband's, their fingers gently interlinked. They seemed more interested in being next to each other than their visitor. Their love was a stark contrast to Timet and Janyce, the latter who was quite pregnant. They sat on completely opposite sides of the room, the suggestion of a practised avoidance of each other obvious in the effortlessness by which this outcome had been achieved. Somewhat uncharitably, Elen-ai wondered whether the child in Janyce's womb had been fathered by Timet. That itself was an interesting possibility to report back to the Family, although the Family preferred certainty over conjecture. Elen-ai wondered whether it was worth trying to confirm that suspicion.

"This certainly is a lovely surprise to have you here, especially after that awful attack on your mother's life," Timet said to Gidyon once everybody had come in to the room and settled themselves. The eldest child of Janyce and Timet, a young man named after his grandfather was sitting by his father. Rania had contrived to sit on Gidyon's other side and was smiling enchantingly at him.

There was a certain niceness and cheerfulness to the room that made Elen-ai want to reach for her knives. If she had thought that she had to be on edge in the Tak household, this effusive outpouring of warmth and hospitality made her feel even less at ease.

"Indeed. It is lovely not only to see your home, but also you, and your family, in a setting outside of the Court," Gidyon addressed his response to everybody, although Elen-ai was certain that the comment had one particular individual in mind, though.

"May we be blunt about what brings you here, though?" Timet clasped his hands together.

"I feel you may already be aware of the circumstances which bring me to you." Gidyon's voice was light and open. His posture echoed that apparent carefreeness, leaning into his chair, resting his arm along the back.

"Your mother has decided to name you her heir," Timet supplied the answer. His thoughts on the matter were not discernible from his tone.

"Quite correct. And I've come to ask whether you will support that decision." Gidyon took his arm from the chair's back and straightened. "I won't play games. I know you've likely already heard that the Katan family will almost certainly offer their own potential heir, and I know your land borders theirs. It's an awkward position, but -"

"My Prince," Timet cut him off. "We have always been loyal to the Queen and her family. That is not something that will ever change."

Gidyon sat perfectly still. He evidently expected that he would have had to do more to get their support. "I don't know what to say." He gave a half-smile, looking around the room.

Lilea leaned forward, her hand still in her husband's, her brown eyes earnest. "My dear, your mother and her mother are people Lindel and I have had the good fortune to know, and know quite well. They are exceptional women and you are the product of them. How could our family fail to put its weight behind you?" The earnestness of her tone made the open declaration of support from her son almost believable. But Elen-ai was a cynic.

She turned her attention to Janyce. Despite her position within the family's hierarchy, the woman had said nothing, watching the exchange with a neutral expression. Elen-ai could see tight anger underneath that veneer of neutrality, though. If Elen-ai recalled correctly, Janyce had been born into the Katan family. Despite the fact that anyone who married was supposed to forgo loyalty to the family of their birth, it was a difficult thing to do in practice. Elen-ai decided that she would definitely look further into Janyce when the opportunity presented itself. She couldn't dismiss the possibility that Janyce had her own allegiance that did not mesh with that of the people surrounding her.

"You are far too kind, Lilea. I don't know how to express my thanks." Gidyon's response cut into Elen-ai's musings.

"Will you be staying with us for long?" Rania asked, the enthusiasm with which she asked grating on Elen-ai's nerves.

"At least a few days." Gidyon smiled at her. "If that's alright?" He turned to Timet.

"Please, you and your companion are welcome to stay with us for as long as you would like."

Rania volunteered to show Gidyon and Elen-ai to their room. As they walked through the large home, she maintained an excited chatter with the Prince that conspicuously avoided including Elen-ai. It wasn't so much that the slight annoyed Elen-ai, it was the abject lack of any subtlety on Rania's part that offended her sensibilities. Elen-ai may not have been one for the political game played by members of the seven families and the Court, but she nevertheless appreciated nuance and a well-crafted approach, and this girl seemed to lack either. What was particularly offensive on top of this though, was that Gidyon seemed to not realise or mind, ogling the girl's figure as they ascended the staircase to their room on the second floor of the five-story building.

At the doorway of the room, Rania paused. "We've made up the one bed..." she said, flicking her long brown hair as she spoke. The impracticality of all that hair simply hanging there irritated Elen-ai beyond measure. She couldn't take it any longer.

"That will be fine, thank you," she said, breezing past the girl and into the room.

"I'll leave you to clean up then. I'll just be in the music room, if you want me." It was very clear that Rania's offer was not directed at Elen-ai.

"What do you play?" Gidyon asked, his voice warm.

"Oh, I'm not very good!" Rania exclaimed. Elen-ai thought that if she fluttered her eyes any harder she may lose them.

"I'm sure that's not true at all," Gidyon assured her. "Will you play for me?"

"You'd have to promise not to be too critical. I'd be terribly nervous if you watched me." Her breathy demeanour made a reappearance, and she even coiled a lock of hair around one of her fingers as she looked demurely at Gidyon.

Elen-ai threw herself into a chair to observe the spectacle. The deliberate thud did not appear to be noticed by either of the adolescents caught in what she presumed they believed to be a terribly romantic moment.

"On my honour, I'd never be too critical of you," he promised.

"Well I look forward to you finding me, then." With one final sly smile, Rania set off along the corridor.

Gidyon closed the door and turned to Elen-ai. "Well that went very well I think," he commented cheerfully.

"Are you referring to the discussion with the Harete family or your efforts to impregnate their daughter?" Elen-ai asked casually, crossing one leg over the other.

"What?" For someone who was very skilled at concealing his real thoughts, Gidyon did a terrible job of feigning ignorance.

"My Prince, if I may offer you a piece of advice: beware of the charms of an attractive and interested person. More people have been brought to ruin by lust than I can possibly count."

"She's nice. Nothing beyond that," he protested.

"Just because the Harete family has pledged their loyalty to you does not mean they are without ambition. Being related to the wife of a ruler is a great coup," she cautioned.

"Really, Elen-ai, don't be ridiculous." Gidyon shook his head dismissively.

"Have you ever been with a woman?" Elen-ai asked as the thought occurred to her. It would certainly explain why he was so blind to this painfully obvious ploy.

"That's none of your business!" Gidyon stuttered.

She put a hand to her forehead. "That's all I need. Someone who can be led by what's between his legs because he knows no better," she muttered.

"I'm not going to be led by my groin," Gidyon countered, a blush creeping its way up his neck.

In response, Elen-ai offered a poor imitation of Rania's breathy laugh and flick of hair - difficult given that Elen-ai had very little of her own hair to flick.

"Now you're just being mean," she was told sternly.

"Gidyon, if you want that sort of pleasure, find someone who will want nothing other than coin in exchange for it. That girl can cause you more problems than the entirety of the Katan family's so-called heir," she said.

"That's crude." Gidyon shook his head and turned away from her.

"I can stop a knife coming to you. I can't stop the damage if you misstep with her," Elen-ai told his back.

Gidyon chose not to respond, walking into the adjacent washroom and closing the door.

He walked out several minutes later, his hair wet and clothes changed. Elen-ai rose and went in for a wash of her own to discover that he had used all of the warm water, almost certainly on purpose.

After she had finished washing in the cold water, she moodily accompanied Gidyon to the music room on the uppermost level of the house, where she was forced to listen to Rania plucking away at a harp and trilling several songs in a rather bland voice. It seemed however, that Elen-ai and Gidyon heard completely different performances, as he effusively praised her every note. Elen-ai would have loved desperately to be anywhere other than by the side of the infatuated Prince, but she could not justify the risk of leaving him alone.

Dinner was slightly less painful, although Rania sat herself next to Gidyon. Thankfully, he was not so foolish as to exclusively pay attention to her, but many of his comments and jokes were clearly not made with her in mind, causing eruptions of giggles or sighs from the girl.

The food was wholesome and good and Elen-ai even enjoyed listening to the conversation when it wasn't between Gidyon and Rania. Clearly, Lilea and Lindel had a close relationship with their son and grandchildren, and the good-natured banter that was flung around the table was a testament to that. Timet's sister and her husband were also present, engaging in the repartee with great abandon, while frequent references to their other sibling - from what Elen-ai could gather, this was the youngest boy, who had married into the Rasatan family - were made. The clear affection that they held for each other would have been quite touching were it not for Janyce's silence. While not conspicuous, it nevertheless was noticeable. There was almost a space around the pregnant woman, as though she were invisible to everybody else. But she did not seem unhappy with her solitude. Indeed, she seemed to have constructed this isolation. She maintained it with a sourness that repelled anyone who may seek to speak with her. The pale blonde hair that framed her face further differentiated her; the rest of the family had curly brown hair. Even her own children did not direct any comment to her. Elen-ai wondered if the woman's distance was because she was hiding something from them, such as an involvement in a plot against the Prince. Certainly, it was the one discordant note in the otherwise perfect harmony that the Rasatans appeared to embody. Something about sitting at the table gave Elen-ai the same discomfort that she felt when holding a fruit that was overripe, sweetness and rot unpleasantly coexisting until the decay won out. Elen-ai resolved to find out more about Janyce Harete as soon as possible, to find out what exactly this family was hiding behind their smiles.

For that reason, much later in the evening after Gidyon and Elen-ai had returned to their room following the bidding of effusive goodnights between Gidyon and Rania, Elen-ai slipped out of the bed she shared with the Prince and out into the house.

She knew that she should probably stay with Gidyon, but she had checked the room and kept her ears out for the sound of anybody moving about the house. The large timbers from which the house was constructed - from the forest surrounding the house - meant that she was able to hear the comings and goings of people within it at this time of night. Wooden floors required far less finesse than the apex of a roof, but wood did have a propensity to squeak when least expected. It gave Elen-ai a confidence that the Prince would not be ambushed without her knowing about it well in advance.

Staying close to the shadows, she made her way to the third level of the house where Janyce and Timet's bedroom was. As she neared it, she could hear the sound of a heated discussion taking place. Curiosity burning, she snuck to the door, flattened herself against the wall, and listened.

"...I'm so tired of you." Janyce's voice came through quite clearly.

"Not as tired as I am of you." Timet's response was infused with a malice that Elen-ai wouldn't have thought possible given the cheerful demeanour he had demonstrated that day. It was satisfying to know that she had been correct about there being something unpleasant lurking behind that open and pleasant manner.

"At least you only have one person to be sick of." The comment was accompanied by the sound of a thump, as though something heavy was being put down. "I'm surrounded here by your parents, your sister and her insipid husband, and our children who your whole family has kept from me."

"If it's that much of a burden for to you to be here surrounded by my family, just leave then!" The explosive delivery suggested that this was an argument that had been conducted a number of times in a variety of ways. The conclusion was foregone and the grievances were always the same; a well-worn path eked out over years and years of bitterness.

"I can't just leave. I have to bear you your final brat," Janyce snarled.

"Yes, well I'm not so certain that it even is my child you're carrying."

That comment was followed by the sound of a sharp gasp. "How dare you." Janyce's voice was low. A different sort of anger was behind it now.

"I wouldn't be surprised if none of the children you've birthed are mine."

"They're more yours than mine. Your parents saw to that, taking them away from me, keeping them close. I was a stranger to them the second they left me."

"You never wanted to be part of my family," Timet accused.

"I was never given the chance," Janyce raged back.

"You never tried. And now you sit in the room like some dark cloud, shaming us all. The Prince and his companion must have noticed that you didn't say a word at all today."

"And pretend that I was listened to when the matter of his position was discussed? Or the decision to encourage Rania to bed him?"

"You don't support him because you want to further your family's ambitions rather than the family to which you pledged your loyalty when we wed." Footsteps sounded on the other side of the wall, coming closer to the door.

"You're despicable." Janyce was the one who had moved, her voice closer to the door.

"And you're just like every Katan I've ever met. Nasty and self-interested. Where are you going?"

"None of your business!" Janyce declared, flinging open the door and stepping into the corridor.

Elen-ai gathered the shadows about her to shield herself from sight. She almost certainly wouldn't have been noticed, though. Janyce was too intent on her dramatic exit than looking at her surroundings to spot an inconspicuous assassin.

"I hope the Divine One curses her," Timet growled once his wife was definitely out of earshot, stomping over to the door and closing it.

Elen-ai followed Janyce, creeping down several flights of stairs and out into the garden in pursuit of her quarry. Nobody else was out of their rooms. Elen-ai heard one or two murmured conversations, even one sigh of desire, but she paid them little heed. She had been in many houses at night and every sound that reached her ears was the sound of a house at peace, with one very significant exception.

The night air held no chill, but it held no warmth either. Janyce rubbed her upper arms in an effort to warm herself. She had neglected to bring a shawl or coat to put over the thin bedclothes she wore.

Elen-ai stood clothed in shadow a few paces away, watching as the unrelenting rigidity that she had seen in the woman's posture melt away, leaving a very human, very alone person.

Janyce paced idly around the small patch of grass that was edged by perfectly maintained flower beds. She didn't seem to have any particular plan in mind. Elen-ai wondered if she came out here often, but it seemed unlikely given the lack of foresight to bring something to keep her warm.

Her arms still wrapped around herself, Janyce's orbit brought her face clearly into Elen-ai's view, illuminated by a ray of moonlight coming down through the clearing in the trees. Elen-ai had never seen such profound loneliness as she saw etched on the face of the woman before her. The intense emotion made her look both terribly young and impossibly old, made more so by the whiteness of the moonlight. It made Janyce's pale hair look luminescent, making her seem almost otherworldly.

Elen-ai was not certain that she could understand what she saw, but she was transfixed by it. It was a sentiment so profound, so intense, that all she could understand was that it had locked Janyce away from everybody around her. The lonely woman paced the small garden. One hand went occasionally to her stomach in the reflexive manner of all pregnant women.

Eventually, Elen-ai decided that she would not glean anything more. No words would be uttered, and no great secret would be revealed through this aimless pacing. Whatever allegiance she may have to the family of her birth, Elen-ai's instinct told her that this woman was too preoccupied with her loneliness to be a part of any particular scheme against Gidyon other than as a reluctant observer as her husband encouraged their daughter to seduce the Prince. Taking one last look at Janyce, she moved back into the house, climbing back up the stairs to the room she and Gidyon shared.

As soon as she entered the bedroom, she knew something was wrong. She went over to the bed to verify that she wasn't, but as she had known from the instant she came into the room that it was empty.

FIFTEEN

Panic threatened for one horrifying, unending moment to overwhelm Elen-ai. It took all the discipline and training she had to quash the sensation and stand completely still, listening to the house. She hadn't been away from the room for long, he couldn't be far away. She could hear everything throughout the house from the sound of the grass being crushed under the feet of the sad Janyce to the breathing of several people, most of them asleep. Amid this, she heard from high up, likely somewhere in the music room, the sound of whispers, of a gasp. As quickly as she could, she climbed the stairs of the house, her feet making no sound. Recriminations swirled in her mind. She should not have thought it safe or wise to leave the Prince, yet she had become lax at the fact that little had happened during the few times when she had previously left his side. At the door to the music room she paused, hearing a furtive rustle of cloth, then she opened it to find Gidyon and Rania locked in a passionate embrace.

At her sudden appearance, they sprang apart guiltily. Elen-ai stood in the doorway, her slight frame nearly blending into the shadows of the house but for her face, illuminated by a candle in the room.

"Elen-ai," Gidyon began, but she stepped into the room toward the two.

"Stop." She cut off whatever he may have been about to say. "You and I will speak later."

Perhaps for the first time, he did as she bade and fell silent. She turned to Rania who was looking at Elen-ai apprehensively.

"Gidyon can be with who he chooses," the girl said, a semblance of defiance peeking through her uncertainty. She lifted her chin, the shadow of a look of pride on her features. Of course, she thought that Elen-ai as someone of common birth, was a lover the Prince could thoughtlessly discard in favour of another woman.

"Why don't you tell Gidyon what your parents instructed you to do," Elen-ai suggested. The soft menace in her voice was terrifying.

To Rania's credit, she did not flinch. "I have no idea what you mean."

"Don't play games with me, little girl. Your parents were enjoying quite the argument just now, and what you had been told to do was mentioned for anyone listening to learn about." Elen-ai advanced on her, her face a grim visage.

"What do you mean?" Gidyon's head whipped from Elen-ai to Rania.

"Tell him," Elen-ai commanded the girl.

"Tell me what?" Gidyon echoed when no words were forthcoming.

"They just thought we may get along," Rania whimpered, her eyes wide and pleading.

"What do you mean?" Gidyon took a step toward her. He was now no longer the lust-struck boy, but once more the Prince, and his words carried an authority that even Elen-ai's menace could not match.

"They said that if you liked me, I should try and..." Unwilling to say the words, she hung her head.

"And what did your family expect to come of this?" Gidyon asked, his face as unmoving as stone. The sudden change in his demeanour was frightening.

"Nothing. I swear." Rania looked up her, her face a mask of wide-eyed honesty.

"The word marriage was never used?"

"Well, maybe once," she admitted.

Gidyon took a deep breath. Elen-ai noticed his hands clench very briefly into fists. "You love your family, don't you, Rania?" he asked.

She nodded, her gaze averted.

"Look at me, please," Gidyon said.

Her reluctance obvious, Rania brought her gaze to him. The vivacity that she had earlier espoused had disappeared and in its place was an uncertain young girl.

"Now answer me. Do you love your family?" Gidyon asked again.

"Yes." Her voice was barely above a whisper.

"Of course you do. Family is the most important thing. Isn't that what we are all told here in the Second Country from birth?"

"Yes."

Elen-ai wondered where he was going with these questions, but stayed silent.

"You marrying me would be very good for your family, wouldn't it? It would bring them much prestige, as well as perhaps a favourable place when it came to dealing with their business. Perhaps it would even bring the ear of the Queen - or the person who succeeds her." Gidyon reached out and took Rania's hand in both of his. "Now I want you to listen very carefully to what I am about to say, Rania. Because I will only say it once. Are you listening carefully?"

"Yes, Gidyon." She sounded almost hopeful.

"If your parents ask you how your efforts with me went, you will tell them that they failed. That you tried your hardest because you did not want to let them down, but I did not accept any of your advances."

Rania nodded obediently. Her hand remained in both of Gidyon's.

"And you will never tell them that I did in fact accept your invitation to meet you here tonight, or that anything transpired between us."

"Of course not," she breathed, a slight smile drawing the corners of her mouth upwards.

"Do you know why you will never breathe a word of this?" Gidyon continued without pausing to allow her to answer, his voice almost gentle. "Because you love your family. And you have the best interests of your family at heart. And if I ever hear a rumour about you and myself, I will ensure that your family is ruined. Taxes, tariffs, a conspicuous absence of invitations to the Court, an absence of blessings on any marriage that may occur between a member of the Harete family and one of the other six families. I will ensure that it is cheaper to buy timber from other countries than from this lovely forest. No, Rania, look at me." His voice retained that gentle quality. Rania's eyes had filled with tears and she had looked down. Elenai almost felt sorry for the girl. She saw Gidyon's grip on Rania's hand tighten.

"Your family has pledged their loyalty to me, and your parents offered me their hospitality. And I do not want to harm you or them. But my trust has also been abused, and that I cannot forget or forgive. Do not cry, Rania. Nothing bad will happen to you or your family if you stay silent. You have my word on that."

Tears spilled unchecked down her cheeks as she looked at him.

"Do you understand?" Gidyon asked, his gaze on her unwavering.

She nodded.

"Good girl. How about we all head to bed, then," he suggested.

She nodded again. Only then did Gidyon release her hand. She fled the room, not even seeming to notice Elen-ai, and went down the stairs to her own bedroom. Elen-ai heard the door open and close, and the sound of quiet sobbing commence. She turned her attention to Gidyon who had put his hand to his mouth and looked as though he were somewhere between being deeply abashed and lost in thought.

"Thank you," he said. The fearsome person he had become to deal with Rania had vanished.

The fury that she had been holding in check while he spoke with Rania uncoiled itself. "How could you be so stupid?" she hissed.

Gidyon at least had the good grace to blush. "I thought..."

She cut him off. "No Gidyon, that's exactly it. You didn't think. At least, not with your head."

"I wouldn't have come here if you hadn't been gone when I woke up," he protested quietly.

"Don't you dare try and make this my fault," Elen-ai fumed, keeping her voice low so as not to wake anybody else in the house. "I warned you. I *told* you to be careful. And you still went chasing after her because she promised you – what?"

"I was never going to do anything serious," Gidyon said.

"You and she were alone, here, in the middle of the night. How can you say that?" Elen-ai threw up her hands. "Shadow God, you're just like your parents!"

Gidyon's face froze into place and his expression hardened. Perhaps anger at himself for being so easily fooled by Rania was coming to the surface, lured there by her comment. There once more though was the cold, furious Prince who had so suddenly appeared to reduce Rania to tears. "You have no right to say that," he said. His voice and his eyes were dangerous, but Elen-ai was too busy nursing her own fury to care.

"I have every right. *I* found out that Zekken was your father, *I* found out that Rania had been told to seduce you, and *I* stopped you from doing anything stupid with her. And here you are throwing everything away because some stupid girl bats her eyelashes at you. Did you really think that she wanted nothing from you? Did you really think that the pleasant picture of to-day was all there was to see?" She made no effort to hide the anger or scorn from her voice.

"Why do you care? Your job is to keep me alive, not to keep me as heir to the throne. That's what you are being paid to do. You are like any other servant. Don't forget your place." Gidyon spat the words at her like bile, his own careful control lost in the heat of his anger and humiliation.

Elen-ai glared at him, the candlelight flickering across both of their faces. "I'll await your orders then, your High-ness," she said, turning from him to blow out the candle so that he didn't see the hurt his words had caused across her face.

In darkness she found herself able to speak again. "Is it your wish that we retire for the evening, or do you have other commands?"

Gidyon did not reply, instead leaving the room that had been the site of so much drama and making his way quietly back down to their room. Elen-ai followed him after extin-guishing the candle, wordless and distant, suddenly returned to being a stranger to him.

That night, neither she nor the Prince slept. She could not begin to know what was in his thoughts. His cruelty had hurt her deeply. She had not realised how much she had come to view the Prince as a friend, nor indeed how incredibly slender the thread that bound them together was. That was the truth about family; a cruel word or an unkindness between kin could be surmounted with time and an apology. Family was bound together by something intangible but impossible to break. It was why Elen-ai had vowed never to leave the Family. There she would be loved and accepted, regardless what mistakes she may make. Certainly, no family was perfect, and sometimes families did terrible things to one another, yet there was nothing so powerful nor so strong as the ties between members of a family. Gidyon himself had exploited that in his threats to Rania.

Elen-ai chastised herself for thinking for a moment that her friendship with Gidyon was something real, something possibly even enduring. As he himself had reminded her, she was just another of his servants.

Morning dawned. Elen-ai shrugged off the fatigue, accustomed only to a few hours of sleep. Gidyon looked less fresh, the smudges of exhaustion visible under his eyes and in the drawn lines of his face. Perhaps that exhaustion was added to by the betrayal of the previous evening. Elen-ai still could not understand how he, an adept reader of people and their motives, had been so tricked by the simple charm of a girl, but a part of her wondered if he had wanted to believe for a moment that he was just a boy who could engage in a simple dalliance. For anybody else, a romantic meeting with Rania would have been perhaps a little unusual but not something to bring them to ruin. For Gidyon, it was his reputation, his name, his legitimacy, that was at stake. The weight of such an expectation, to be always perfect, to have not the slightest mark against him that might call his capacity to rule into question, must be crushing, even though he never spoke of it. But Elen-ai was not feeling charitable towards the Prince, so she pushed that explanation to the back of her mind and instead labelled him a spoiled, graceless brat.

Despite whatever personal feelings he may have felt toward the family who had sought to leverage influence over him through their daughter, Gidyon was perfectly charming at the breakfast table. Timet had appeared briefly, grabbing a hunk of bread and hurriedly apologising for a speedy departure, citing the need to attend to some logging operation. He also offered an apology for Janyce, claiming that she was not feeling well.

Lindel and Lilea were both in attendance, sitting content-edly at the table, their wizened faces focused intently on the successful passage of food from their plates to mouths. Gidyon made very polite, and patient, conversation with them as he picked at his own food. Elen-ai stayed silent as was her cus-tom, occupying herself with her food and observation of the room.

Rania entered when they were about halfway through their meal, her own face looking as though she had not enjoyed much sleep during the night. Elen-ai had heard her sobs sub-side after a few hours, but it seemed that the girl had not got-ten much more sleep than Elen-ai or Gidyon. Gidyon greeted her with the same charm he had on the previous day. To any-one who was unaware of what had transpired during the even-ing, there was no difference in his demeanour. For a moment, Rania looked surprised, then she cautiously offered her own smile and greeting.

"Did you sleep well? You look a touch pale." Gidyon's concern sounded so genuine that even Elen-ai believed it for a moment.

"I'm afraid I found it very difficult to fall asleep," Rania confessed hesitantly.

"I hope that you have not been disturbed by my and Elen-ai's presence or our impact on your family," Gidyon said. The veiled warning was evidently not lost on her. She turned an even paler shade of white.

"N-no, your highness. Perhaps I overindulged at dinner," she stammered.

"Hopefully the unease will pass," he said, his face com-pletely sincere.

"I'm sure it will." Rania lowered her head as she scurried to her seat – one as far away from Gidyon as possible.

He appeared not to notice her careful avoidance of him, instead simply returning to pick at his food in apparent con-tentment.

The morning passed with Gidyon taking a walk through the house's gardens and Elen-ai following him from a distance. What she had briefly glimpsed of the Harete gardens the previous day had only been a fraction of their scope. They were quite spectacular. Were she not still so upset by Gidyon's cruelty and stupidity the evening before she would have quite enjoyed discovering the meandering paths, or even simply sitting in some of the different areas. Hedges were pruned to guide the walker into different sections, some alive with the violent blossom of late spring flowers. Even the kitchen's gardens were artfully arranged, neat lines of vegetables and herbs forming beautiful patterns in the soil.

Some people brush past arguments, not letting words flung at them in anger achieve the objective of getting under the skin. Gidyon and Elen-ai were the other type of person; the one for whom such comments, even though said in the heat of the moment, could not be forgotten or forgiven. It seemed to Elen-ai as they each made their careful way through the gardens as far apart from each other as possible, that whatever friendship may have existed between them was almost certainly destroyed.

Still no word had been exchanged between them when they went inside for lunch. Timet had returned from the work that he was overseeing and Janyce had emerged with her impenetrable sullenness in place. Elen-ai spared her a lingering glance, but there was no sign of the deep distress that Elen-ai had witnessed the previous evening. Her cool mask of indifference was as it had been the previous day. Hiding genuine emotion seemed necessary in order to be a member of a family with wealth and power. It seemed an exhausting task to Elen-ai.

As had been the case with breakfast, Gidyon chatted cheerfully with everyone at the table, even Rania. Elen-ai felt a momentary pity for the girl. After all, she had merely been doing what her family had bid her. As disgusted as she may have been with Gidyon for his blindness to the plan, she was more repulsed by family members who would use their own so callously. It was a timely reminder that the world through she accompanied Gidyon was not her own, governed by a certain ruthlessness that she, an assassin, found left a bitter taste in her mouth. She would be glad to leave this life.

Whatever she may have thought of the Harete family though, when she took a bite of the luncheon dessert, she thought that she had never tasted anything so delicious in her entire life. Gidyon's effusive words of appreciation for the dish echoed her sentiments.

"It's because it's made from fruit which we picked today from our orchards," Timet explained with a disarming smile. "Nothing can beat freshness."

"But it's the recipe, too!" Gidyon exclaimed.

"A secret of the household." Lilea leaned forward in a conspiratorial manner, a smile on her face.

"Forget timber, you should just sell this," Gidyon joked between mouthfuls.

"We're so glad you like it," Lilea reached her gnarled hand across the table and patted the Prince's forearm. Elen-ai wondered how sincere the old woman actually was, or if she too had been a part of the scheme to entrap the Prince.

"I shan't forget your hospitality, or the efforts that the members of the Harete family went to." Gidyon smiled, turning ever so slightly to look at Rania. It seemed unnecessary to yet again remind the girl of Gidyon's promise to her. His comment clearly struck home, she caught the quiver of her lips quickly, pressing them together tightly. However, he made no other such comments to Rania during the rest of the luncheon, simply announcing at its conclusion that he and Elen-ai would depart the following morning. Polite lament over the brevity of his visit was offered, with the return of promises to return and stay longer – delivered with equal politeness.

The rest of the afternoon was an exercise in a similar silence to the morning. This time however, Gidyon spent the
time inside, seating himself in the house's library and perusing
the books there. The Harete catalogue did not come close to
rivalling the collection of the Veertaks, but the bookshelves
were filled with a respectable number of texts nevertheless.
Elen-ai read on the other side of the room to Gidyon, casting
the occasional glance at him, but he refused to so much as look
in her direction. She refused to be the one to speak first to try
and bridge the gulf that both of them had created the previous
evening. She remembered the words of her Father so many
weeks ago, about learning from her mistakes. She resolved to
not make the mistake again of thinking she and the Prince
were friends. Remembering that day, the advice of her Father
was inextricably linked with the bustle and sound of the market. Even though she preferred silence and shade, she wished
she were back in the market, in Herran, close to the Family and
everything that she knew.

SIXTEEN

Gidyon maintained his silence throughout the evening and into the entirety of the carriage ride the next day. In reply, Elen-ai retreated into herself, pretending that he wasn't there. They remained in their respective silences for the entirety of the week that it took them to get to the Bertak family's home, speaking only for the most necessary of communications. There were no more evening lessons on the art of fighting, no more light-hearted banter, no more easy companionship.

Elen-ai watched alone as the Harete forest thinned out until it turned into the flat farmlands that were in the footlands of the Bertak mountains. Despite the expansive number of farms, farming was not really where the Bertak fortune came from. The Bertak lands encompassed a small cluster of mountains in whose bowels were precious metals. Indeed, the metal that formed the cuffs which the Queen always wore at her neck and wrists came from the Bertak mountains. However, despite controlling this resource, the Bertak family's wealth and power did not rank among that of the Aadran, Tak, Katan or even Harete families. An uncharitable soul, and Elen-ai did not consider herself particularly generous, might say that it was because the Bertaks had never put much time or effort into cultivating craftspeople loyal to them to work the resource that they controlled, instead simply seeing the short term benefit to selling off the metal they withdrew from their mountains. Regardless, as a result, the fertile soil in the rest of their lands had been turned into farms that generated extra revenue for the family. This was hardly a singular practice. Any land within the Queendom that was suitable for farmland and not purposed for some other use had foodstuff grown on it. However, it was known that the Bertaks found it particularly egregious that they needed to support their wealth with farmland rather than to simply extend their wealth. This petty embarrassment was compounded by the fact that everybody knew it. The conditions for those who worked in farms on the Veertak estate were markedly different to the other lands they had traversed. Elen-ai watched Gidyon's face as he observed the pitiful existence of the people who worked the farms scattered along the Bertak lands. Perhaps had the Bertak family established a community of jewellers or metalworkers, similar to the scholars in Atak or the clayworkers in the Katan lands, the Bertaks would be wealthier and the people who lived on their land would live in better conditions.

People barely paid the battered Veertak carriage any mind as it passed by. Late harvests were being conducted, or the land was being tilled in preparation for the next planting. Nobody realised that the ignominious carriage carried their future ruler, likely they didn't spend any time wondering who passed by them. Their clothes spoke of the pittance paid to them by those who owned the land on which they worked more eloquently than they ever could have.

The days were clear and warm. Summer had suddenly gone from being a hint on a breath of wind to possible. As they trekked through the Bertak farms on the first day, Elen-ai spied a bird climbing almost vertically into the sky. It looked as though it would fall out of the air, its ascent was so high and so steep. Then it suddenly turned and swooped back down with a reckless speed, lost from sight as it plummeted close to the ground, blending against the faint outline of the mountains' blue backdrop. Elen-ai assumed that the bird was catching some prey, but she preferred to think that it was enjoying the ability to perform such a remarkable feat. She almost turned to say something about it to Gidyon, but caught herself, remembering that he was not her friend. Such comments, such conversations, did not take place between a servant and master.

Elen-ai did not know with what thoughts Gidyon occupied himself during that week. He seemed to draw in upon himself, to be constantly musing on some idea or another. Yet with whatever conclusions he may have drawn, he never seemed satisfied. A look of pensive worry crept onto his face as they entered the Bertak land and never departed, even in his sleep. The absence of any answers as to who had tried to kill Gidyon and the Queen bothered Elen-ai, too. With a would-be killer still at large, it meant she had to continue to stay as close to Gidyon as possible, which was particularly unpalatable given his obnoxious silence.

Due to the absence of any taverns or inns within the Bertak lands as a result of the family's well-known disapproval of 'houses of ill repute', Elen-ai and Gidyon had no opportunity to bathe or sleep anywhere other than under the stars. The closest they came was a small settlement that they encountered on the second day where Elen-ai merely bought some more food to last them until they reached the seat of the Bertak power; the family home. Taverns and tiny townships were scattered throughout the other territories of the Queendom, but not here. The family did not encourage such things, going so far as to prohibit the conglomeration of more than ten abodes three generations ago. The only settlement allowed by the Bertaks in their lands was right outside the entrance to the mountain mines.

They followed the shore of lake Bertak during the last two days of travel. That section of the lake had no shore, merely high cliffs with a significant drop down into waters that moodily broke upon the point where stone met the waves. For those two days, Elen-ai spent much time glancing uneasily at the crumbling edge of the road and the drop into those unwelcoming waters. She kept the carriage as far away from the edge as possible, maintaining an inward commentary of colourful descriptors about the family who seemed not to deem it necessary to maintain the roads within their lands.

These uncharitable thoughts were at the forefront of her mind when they arrived at the Bertak home. It was built from the same stone that made up the mountains, and the cliff on which they had driven. However, unlike the stone which in its natural environment had a vaguely pleasant colour, the slabs of the house had been polished so that they shone a dirty off-white. The house itself was architecturally magnificent; half of it nestled in the mountain at whose foot it had been built, the other half extended almost to the edge of the cliff. Despite the visual spectacle that the house offered both to someone observing it, as well as someone looking out from it, Elen-ai found it a tad ugly, pretensions of grandeur too obvious in the lines of the design. She had no idea for what purpose an observatory on the uppermost level had been built – the mountain would block out much of the sky – but there it sat, a testament to the family's supposed status as intellectuals.

Elen-ai drew the carriage to a stop. Nobody came to greet them. It was as though the house was deserted. She and Gidyon stepped down off the carriage and walked around, waiting for someone to notice their arrival. Eventually, Elen-ai went up to the grand doors, elaborately carved timber that looked as though it were Harete wood, and knocked.

The door was answered by the thinnest woman Elen-ai had ever seen. Despite the warmth of the day, she was dressed in a high-necked full-length dress with sleeves that came all the way down to her wrists. "May I help you?" she asked.

"Are the heads of the family in?" Elen-ai enquired.

"Who wants to know?"

"The Royal family," Elen-ai responded, reining in her temper so that she did not simply snap at this emaciated creature.

"One moment, please," the woman replied, shutting the door in Elen-ai's face.

Gidyon, who was standing a few paces, away gave snort. "Amazing," he said softly. Elen-ai couldn't help but agree with the sarcastic sentiment. It was the first time one of them had spoken to the other without having to.

A few minutes later the woman returned, opening the door wide – quite a feat given the size of the door relative to her. "Please come in," she said.

Elen-ai and Gidyon walked through the huge doorway and into the entrance hall. Various weapons were mounted on the wall, glinting dully in the dim light. As they followed the woman, Elen-ai counted at least thirty different types of sword, twelve spears designs, and sixteen daggers.

They were led through several dark corridors and into a room which overlooked the lake. Here, in contrast to the darkness of the halls through which they had passed, the light poured in, almost too bright.

"If you will be seated, Lady Julyana will be with you shortly," the woman informed them, exiting the room.

Elen-ai and Gidyon exchanged a look of raised eyebrows, their first actual interaction in over a week.

Gidyon wandered over to the window and looked out at the lake below. The sun glinted off its surface, the blue of the water lost in the sparkle of the sunlight. Elen-ai had no idea how he could remain squinting into the glare for so long without his eyes becoming sore. To save her own eyes, she turned her attention to the room's interior. Only two weapons graced the walls in here; a matching dagger and sword. Aside from chairs, a few tables, and a cabinet of bottles filled with what Elen-ai presumed were liquor, there was nothing else in the room.

They were waiting for several minutes before the door opened and a plump woman in her middle years entered. Her fingers were bedecked with various rings and around her throat was a cuff similar to the one worn by the Queen. Unfortunately, while around the slender column of the Queen's neck the cuff was quite striking, it merely emphasised her jowls peeking over the top. The only thing about her which was not rotund was her nose which was curiously delicate in stark contrast to the rest of her. Her mouth had been stained a dark crimson, standing out against her powdered face. She looked somewhat absurd given that only in the capital did people really paint their faces, and even then, only on particular occasions.

Gidyon had turned from the window and crossed the room to greet her. "Lady Julyana. It's so wonderful to see you again." Despite the fact that he hadn't bathed in several days and was covered with dust from the road, Gidyon still managed to be disarmingly charming.

"Master Gidyon." The woman's round fingers enveloped Gidyon's outstretched hands. "Or should I call you Prince?" Her question was delivered with a sly emphasis which had Elen-ai double checking that all of her blades were within easy access.

Gidyon did not seem at all perturbed by her comment. "It seems that news has a way of reaching everyone."

"And I presume that this is your companion who I've heard much about. Lady Elen-ai." Her emphasis of 'lady' made clear her scepticism on the subject of Elen-ai's character.

"Lady Julyana, it's a pleasure to meet you. I am most impressed by your weapons collection," Elen-ai murmured, her anger in check – just.

"Ah yes. All the women in my family have a love affair with weapons of any form. The collection was started by my grandmother, a custom that I have continued." Julyana responded with a dismissive airiness.

Elen-ai bit down on her incredulous question as to whether or not Julyana herself was even remotely adept with any blade other than one that was part of a cutlery set.

"Please, let us sit." The outermost limits of politeness met, Julyana addressed Gidyon, lowering her girth into an armchair. She did not offer him or Elen-ai anything to drink or eat.

"I presume if you are aware of my new title, and even my companion's name, you are aware of why I am here." Gidyon sat after a moment's hesitation. Elen-ai sat beside him, trying to restrain herself from glaring at this odious woman.

"I certainly am. I'm sure it would not surprise you to know that I am also aware of the responses that other people have given you to the question of whether or not they will support your claim to the throne. It was so distressing to hear of the attempt on you and your mother's lives all those weeks ago before, by the way." Julyana interlinked her pudgy hands together, the rings clinking softly. She paused, a look of relish coming over her face. "It has been a long time since the crown has truly needed our support on something. We know you have the support of the Harete family and the Veertaks. And the rumour of a Katans' alternative heir has certainly reached our ears, alongside the possibility that the Rasatan family will throw their support behind this claim. I personally found it interesting that the Tak and Aadran families declined to state their support for you." Her brown eyes looked at him keenly.

"Families as large and powerful as the Taks and Aadrans have the luxury of being able to make such a decision. But even they must tread carefully," Gidyon replied.

"And yet you have one of the other largest families in the Queendom poised to oppose your claim," the large woman pointed out.

Gidyon shrugged. "At this point, it is mere speculation. But if they were to do so, I'm sure that they have their own reasons. Even so, to do so would be a risk. I currently have more supporters than I have opponents."

"The way the Bertaks speak may alter that," Julyana said.

Gidyon inclined his head in acknowledgement of that truth.

"Tell me your Highness, if the Bertak clan were to support your mother's decision to put a man on the throne, what would that mean for our corner of the world?" Julyana leaned back, her fingers still clasped. It looked very much as though she was enjoying this conversation.

"That I could not tell you," Gidyon said. "One would have to wait and see what the future holds."

"Hmm." Julyana looked down at her hands. "I hear you have pledged to marry a woman of common birth in order to ensure your neutrality."

"You hear correctly."

"Yet measures taken to protect neutrality do not always work."

A look of confusion swept across Gidyon's face almost too fast to see. "It's the best I can offer, I'm afraid," he confessed, spreading his hands.

Julyana unlinked her fingers, placing her palms flat against each other and bringing her touching hands up to her face. She performed the act of thinking well, gently tapping her fingertips against each other, with a slight frown drawing her eyebrows downward, creasing the powder on her face. Eventually she straightened up, her pretence of deliberation complete. With a regretful sigh, she raised her eyes to meet Gidyon's. "I am terribly sorry your Highness, but I'm afraid that the Bertak family cannot support your claim to the throne. We must follow the lead of the Tak and Aadran families and remain neutral in this matter. I'm sure you can understand," she added with an insincere smile.

Gidyon's pleasant smile did not waver. "Lady Julyana, you and your family must of course protect yourselves in uncertain times," he told her, his tone warm and understanding.

"I should note that I of course personally wish you success in your claim," she said.

"That is very kind of you," he told her.

"Would you and your companion like to stay awhile with us?" she offered after Gidyon said nothing more.

"It's very generous of you to offer, but I'd hate to impose upon you any further than we already have." Gidyon stood, Elen-ai echoing his movement.

"Perhaps on another trip, then?" Julyana levered herself to her feet with no little effort.

"Of course," Gidyon assured her.

She waddled with them to the front door, back through the dark corridors, their gloom punctuated by the gleam of the carefully polished metal of the weapons on the walls. "Can I offer you anything else?" She made one last cursory effort at the front doors.

"No Julyana, I wouldn't want to take anything from you." She was clearly unable to discern whether or not his response was a barb due to the warmth with which spoke. Elen-ai was.

Julyana waved them off from the front steps, disappearing back inside her ugly ode to the Bertak's perception of their place in the world before the carriage was even out of sight.

Once it was certain that they were away from the Bertak house, Gidyon's anger revealed itself in the most magnificent fashion.

"How dare she!" he exploded.

"Was she ever going to support you?" Elen-ai asked, her own anger only a pace behind his.

"Not unless I promised to marry a member of her family," he replied, the stony wall of silence between them temporarily dismantled in the face of his outrage.

"Her as family? What an awful prospect," Elen-ai commented viciously.

"I'd rather see the Katan girl on the throne than call that fat creature family," Gidyon spat. "Do you know what was the worst thing? The lack of any politeness. We were made to knock on the door. She was playing games with us."

"I could go back and kill her, if you liked," Elen-ai offered, only half in jest.

"It's not worth it." Gidyon shook his head.

"It would be easy. It would appear as though one of her weapons had fallen on her," Elen-ai said.

Gidyon looked at her, his face suddenly wary. "Do you always see the world in ways to kill people?" he asked.

Elen-ai shrugged. "I suppose I do." Uncomfortable with whatever he might have said next, she returned the subject of the Bertaks. "Does she know about Zekken?" Elen-ai asked, recalling the comment about impartiality.

"I don't think so." Gidyon shook his head. "I think she heard it as a rumour but she doesn't know whether or not it's true."

Elen-ai thought back to the look of confusion that had crossed Gidyon's face. Of course, it hadn't been confusion, it had been designed to leave Julyana assuming he knew nothing of any such rumour. An alternative path as an actor would pay him lucratively if he was ousted from the Palace.

The detente between them as a result of Julyana Bertak lasted into the evening. They set up their modest camp and lay on the grass looking up at the sky side by side. While they still hadn't had an evening fighting lesson, it was a marked difference to the previous week.

"You can't get a view like this in the city." Elen-ai gestured to the sky. The still, cloudless night of the early summer meant that a band of yellow lingered on the horizon, the sky above it a light blue tapering into darkness above them, punctuated by emerging stars.

"It is beautiful," the Prince agreed.

"Do you think that they may have been behind the attack on you and your mother?" she asked after a pause.

Gidyon was silent for a moment, contemplating the possibility. "I've been wondering a similar thing myself," he confessed. "I certainly think they are the most likely suspects at the moment. She did not do a very good job of hiding her belief that the Bertaks have been overlooked by the crown."

"I don't see how they can gain anything from you and your mother being dead, though," Elen-ai noted.

"I know," Gidyon agreed.

"The only two families we haven't spoken with are the Rasatan family and the Katan family. If you don't think it's someone in any of the families that we've been to so far, it has to be someone from the last two," Elen-ai said logically.

"You could be right," Gidyon said, clearly unconvinced. "I can't help but feel I'm missing something, though," he said. "Something's bothering me, but I don't quite know what it is. How will anyone take me seriously as a ruler if I can't keep my people in check?" he exclaimed. He drummed his hand on the ground in frustration.

"I wouldn't worry yourself about it. It'll come to you," Elen-ai said, rolling her neck to ease a stiff spot. "Where are we going next? The Rasatan lands?"

"We'll go past Herran on the way to their lands. I think I'd like to spend a few days at home before I go on to see them. Besides, I'd like to have a few words with my mother," he said darkly, his anger with his mother obviously unabated despite the intervening weeks since his discovery of her relationship with Zekken.

"Makes sense. Whatever you'd like to do, I'll do," Elen-ai said comfortably.

"Would you really have gone back and killed Julyana if I had asked you to?" Gidyon asked suddenly.

"I would certainly have considered it. She was rude," Elen-ai said.

"Does it ever bother you? Killing people?"

"Once," she admitted.

"Why not more?" He had propped himself up on one elbow to look at her, but she declined to return the movement.

"It just…doesn't." She couldn't explain it to him any more than she could understand it herself. "If I had to guess it's possibly because I've always been taught that death is natural."

"But you bring death early."

"Who are you to say that?" she challenged gently. "People kill people all the time. If the Family didn't exist, some other group would take its place. Because try as we might, we kill each other. It's in our nature."

"That's a pessimistic view," Gidyon said.

"I don't think it's pessimistic or optimistic. It's a fact." Elen-ai turned slightly away from him so that he couldn't even see her profile, only the curve of her cheek.

Taking the hint, Gidyon fell silent.

Elen-ai was occupied by thoughts of the third time she had taken a contract. This time, the Mothers and Fathers had not been kind to her. She had been sent to eliminate the life of a girl who had fallen pregnant to a member of the Katan clan. The man's aspirations of a good post within the trade administration meant that he needed to have a clear history and this girl was a blight on that because it demonstrated a lack of discretion on his part, given that he was married.

Elen-ai had followed the girl for three days. As was the case with most people who lived in the Katan lands, she was a skilled clayworker, pulling beautiful shapes from sticky clods. Elen-ai had only learned of the motivation behind the contract by listening carefully; the man had unusually not offered an explanation for why he wanted her dead when he had approached the Family. It was a curious inversion to her first kill, and from everything that Elen-ai had seen, the girl was perfectly lovely. The child in her stomach was only just beginning to show, and she hadn't told anybody other than her mother and the child's father that she would soon be a mother. However, Elen-ai's role was not to arbitrate on the morality of the contract but to see it completed. She did not ponder the killing of a corrupt merchant or a brutal farmhand, so she should not question this. So she had killed the girl gently as she slept. She would not have felt a thing.

Beside her as she remembered, Gidyon slipped quietly into sleep.

SEVENTEEN

Their friendship had not recovered from the heated exchange at the Harete home despite the fact that they had resumed talking to each other. Both Gidyon and Elen-ai addressed each other with a measure of wariness, of uncertainty as to what barbs each could and would hurl at the other. But, united by their shared dislike for Julyana Bertak, they had returned to speaking terms. That fact certainly made the trip back to the capital go by a little faster than it otherwise would have. The training sessions in the evenings even resumed, and Elen-ai noticed improvement gradually creeping into Gidyon's technique.

Three days after their unpleasant encounter at the Bertak family home they returned to sovereign land and the main road. Elen-ai was glad. Being on the badly maintained roads of the Bertak estate had left her cranky. Her mood was not helped by the fact that each day had been hotter and stickier than the last, promising rain but failing to deliver it. As they approached Herran, the breeze coming from the sea offered a welcome if not fleeting relief from the oppressive heat which clung to them. On the seventh and last day of their travel, desperate to distract herself from the uncomfortable heat, Elen-ai turned to Gidyon. "Are you any closer to knowing who was behind the attack on you and your mother?"

"I have no idea. Nobody that we have spoken to seems to stand to gain anything from the success of such an attack." He made a gesture of irritation. "I need to find out who it was. How can I be the heir to the throne when someone who tried to kill me and my mother remains at large?" His helpless frustration was understandable.

Given they were absolutely no closer to knowing who was behind the attack, Elen-ai could not help but feel that whoever it was might try again. If someone really wanted another person dead, they weren't going to take stop trying because of one failed attempt.

"People don't just kill for their own advancement," Elen-ai commented, squinting to verify that she could in fact see the city in the distance.

"What else do they kill for?" Gidyon slid her a look of curiosity.

"Killing someone either comes from a place of extreme reason or extreme emotion. Reason is generally when people decide the best, or easiest, way to secure what they want is to eliminate someone. Emotion is when you are generally, not always mind you, unbearably angry with someone to the point that their continued existence is a blight you cannot stand."

"You really think that the reason behind the attack could be the second?" Gidyon rubbed his chin thoughtfully as he contemplated her comment.

"The Veertaks seem loyal, and they seek peace. An upset like that would not serve their interests. The Taks and Aadrans – well, Zekken definitely wouldn't want that, but then again, neither family stands to gain anything in the instance of you and your mother's death." Elen-ai did not repeat her earlier suspicion about Arlena. No matter how she looked at it, she could not believe that the Aadran matriarch would use such a crude way to further or secure her family's position. "The Harete family thought they could further themselves by marrying Rania to you. The Bertaks...I again see no way they would benefit from the murder of you or your mother. Maybe the Katans or Rasatans? But it doesn't seem quite right to me. Their best gains are made politically, too. It does seem like the desire to end your life is a very personal one," she concluded.

"I agree." Gidyon sighed in frustration. "I mean, the death of my mother and myself would be an opening for them to put one of their own on the throne, but trying to have us killed is such a risk. It's not what someone who is coming from a place of reason would do." He frowned. "I just cannot help but feel I've missed something."

Beside him, Elen-ai thought to herself that there was some vital piece of information they did not yet have, despite her discovery of Latana's secret relationship with Zekken. The knowledge that she did not know something crawled under her skin along with the heat of the day, an irritant that she could not alleviate. Knowledge that was unknown was dangerous.

The city streets quickly negated any relief the sea breeze offered on the approach to the Queendom's capital. The buildings trapped the heat in while also barring the entry of the breeze that had been so welcome on the road. Nevertheless, Elen-ai was fervently glad to be back in the city. She had missed the crowded streets, the familiar atmosphere, the sound of humanity so crushingly proximate. The intense isolation of the previous few weeks with Gidyon was instantly alleviated by simply being surrounded by the noises, smells, and sights that were inextricably associated with home.

The carriage wound its way through the streets, paid no heed by the inhabitants of Herran who were too preoccupied with the task of surviving the stifling heat to take note of one of the many nondescript carriages which passed them.

The sun was reaching its zenith as Elen-ai drew the carriage into the Palace courtyard where servants scurried out to greet them. Gidyon and Elen-ai descended from the driver's bench to face the gaggle of people who breathlessly murmured welcomes to them.

"Master Gidyon, we can have baths ready for you both in only a few minutes," Gidyon was informed.

"That's very kind of you Mal-et, but I think it may be an offer I take you up on in a little while. Do you know where I might find my mother?"

It was strange to hear the Palace servants not address Gidyon as their Prince. Elen-ai had almost forgotten that the Queen had not publically announced her appointment of Gidyon as her heir due to the attack.

"I believe she is in conference with her advisers. She should be finished-"

"I'll see her now, thank you Mal-et. It's good to be home." Gidyon spared a moment to place a hand on the servant's shoulder and give it an appreciative squeeze, leaving the servant looking at him with obvious affection and respect. His thoughtful nature had clearly earned him the love of many who worked in the Palace, judging by the expressions on the faces of the people they passed as they walked through the grand entrance of the Palace. Perhaps, Elen-ai thought to herself, Gidyon would not be rejected by as many of the people as she had once thought.

Gidyon navigated the corridors until they reached one of the rooms that Elen-ai had surmised from her night time investigation of the Palace was used for the Queen's conference with her brothers and advisors. Without knocking, Gidyon opened the doors to the council room filled with maps, desks, and his mother and two of her brothers, all three of whom had turned to regard the impudent individual who had entered without having the respect to at least knock first.

Anger gave way to surprised delight when they recognised Gidyon, the Queen coming forward with her arms held wide to embrace her son. Elen-ai noticed a light bandage on her left hand – presumably the lingering reminder of the injury sustained during the attempt on her life. Gidyon suffered the embrace for as short a time as was possible, then turned to his uncles.

"Nikalus, Silius, I need a moment alone with my mother." He did not speak as their nephew asking their indulgence but as his mother's son, as their Prince.

The two men immediately left the room, casting curious glances at mother and son. Elen-ai was impressed by their deference to their nephew. Latana regarded Gidyon. For the first time that Elen-ai had seen her, she looked older than a woman just leaving girlhood.

"Zek told me that you know he is your father," she said, her face as neutral as ever.

Gidyon stared at her, his eyes so very blue and so very cold. "How could you?" His voice was soft.

"My darling, it's not that simple." An expression of distress clouded the Queen's lovely eyes.

"Don't you dare tell me that. You and my uncles taught me about the importance of duty, the importance of our family's place; that we are more than ourselves. And I find out when I'm on the other side of the country, after someone has tried to take my life – has tried to take your life, that you have betrayed everything you taught me to value and believe?" Gidyon's voice rose as he spoke, becoming louder and louder until he was shouting at the Queen.

If Elen-ai thought she had seen Gidyon angry, the ire she had witnessed was nothing compared to the utter fury he was unleashing on his mother. Yet the Queen did not waver, facing the wrath of her child as straight-backed as ever.

"You don't understand. One day maybe you will." She shook her head sadly. "I know I have failed my duty. There is no excuse that I can offer."

"Failed? That doesn't even begin to describe it." With a violent gesture, Gidyon began pacing the room. "You realise that if this is known by even one person then my claim is ruined, our *family* is ruined. The best thing that would happen is the Katan family put their daughter on the throne. But far more likely is some kind of civil war. Although I suppose it wouldn't matter. We'd all be long dead by then." Anger he had been storing away over the weeks since he had learned of his paternity was unleashed now and had taken on a life of its own. Elen-ai was not certain he could have reined it in, even with his considerable self-control.

"I know what the consequences could be, Gidyon," Latana said, turning to watch her son as he walked. "Are you going to punish me forever for a choice that I made?"

"A choice that you made would be to have a brief affair with him and then break it off. Clearly, that's not what's happened. Even now!" Gidyon flung his hands up.

"I love him," she said simply.

"That's not enough," he flung back at her.

"You're a child, you know nothing of love," she cried, a slight, self-righteous anger creeping into her voice.

"And you're an adult. You aren't supposed to be overruled by your emotions," he returned.

"Enough! I am still your Queen, and your mother, and I do not need to be lectured by you on how I should be conducting myself." Apparently fed up with Gidyon's tirade, Latana raised her own voice. "Do you have any idea how lonely it is to be Queen?"

"So you wanted me to be lonely, but you could not bear it?" There was something particularly wrenching about the look of anguish on Gidyon's face.

"You'll at least have a wife by your side," she thundered.

"A wife who will be the person best suited to be by my side, not the person I may want to take as my wife. How can you ask me to do what you would not?"

Latana stared at Gidyon, her mouth slightly agape. She remained totally rigid for several seconds, then her composure began to crumble. It started with her shoulders slumping ever so slightly. From there, she seemed to crumple in on herself, her hand coming to her mouth and her eyes filling with tears.

She began to sob quietly. "I'm so sorry," she eventually whispered.

Gidyon watched unmoving as his mother sobbed. He did not relent, his face still contorted with anger at her betrayal. The Queen walked over to one of the chairs and sat, burying her face in her hands and continuing to weep.

Elen-ai shifted slightly. She felt profoundly awkward at witnessing this very personal exchange. "Should I leave?" she suggested quietly.

The Queen raised her head to regard Elen-ai. An expression of resignation settled across her features. "I hadn't even realised you were still here," she admitted. There was something particularly shocking about the lack of regard for her composure.

"Elen-ai has been with me throughout everything. She knows everything," Gidyon told his mother.

In response, the Queen raised her hand in a weary gesture. "I must thank you for keeping Gidyon safe, Elen-ai," she said, an almost unthinkingly polite comment.

"You are welcome, your Majesty." Elen-ai linked her hands behind her back. "Really, perhaps it would be easier if I left, though. This seems like a very uh, personal conversation."

"No. I would like you to stay here." As Gidyon turned to address her, his posture of anger melted away and a look that could have been one of pleading arranged itself on his features.

She acquiesced with a nod, wishing he hadn't asked. Such displays of temper were so intensely personal. She had no business witnessing the innermost feelings of her Queen.

"Have you finished chastising me Gidyon?" the Queen enquired, her composure restored to her aside from the slightest rasp in her voice from her brief but violent sobbing.

"I have nothing more to say to you," Gidyon informed her coolly.

"Divine One, if you want to throw a child's fit, do not lecture me like you were an adult," Latana exclaimed. "Put aside your anger with me and tell me what you discovered. Our people in the households only know so much of what transpires. Or will you refuse to speak to me like an infant throwing a tantrum?"

It was with no small amount of sullenness that he did as she bade. "Elen-ai would you mind interjecting if I miss anything?" he asked, before launching into a recount of their journey.

Occasionally Elen-ai would correct him or remind him of a detail that he had forgotten. By unspoken agreement, neither of them mentioned the evening that Elen-ai had found him with Rania. Latana's face grew sharper as she listened, seeming to recover her footing now that they were onto matters within her domain: political schemes. When Gidyon told her of Julyana Bertak's behaviour she let out a slight hiss but did not interrupt. Gidyon finished by offering a more abridged summation of his and Elen-ai's conversation from earlier that day.

Latana frowned slightly, turning to Elen-ai. "How can killing someone be so simple? Reason or emotion?"

Elen-ai spread her hands in a gesture that approximated a shrug. "I don't claim to know the hearts of the people who approach the Family, but at their most simple, these are the constants."

"The Palace's sources of information around the Second Country have found no trace of anyone hiring a group of people to make an attempt on either my or your life, Gidyon. Yet someone at least knew enough of our movements to direct people so that they came within striking distance of both of us," the Queen said.

"Therefore the plan behind such an attack came from someone who either lives in Herran or is in Herran often," Gidyon mused. "That eliminates the Katan family, I suppose. They are rarely here. I do not even know how long it will take before they answer my invitation. Unless they worked through someone who does come to Herran often. That would give them a certain distance in the even that their ally is discovered."

"Inviting them was a good idea. Especially given it means they will stay here in the Palace where we can watch them, rather than in their own residence. Visiting the families was also a good idea." The Queen smiled at Gidyon. "My wonderful, clever son. You make us so proud."

Gidyon's face closed like a slammed door. "Who do you mean by us?"

"Our family of course," Latana replied.

"Don't lie to me." His voice became sharp, louder.

"I'm not lying to you."

Gidyon shook his head. "You can't fool me with a charming smile like you can everyone else. When you said 'us' you meant you and Zekken, didn't you?"

His mother opened her mouth but was spared responding by a knock on the door.

"Nobody can hear what is going on inside this room," Latana explained to Elen-ai as she stood up and crossed the room to the door from which the knock had originated. Elen-ai suspected that the explanation was offered to avoid looking at or speaking to her son.

"I beg your pardon, your Majesty," the woman on the other side said.

"No trouble, Len-am," the Queen replied calmly, as though her son was not furious with her, or her rule and authority was not being threatened by unknown attackers and political rivals.

"It would appear that you have visitors." There was a certain familiarity in the exchange between the Queen and the matronly servant. Elen-ai assumed this Len-am was as close to a friend to the Queen as anyone could be. The Queen's words about being lonely resonated in her mind.

"Visitors?"

"At the invitation of ah, Master Gidyon." She held out a piece of paper.

The Queen took it and read it. Elen-ai recognised the letter Gidyon had sent to the Katan family from the tavern so many weeks ago. Latana scanned it quickly then handed it back to the servant.

"It would appear that your invitation has been accepted, Gidyon. You have returned just in time." Latana did not turn to look at her son as she spoke.

"It's not just the Katan family," the servant Len-am said. "They appear to be accompanied by two members of the Rasa-tan family."

"On what grounds?" Latana pursed her lips, the only sign that she might have been taken by surprise.

"I believe as part of the Katan retinue."

"Tenuous grounds on which to impose themselves on us, especially as guests rather than merely visitors."

"You don't need to tell me that, your Majesty," Len-am replied, none of the Queen's diplomacy in her voice.

At the obvious disapproval, Latana laughed. "Prepare rooms for them, offer them refreshments, and send word to the kitchen that they will need to prepare a special feast for tonight – please also apologise to them, I know it is late notice."

"As you wish."

"Oh, and I think if we are to welcome our guests perhaps we could take a lesson from the diplomatic wisdom of lady Jul-yana." At this, she did turn to look at her son, a smile of grim purpose on her face. Gidyon, at least temporarily united with her by the diplomatic hostility of the visitors, smiled back at her. The resemblance between them was striking.

"Sorry Len-am, one more thing." The Queen turned back to address the servant as the thought occurred to her. "Double the guards, if you would."

EIGHTEEN

While Julyana Bertak's attempt to assert her authority had only made it look as though she was attempting to impose an authority she did not possess, Queen Latana's efforts had a vastly different effect. Leaving her guests to eat the refreshments she had instructed be offered to them, she changed out of the simple trousers and shirt she had been wearing when Elen-ai and Gidyon had first found her. When they met her after washing and changing into fresh clothes, they found Latana dressed in a deep crimson gown that was a simple sheaf on her slender figure. Her hair had been braided and piled on top of her head, she wore no jewellery other than the simple gold bands at her throat and wrists. She looked magnificent.

The Queen's first reaction was to look at Elen-ai's trousers. "You know, skirts can be just as effective a weapon as any," she commented.

"Not the sort of weapon I really use," Elen-ai replied with a slight tilt of her head.

"I doubt your type of weapon will be necessary tonight." The Queen smiled, her beauty almost too much to look at. Whoever had arranged her hair had done a magnificent job of accenting the sculpture of her cheekbones, the arch of her brow – even the shape of her lips was more somehow pronounced, more lovely than normal. To accent those spectacular eyes, a line of black had been slicked along their rim, sweeping up to meet the end of her eyebrows, but that was all.

"Come on, Sil and Nik are waiting for us," she said.

"Will the Councillors be joining us?" Elen-ai asked.

"They left a few days ago. Things with the Fourth Country are...not good. They are going there with Kaine to try and broker some kind of treaty." The Queen let out a little sigh but elaborated no further.

Elen-ai was sorry to hear that the foreigners were gone. She had hoped to see the Councillor who had saved Gidyon's life on their return to the Palace. Had they gotten to know one another better, Elen-ai felt they would have been friends. She fervently hoped that Freya and Ashtyn were safe and that she would one day see them again.

The trio made their way through the Palace to the blue sitting room, Elen-ai and Gidyon flanking the Queen. Guards stood on either side of the door, chatting to a waiting Nikalus and Silius. As the Queen approached, the guards stood to attention.

"Good afternoon." She smiled at them before turning her attention to her brothers. They were dressed in similar clothes to Elen-ai and Gidyon, understated garments which nevertheless underscored the fact that they were members of the Royal family.

"Ready?" the Queen asked.

The two men looked at their sister and Queen. "We stand beside you," Silius told her.

"Always," Nikalus added.

She paused for a moment to spare them a look of gratitude before nodding to the guards.

The doors were opened wide to admit the Royal family and Elen-ai.

"My dear friends, please forgive our delay." Latana exuded a warmth to match the day. Her perfect presentation was a counter to the slightly wilted guests, all of whom had risen and bowed at her entry. They may have been trying to usurp her, but she was still their Queen.

"Latana it is so reassuring to see you well after that awful attack. I'm sure our visit took you by surprise, and that you were of course in the middle of something." A woman who shared Latana's liquid gold eyes spoke first.

"Darling Liita. It has been so long since you left the Palace. I am so glad to see you again, and to have you staying here under our roof, too." The Queen crossed the room to embrace the woman. Once they released each other, the woman turned to the rest of the Royal family.

Elen-ai presumed this must be the Queen's sister - Gidyon's aunt and the mother of the would-be Queen. She had lived with the Katan family from the age of eight as was the custom with any woman other than the heir born into the Royal family. It meant that while she may have been their sister by blood, she was more a Katan than a member of the royal family. Elen-ai wondered if resentment festered within the woman who had been sent away by her family because she was not born early enough. Was it enough resentment to try to extinguish the lives of her sister and nephew?

"Of course you, you remember my daughter Serenah. Although it's been so long since you last saw her, I doubt you'll recognise her." The slight barb was swept aside by the fact that a young girl strongly resembling Liita stepped forward and bowed to the Queen.

"Such a beautiful young lady. And of course, I am sure you all remember Gidyon. My son and heir." Latana's smile dared anyone to raise an objection.

On cue, Gidyon bowed to the room, forcing its inhabitants to return to the gesture.

"And Erek and Keela. It's such an unexpected pleasure to see you both." Latana turned her attention from her sister to the representatives of the Rasatan family. She gave just the barest emphasis to 'unexpected', although it was doubtless noticed by everyone.

"When we received word that Halen, Serenah, Liita, and Enges were coming to court, we thought it would be the perfect opportunity. We are in negotiations for a marriage between our families and seek your blessing." Erek spoke rather than Keela, despite the fact that she would have been the head of the Rasatan family at court. He was just as handsome as Elen-ai remembered. Perhaps more so.

"Does this spell an end to your days as an unwed man?" Latana asked playfully, seemingly not immune his good looks.

"For me, no, but my youngest brother, yes," he replied, his eyes focused totally on the Queen.

"Well you would make a woman very lucky, Erek," Latana told him.

"But my heart beats only for you, my Queen," he said with a sincerity that would have been disconcerting were it not for the easy charm of his delivery.

Latana gave Erek a smirk of amusement before she addressed the room. "Please, let us sit."

More drinks were brought in along with another selection of the exquisite treats that Elen-ai remembered from her first time in the Palace. Meaningless conversation flowed back and forth in an exchange of trivialities and pleasantries. Later would come the reason for this visit, but this was a prelude, an opportunity for the two sides to gain the measure of one another before such a battle. Elen-ai tried her best to remain unnoticed, but her efforts were foiled when Erek came to sit beside her.

"You look as though you've gotten some sun since last we met, lady Elen-ai." He looked at her with those impossibly blue eyes. She felt as though he were looking into her very soul.

She smiled demurely. "Gidyon and I have been on quite the journey," she said.

"I was not aware when we last met that you were a companion who warmed his bed," he said, still looking intently at her. "Although I admit I was curious at the time about what exactly your role was in accompanying him."

She shifted slightly, uncomfortable with the directness with which he spoke about the supposed intimate relationship she shared with Gidyon. She couldn't help but feel he got away with a great deal that others may not as a result of his extraordinary good looks. "He is a remarkable young man," she said by way of response.

"Am I wrong in thinking you are a more worldly individual than he?" Erek asked. It was definitely a question that a less handsome, less charming person would not have even dared ask.

"In some ways." Rather than meet his eyes, Elen-ai looked at the sharp plane of his nose, forming a perfect shape in concert with the angle of his cheekbones and jawline.

"Does that mean he has your loyalty?" His voice was soft enough that nobody else could hear what he was saying. Even if their conversation would have been audible, everybody else seemed occupied by their own conversation. Gidyon, Halen – the patriarch of the Katan family – and Keela Rasatan were engaged in a discussion, although Keela was sitting and nodding for the most part. She seemed terribly unassuming, with a certain hunted look about her, as though she expected someone to jump out and yell 'boo' at any moment. Her timidity made it surprising that she was the mother of Erek. The Queen and her brothers were similarly engaged, speaking with much delightful laughter to their sister and niece, maintaining a pretence that they were a loving and united family. Elen-ai wondered what exactly Erek was asking her. For a fleeting moment, she wondered if he was propositioning her.

"I am but a loyal subject," she answered eventually.

"Aren't we all," Erek muttered. The comment and the edge to his tone piqued her curiosity. Despite his casualness, there was an intensity, an undercurrent of emotion, that he could not completely conceal.

"I'm not so sure I understand your meaning."

He shook his head slightly as if to clear it of a thought. "Do guard your heart carefully, Elen-ai. The Royal family has its own agenda and you may not fall into it," he said, his eyes on the Queen as she laughed at some joke or comment.

"She's very beautiful," Elen-ai commented, seeing the direction of his gaze.

"The most beautiful woman I've ever laid eyes on," Erek replied. "Sort of spoils all other women, begging your pardon."

"I can't disagree," Elen-ai told him honestly.

Erek turned back to regard her with that piercing gaze once more. "You're an unusual woman, lady Elen-ai," he said.

"I'll choose to take that as a compliment," she muttered as she bit into a pastry layered with nuts and vegetables.

He laughed, a charming noise, the accompanying smile oddly, not making him more but less handsome.

The gathering finished shortly, the visitors finally allowed the opportunity to bathe and rest in preparation for the dinner to follow in a few hours. The Queen and her brothers went off to conclude the matter they had been discussing when Elen-ai and Gidyon interrupted, leaving the two of them with free hours until the meal. Elen-ai followed Gidyon out to one of the Palace's courtyard gardens. The air felt almost like liquid enveloping them as soon as they stepped outside.

"Are you alright?" Elen-ai asked.

He shrugged. "I have to be."

"I think it may rain soon," Elen-ai commented idly.

"Blessing of the Divine One. I hope so," he replied.

"What do you think they'll say tonight?" Elen-ai asked, wandering over to a stone bench and sitting on it, stretching her legs out and leaning back to look up at the sky. Sure enough, she could see that fat clouds the colour of a two-day-old bruise had begun to reach across it. Soon they would be above the Palace.

"I still think they plan to challenge my claim. I'm not sure if they will come out and say as much, though," Gidyon answered, coming to sit next to her.

"Your mother was impressive this afternoon."

Gidyon chuckled. "She certainly was. I will not say as much to her, though. I'm still too angry."

"Do you think that you'll get over it?"

"I am sure I will, but right now it doesn't feel like it," he admitted.

"She's only human," Elen-ai offered.

"But she's the Queen. She supposed to be more than just human. How else can she claim people should be ruled by her?" Gidyon said.

Elen-ai said nothing. Gidyon had a point.

The clouds were creeping over the sky now. The contrast between the dark sky and the golden light shining on the courtyard's walls was quite striking.

"I can't say I'm looking forward to tonight," Elen-ai admitted.

"Neither am I," the Prince confessed. "At least the food will be good."

They sat together in silence until the first raindrops started to fall, forcing them to retreat inside.

Gidyon was correct. The food the Palace kitchens had produced was spectacular. Tenderly cooked meat, crisp vegetables, exquisite sauces. Elen-ai had no idea what she ate, she just knew that the display of power and wealth in every bite had certainly convinced her. There was some irony in the fact that the Katans were served a meal that emphasised the power and richness of the throne on plates made in their own lands. However, if Elen-ai had thought the Katan plates she had encountered before were of fine craftsmanship, these were in a completely different class. So thin she feared the servants would break them by simply handling them, the beautiful painting on each was a triumph of artistry. Even a single plate would be worth a small fortune.

The drumming of the rain was a constant noise in the background of the meal. The windows of the dining room had been opened to allow the rain-cooled air in. The breeze swirled gently around the room, doing nothing to alleviate the tension that was slowly building inside.

The Queen remained in the same dress she had worn to the afternoon tea, the only change a little jacket over her shoulders in concession to the sudden coolness, and red stones to match her dress in a line up the outermost cartilage of her ears. The simplicity of her outfit was a contrast to the opulent finery and heavy face paint that her guests had donned. It had the effect of making them look foolishly extravagant and desperate to prove their importance – which of course, they were. The only exception was Erek who wore a simple shirt of deep blue that accented the violent colour of his eyes in concert with the simple black lining them.

Gidyon had changed into a red shirt to match his mother's dress, and he too had opted for simplicity over extravagance. When Erek came to greet the Queen and heir, the three of them looked like an impossibly attractive family thanks to the trick of their garb.

The pleasant conversation of the afternoon was duplicated at the dinner table, punctuated by the occasional toast. Only once the final dish had been cleared from the table did the focus turn to more serious matters. Elen-ai had noted that nobody had drunk more than one or two glasses of any form of liquor despite the abundance proffered to the guests. It seemed everybody wanted their wits about them.

Latana initiated the shift in tone, reclining in her chair with a tall flute of some blue liquid twirled idly between her fingers. Despite the bandage still on her hand, the injury had not caused any her obvious trouble as she ate.

"Now Halen, what is this I have heard about your discontent with recent choices I have made?" she called to him from the other end of the table.

Clearly thrown by the direct nature of her question, the head of the Katan family gaped at her for a moment, the white cream coating his face making him look almost comical. "That is a very strong wording, your Majesty," he said eventually.

"How might you put it then?" She smiled, but it was a smile without any warmth.

"I am concerned by recent decisions. Concerned of course for your wellbeing."

"Come now Halen, you do not need to be coy," the Queen encouraged him.

"I am a loyal subject of the realm," he replied.

"Not a loyal subject of mine?"

His hesitation gave away his position, although nobody had ever really doubted where his loyalties truly lay. "I seek what is best for the people of the Second Country," he said finally.

"And do you believe that the Second Country would be better served with your granddaughter on the throne?"

The silence that followed the Queen's question hung heavily in the room. Shock had stolen the breath from the observers of the conversation between the Queen and Halen. That she would actually ask such a direct question in a world governed by polite side-stepping was without precedent. The only sound in the room for several moments came from the rain outside.

Finally, Halen cleared his throat. "It has been suggested to me that Serenah's claim to the throne may be stronger than Gidyon's, begging your pardon." He inclined his head to Gidyon.

Before Latana could speak, her son did. "I am afraid I will have to take issue with your comment, Lord Katan." He sounded quite amiable. "Not only is she a Katan by birth, but I would also add that being suitable to rule is not simply about birth. Serenah," he turned to address his cousin. "Can you tell me with whom the Second Country's largest amount of trade is conducted? Do you know how many people live within the Second Country? What is your opinion on the laws relating to thievery in place of an unpaid debt? What do you think we should do first and why; repave the sovereign road, rebuild Herran's marketplace, or draft orders for a standing army in case of an attack from belligerent external forces? An answer to any of these questions will do."

The girl looked at Gidyon, her eyes wide and terrified. Her face had been powdered with bronze pigment. It made her look almost like a statue. She opened and closed her mouth several times, but nothing came out. Finally, she looked down at her lap. "I don't know," she admitted in a whisper that was almost drowned out by the rain outside.

"How would you have her rule, Halen?" Latana challenged. "Or would you generously guide her with your wisdom? Please do not take this personally," Latana directed her final comment to Serenah whose eyes had quietly filled with tears.

"She's four years younger than Gidyon." Enges, the girl's father spoke up. "In four years she could learn these things, too."

"I started learning the fundamentals of the Second Country's legal system when I was eight," Gidyon said, almost gently.

"Surely she would also be able to call on her uncles for advice on how to guide the Queendom," Halen pointed out.

"Perhaps, although we would note that the best thing for the Queendom is to have Gidyon or Latana ruling it," Silius said, making no effort to hide his hostility. Elen-ai wouldn't have been surprised if he threw a punch at the older man. She hoped he would.

"I am curious to know what our friends from the Rasatan family think on this matter." Latana interrupted whatever

Halen was going to say, turning slightly in her seat to regard Erek and his mother.

Erek leaned forward. "My father has instructed me to convey his concerns about the effect a man holding the throne may have on our country," he said.

"And do you share those concerns?" Latana asked, her head cocked slightly as she met his gaze.

"My Queen, as I am sure you already know, I am in Herran rarely for my own purposes. I am a vessel for my family's wishes." His face was a mask of regretful sincerity.

"You do come to the capital often, and always on the business of your family. You are very lucky to have such a devoted son, Keela," Latana said.

"I am." Keela smiled timidly at the Queen. She seemed shocked at being directly addressed. Indeed, the fact that Erek referred specifically to his father's views on the matter of Gidyon's position rather than his parents' spoke to the utter domination of the poor woman.

Latana surveyed the people sitting at the table, her lips slightly pursed. "If I did not know any better, it would seem that you were planning to move against me, Halen, and that the Rasatan family is in support of this. That sounds like treason to me."

"Your Majesty, your sister is married to my eldest son. Your niece is my granddaughter. We are here as guests at your table. Such a phrase is ugly and unnecessary." The boldness with which he contradicted the Queen validated her words even as he proclaimed otherwise.

"I must say, that is a great relief to hear, Halen." She bestowed on him one of her lovely smiles. "I was always certain that you were a loyal subject of the Queendom rather than a pathetic usurper, trying to eke out more power in the guise of acting in the best interests of my people."

Elen-ai was amused to see him turn a shade of light purple underneath the white face paint as he struggled to find a way to respond to the Queen's insult without proving her correct. She heard Gidyon give a little cough that she would have bet everything she owned was in fact a concealed laugh.

"Well, yes," Halen said eventually in a most inelegant manner.

Liita smoothly interjected. "In any case, I am sure that the question of Gidyon succeeding you is not a serious possibility for a great many years. I'm certain that all of us at this table wish on you the blessings of the Divine One for many more years of your reign."

It was impossible to know what the Queen truly thought of her sister's comment, but she smiled and nodded. "You are quite right, Liita. I must confess, I always assumed there would be some consternation in the immediate aftermath of Gidyon being named my heir. I am sure that with time, any concerns that may be felt will be allayed, one way or another."

The finality of her words moved the conversation on, but Elen-ai saw the slight tightening around Halen's jawline and the briefest of glances between Liita and Enges. The matter was most certainly not finished.

The dinner dragged on for a little while longer, but following the diplomatic altercation between Latana and Halen, the mood had changed completely. The rain continued to fall, an unabated patter that sounded outside the windows, intruding into any pause in chatter. Eventually, the Queen stood and bade all of her guests a good evening, which concluded the meal. Elen-ai followed a pensive Gidyon back to his room.

"I assume that they won't give up, then," she said once they were in his sitting area.

"I would stake a significant fortune on that, yes," he affirmed.

"How?" she wondered aloud.

He sighed, falling into a chair and running a hand through his hair. "I imagine several legal claims challenging my right to rule, put up by someone else of course, attempts to generate popular support for Serenah as an alternate ruler to me, and a variety of other petty schemes." He lowered the hand that had been entangled in his hair to run a finger up and down the bridge of his nose. "It just makes me so angry that they think Serenah would be a good ruler. She clearly knows nothing about anything related to statecraft. I don't even know if she really wants to be Queen. It's not right." He made his hand down in a fist and brought it down to thump on his knee. "And what's this about the Rasatan involvement? I don't understand what they're playing at," he exclaimed, his speech unusually inelegant. "Might they have somehow been behind the attack on me and mother, on behalf of the Katans?"

"I've been wondering that myself," Elen-ai commented. "I can only assume that they've been promised something if they support and aid the Katans."

"I wish I knew what's going on," Gidyon said, clicking his tongue in frustration as he stared at his still-clenched fist.

"There may be a way to find out," Elen-ai offered.

His head snapped up to look at her. "I'm listening."

"I could get into their rooms now and see if I could find anything."

Gidyon pursed his lips, seriously considering the offer. "Are you certain you could get in and out unnoticed?" he asked.

She snorted in response, giving him a look of mild offence. In reply, he held up his hands, palms outwards. Then he grew serious. "Do it," he told her. "You should be able to get to their rooms through here." He got up and fetched a paper scrap, sketching a rough map of the Palace for her.

It took her one minute to change her clothes and slip out of Gidyon's room, the sound of the rain surrounding her as she moved through the Palace.

NINETEEN

The rain had well and truly settled in. It was a gentle beat that would have masked Elen-ai's footsteps, had they made any sound. She made her way to the visitors' wing, easily remembering the Palace's layout from her first night time expedition. Leaving the corridor, Elen-ai slipped outside to one of the small gardens within the wing. Recalling where Gidyon had told her Erek Rasatan's room was, she found the window and swiftly scaled the wall. The window was open. The stone walls of the Palace had soaked in the heat of the previous few days and every room was still stiflingly hot without the respite of the cool night air. It was almost too easy.

The sound of discussion between Erek and his mother surprised Elen-ai, not because she had not expected them to confer at this hour, but because it was very clearly a heated argument that she heard. Elen-ai slipped through the window, conscious of the water clinging to her clothes. Fortunately, a little rain had been blown into the room already so the drops from her clothes joined the ones already there unnoticeably. It didn't really matter though. Erek and his mother were too engrossed in their exchange to notice some extra water in the room.

Elen-ai stared in wonder at Keela as she addressed her son. Gone was the timid woman who had barely uttered two words throughout the afternoon refreshments and dinner. In her place was a bastion of terrifying authority. She wore the same face, but the features were arranged in a totally different way. Her mouth was a snarl, her eyes were suddenly narrow and focused, and flashing with malice. Elen-ai had entered the room midway through Keela administering a spectacular beration to Erek.

"...and you just sat there moping at that stupid creature for most of the night. You said none of what we planned you would."

Erek who normally seemed so supremely confident was sitting looking up his mother, an abashed expression on his face. "I'm sorry mother," he said, his voice plaintive and pathetic.

"Sorry? There are bound to be questions about our loyalty to the Katans now. We were supposed to present a show of solidarity with them to secure our allegiance," she snapped.

"I had to respond to what was being said. When we discussed how the evening would go, we didn't expect Latana to discuss the situation so plainly," he whined.

"Don't think for yourself, it never ends well," she told him nastily.

He looked down, the hurt obvious on his face. "Father told me that in such situations..."

"Your father is a bigger fool than you." She cut him off, flapping a dismissive hand at him. "Be quiet for a moment. I need to think." She put one hand on her hip and brought the other to her chin, turning away from him and pacing the length of the room. She came within a hand span of Elen-ai but turned around before she actually touched the assassin. "Why didn't you tell me about Latana and Zekken as soon as you found out?" She sounded exasperated, the raw bite of her anger lost in contemplation.

"I...I don't know." Erek kept his eyes on his mother as she returned to her previous spot in front of him.

His response seemed to rekindle her anger. "Well I do. It's this ridiculous infatuation you've had with her ever since the first Season. It's made you blind to her incompetence as a ruler and what should be done to stop her, and to put our family in a position to be strong."

"I'm not in love with her," he protested, but again his mother cut him off. From the look on his face though, Elen-ai had to agree with Keela's assessment that Erek was infatuated with the Queen.

"Why else would you spend so much time and coin tracking down half the servants and messengers in the land to put together something that has been so well hidden?" Poison dripped from her tongue as she addressed him.

"I knew she was doing something she shouldn't have been. I knew it," he exclaimed.

"Because she wouldn't take you to her bed again? Really, Erek, I don't know why you think you're so special." Keela's contempt for her son made Elen-ai's skin crawl. None of her Mothers or Fathers would ever speak to one of the Family's children like that.

"You see the way she treats me. She flirts with me, she acts as though I'm one of her favourites, but aside from that first time, she has never invited me back to her bedchamber. I knew just knew something was wrong. I knew she was hiding something."

Keela snorted. "Well I suppose your obsessive snooping did uncover something we can use. Why you had to be so impudent in that attempt on the life of Latana and that...." The sound of sobbing cut her off. She lowered her gaze to her son.

Erek Rasatan, the most handsome man Elen-ai had ever seen, was crying like a small infant. "He's just as likely to be my son, and they took him from me, mama. Being by her side, being the father to her son, it should have been me. I just wanted to take him away from them and scare her," he gulped in between sobs.

His mother stepped forward and pressed his head to her stomach, rocking him gently back and forth. The abruptness of the shift from vindictive spite to maternal care was disturbing.

"I know my darling, I know. It's alright. I've always said you were destined for great things. You're right, it should have been you she took as a lover. There now, there's no need to cry." She murmured the platitudes to him with disconcerting intensity.

Gradually he stopped crying, quietened by Keela's soothing. She took his face in both of her hands, leaned down so that she could look directly in his eyes and spoke with the firmness of someone addressing a small child. "No more of your own plans, hm? If we decide that the way forward is to kill that fool and her child, you wait for me to organise it. From now on you'll do what I tell you?"

He nodded obediently. She kissed his forehead gently. "That's my boy," she crooned.

Elen-ai had seen enough. She climbed silently out of the window and returned to Gidyon's rooms.

"Well?" he demanded the moment she came in.

"I suggest you sit down," she advised him. When he had done as she bade, she continued. "I know who was behind the attack on you and your mother and why." She held up a hand to forestall his questions, searching for the best way to explain what she had learned.

"It would seem that Zekken may not be your father. The uh, the Season in which you were conceived was the only time the Queen was with someone other than Zekken."

"Erek," Gidyon surmised quickly. He did not seem to be particularly upset by the revelation, but Elen-ai expected that may come in time. For now, he was too busy trying to see how this information might change the situation.

She nodded. Now that she knew, she thought she could even see a physical resemblance between the Prince and Erek. Certainly, he didn't look like Zekken in the slightest.

"How did you find this out?"

"Luck, really. He was talking with Keela. She's not at all what she seems, by the way. She's awful."

Gidyon raised an eyebrow at this news but said nothing. Elen-ai continued, still choosing her words with care. "From what I gathered, Erek is quite in love with the Queen and he couldn't understand why she had never invited him back to her bedchamber. It seems he spent quite a lot of money finding a number of servants, or people who might know something, to try and learn what your mother was doing and why she may not want him to uh...well, you get the idea.

"I suspect he spoke with enough people to realise the existence of the relationship between Zekken and Latana. I can't exactly know his thoughts, but from what I heard, discovering that the Queen had taken a lover that was not him prompted him to arrange an attempt on the lives of both you and your mother."

Gidyon was silent for a moment as he considered the information. "He is in the capital often on family business. He would likely have enough knowledge of the goings-on within the Palace to give any assailants the information that they used to get to us. But I don't understand. Why would he try to kill me if he might be my father?"

"The way Keela was treating him, and the way he was behaving...I'm not sure that he's entirely sane." Recalling the sudden change from Keela's nastiness to her cossetting of Erek made Elen-ai feel vaguely nauseous. "He's a terrific actor, able to seem normal in public especially because of his looks, but I think, if what I saw was any indication, he's not quite right. The most unstable of individuals can be the most deceptive," she elaborated.

Gidyon was silent for a moment longer. "We need to go to mother with this. Now. Not only did he try to kill us, but he knows about her and Zekken." He got to his feet.

As she followed him through the Palace, Elen-ai wondered if Gidyon was seeking action to distract himself from thinking too much about these recent revelations. The rain pattered softly outside. Its gentle tap-tap generated a sense of understated urgency that nestled itself somewhere in Elen-ai's stomach.

Gidyon knocked sharply on the door to the Queen's chambers, ignoring the curious looks that he was given by the two guards outside it. Latana answered almost immediately. Evidently she too had not been asleep, although she was wearing bed robes and her hair had been let loose from the elaborate braids it had been piled into that afternoon and evening. Even her collar and cuffs had been removed, giving her a certain look of delicacy.

"Gidyon." Her surprise at her son's sudden presence was undisguised.

"Elen-ai found out something." The seriousness of his tone had her immediately stepping aside to admit them. The room looked exactly as Elen-ai remembered it, barring a few papers strewn about rather than neatly stacked and put aside.

"I was just reading over some petitions for new buildings in the market district," Latana explained distractedly, gesturing to the pages on the couch.

"Why didn't you tell me Erek might be my father?" Gidyon's question cut across her demeanour, freezing her in place.

"I didn't think it was important. We never thought it likely. How do you know he was the other?" Her words were careful, like she was picking her way across a floor strewn with burning coals.

"Elen-ai overheard him speaking with his mother. He knows about you and Zekken."

Latana's face turned quite white. "How could he possibly know? We've been so careful."

Gidyon was obviously unimpressed. "He's obsessed with you."

"If I understood what I heard, he sought out a number of servants and messengers. From there, I would imagine he tracked your respective movements and figured it out," Elen-ai interjected before Gidyon could launch into another tirade against his mother's relationship with Zekken.

If possible, the Queen paled further. "I always just assumed he was being unnecessarily exuberant," she mumbled, putting a hand to her mouth and turning slightly away, as if to give herself space to think.

"We can consider the whys and hows of it later, mother." Gidyon cut off her musing. "There is a problem in front of us as well as an opportunity, but I think we need to act quickly."

Latana turned back to face her son, her eyes devoid of the confusion and shock that had filled them only a moment before and instead sparkling with purpose. "Someone taught you well, to see opportunity within a problem." She smiled at him, never once losing that focus.

"I learned from the best."

She reached across the space between them and placed a hand on his arm, letting it rest there for a moment before crossing the room to summon a servant. "Please bring Erek Rasatan here," she ordered once her summons was answered.

While they waited for him to arrive, Gidyon cleared his throat. "Are you sure this is the best way to deal with him?"

The Queen threw her son an amused look as she went into her bedchamber, returning with a deep purple robe which she tied firmly about her waist. "He will be uncertain about why I called him here due to the late hour. Now is the perfect time to confront him and bend him to our purpose. Besides, he is only a man." She ran her fingers through her hair to remove any knots, shaking it out behind her. "Thank you, Gid," she added, the only moment of hesitation in her certainty.

"I still don't forgive you. We will be having many words once this mess is sorted out. You do realise we wouldn't be in this predicament were it not for you?" He folded his arms across his chest.

"I will not apologise for my choices," Latana told him sternly.

He shook his head. "I pray to the Divine One I will not be so arrogant when I rule."

"The very act of you taking the throne is arrogance incarnate, my son," his mother retorted, turning away from him to address Elen-ai. "You have done the Second Country a great service not once, but many times over. I do not know how to thank you."

Elen-ai suffered the gaze of the Queen, feeling herself falling into pools of liquid gold. It was little wonder that Erek was so desperately infatuated with her. There was something utterly irresistible about Latana. "I am simply fulfilling the Family's contract, your Majesty. But perhaps I should not be here for this," she suggested.

"No, I think you have earned the right to stay," the Queen countered. She offered Elen-ai a smile that set her whole face alight.

"As your Majesty wishes," Elen-ai acquiesced.

Erek arrived quickly. Since Elen-ai had left his room, he had changed his clothes, wearing casual attire that one may don in the hours after dinner and before bed. From what Elen-ai had seen though, he would have chosen those clothes carefully despite the casual air they exuded.

In the man who strode into the room, there was no sign of the cowed, child-like being who had been subject to his mother's abusive tirade. The charm and confidence were as ever. The difference was unnerving.

"Your Majesty." He bowed low as he entered. Seeing Gidyon, he offered him a bow too. "To what do I owe this pleasure?"

From her inconspicuous place in the corner, Elen-ai watched as the Queen put on her most charming smile. "After the events of this evening, I thought it may be worth having a more intimate discussion over the matters at hand."

His smile did not waver in the slightest. "I am sure Gidyon has told you what I said to him in the Veertak home. I personally think he would make a superb ruler, although I do wonder about his decision to marry a lowborn woman. Nevertheless, my father's word is what I ultimately must respect."

"What about your mother's?" Gidyon chimed in, his eyes – so similar to Erek's now that she looked – wide and innocent.

Erek gave a little laugh which he accompanied with a dismissive shrug. "I love my mother dearly, but she doesn't really have the head for such matters."

Latana smiled but the warmth had left her face. "Of course."

"I'm sure there must be something I can do to help you both, though." Erek took a step toward the Queen and took her hands in his, looking earnestly into her face.

"You could start by not making any more attempts on the life of Gidyon or myself." Latana did not move, nor did she alter the polite lightness of her tone.

Erek's reaction was almost imperceptible to the casual observer, merely a slight stiffness stealing across his face before the charming mask slipped back into place. However, he was not in a room of casual observers. He was in a room with three individuals who were accustomed to watching and reading people. "How can you think I would do such an awful thing?" He sounded genuinely bewildered.

Latana yanked her hands from his. "I am aware of everything. Please do not try and lie to me, Erek. How could you?" Her question was soft, almost gentle.

His face crumpled. Such small pressure from the Queen and he was suddenly just as he was with his own mother. "How could *you*? What does he have that I don't? That you would think of him as Gidyon's father even though it could just as easily be me?"

Elen-ai watched Gidyon's face as he regarded the man who may have sired him whine at the feet of his mother. As usual, she was unable to discern what he was thinking.

"Is that was this is about? Why I did not take you as my lover?" A note of disgust crept into Latana's voice.

Erek grasped for her hands again, but she drew them out of his reach. "Please just tell me you care for me too," he begged. It was uncomfortable to witness this display. Elen-ai found that she could not look at the pathetic spectacle directly.

Latana allowed her disgust to show on her face. "I will tell you no such thing. Instead, I will tell you what you are to do now if you do not want me to imprison your entire family."

Elen-ai didn't see Erek draw the knife. The discomfort that his desperate mewling instilled meant she had averted her gaze, choosing instead to try and gauge how Gidyon was reacting to this display. She only saw the glint of the knife out of the corner of her eye as he drove it all the way into the base of the Queen's unprotected neck.

The skills of the Family gave her a speed none could match, but even she couldn't make it across the room in time to stop the knife from plunging into Latana's delicate flesh. Gidyon's cry rang in her ears as she wrenched Erek off the Queen and violently twisted his neck to end his life. His body hadn't even hit the ground before she had wheeled back to the Queen.

Gidyon pushed her aside to get to his mother, paying no heed to the red, red blood that soaked into his clothes as it poured out of the wound in her neck. He screamed for help as Elen-ai came to the other side of the Queen, placing her hands on the wound in a desperate attempt to stop the blood as it gushed out.

Somewhere, members of the Royal Guard called frantically for someone to come and prevent the Queen's death, but all

Elen-ai could focus on was the softness of the Queen's hair as she cradled Latana's head. Beside her, Gidyon was whimpering, or perhaps he was just repeating 'no' over and over again. The look of surprise on Latana's face unsettled Elen-ai the most.

Hands pulled her away as a number of people descended on the Queen to try and save her, but Elen-ai was too familiar with death to cling to false hope. She knew the Queen's end was inevitable.

TWENTY

Gidyon's howl of anguish signalled the terrible truth: Queen Latana was dead. Elen-ai fought her way through the shock that was threatening to engulf her and crouched next to Gidyon. The boy was sobbing as he held his mother's body. Tears had yet to make their way to his eyes despite the cries that wracked him. Somehow it made his grief all the worse to witness.

"Gidyon, look at me," Elen-ai said. When he did not seem to hear her, she repeated herself.

The room was a maelstrom of activity, yet a space around the Queen, her son, and Elen-ai still existed. The horror of the Queen's murder was keeping people away, but that would not last for long. The Prince looked up at Elen-ai, his eyes dulled by the momentousness of the events that had transpired so quickly.

"Gidyon," Elen-ai spoke urgently. "Erek attacked the Queen, you don't know why. It seemed he just became mad out of nowhere. You pulled him off, not in time to save your mother. In the struggle, his head was hit. Do you remember?"

He looked dully at her and she feared that he would not understand what she was telling him. He nodded slowly.

"Tell me what happened," she instructed. Her heart broke for what she was doing to him, but she didn't have the time to be gentle. Her duty was to protect the Prince and this was the only way she could do that now.

"Mother and I met with Erek to try and convince him to support my claim. Suddenly he went crazy. He pulled out a knife and stabbed her before I could do anything. I fought him, he hit his head and he fell down." He even managed to sound as though he believed it.

"Good," she told him. She rose to leave but he reached out a blood-soaked hand and grabbed her sleeve.

"Please don't go."

"I'll be right back, I promise," she told him.

"Where are you going?"

"To take care of something."

He didn't understand, he just stared at her, his hand still clinging to her sleeve. "Gidyon. I'll return quickly," she reassured him. "Trust me," she added when he didn't move.

He nodded and let her go, dropping his head back to look at the Queen's lifeless form.

Elen-ai slipped out of the room as Silius entered it wearing a dressing robe the same colour as the Queen's eyes.

Catching sight of his sister's corpse, he let out an oath. "Divine One, what happened? Tana!"

Amid the new commotion Silius' arrival had caused, Elen-ai sought out the maid Len-am who had brought the message of the Katan's arrival to the Queen earlier in the day. She was taking a risk in trusting the woman, but it was a calculated risk. Dressed in her own bedclothes, the servant had come running quickly to answer the cries for help. She stood, looking in stupor at the Queen's body, still cradled by the Prince.

"I need your help," Elen-ai said.

She looked at the still-wet blood on Elen-ai's hands and clothes. "What happened?"

"I didn't think he was a real threat," Elen-ai said simply, indulging herself for a moment and wallowing in guilt. This was twice she had become complacent. This time though, that complacency had cost a life. "But I need to make sure this is all that happens. For the Queen's sake."

Len-am nodded despite her obvious confusion. "What do you need?"

"Show me where Keela Rasatan's room is."

Len-am threw a glance at Erek's body, at the present paid no heed by anyone. Whatever suspicions she may have had, she kept them to herself as she turned and led Elen-ai through the Palace, winding through the servant's staircases and corridors where they remained unseen. The rain pattered down outside, muffling the servant's footfalls. Elen-ai's were as ever, silent. She could hear the sound of running in the grand corridors of the Palace. As news of the Queen's death spread, it seemed people were taking the fastest rather than the most discreet route.

Nobody was in the corridor outside Keela Rasatan's rooms.

"I need your shirt," Elen-ai said, stripping off her own soiled shirt. Len-am did not even hesitate. She took off the requested garment, holding it out to Elen-ai who used it to meticulously wipe all the blood off her hands. She looked at her trousers for a moment then stripped them off too. The air was still warm enough that even in her underthings, she was not chilled in the slightest. Len-am did not seem to be concerned that she was in her own undergarments. Instead, she simply held out her hands expectantly for the dirtied clothes.

"Wait for me here," Elen-ai told her, opening the door and slipping into the bedchamber. Using the skills of the Family it was easy to see the room in the dark and find the slumbering form on the bed.

Elen-ai crossed the room and regarded Keela for a moment. In her sleep her face held a certain malevolence that was masked when she was awake. Keela's breathing was smooth and even, undisrupted even as the assassin stood over her.

Elen-ai gave a swift and merciful death, smothering Keela Rasatan as she slept. Unlike the Queen who died in confusion and pain, Keela felt nothing. It seemed unjust. Once she was satisfied that the woman's life had departed, Elen-ai cast about the room for a way to conceal the fact that her hand had brought this death.

Fortune was with her. Keela had a room several floors up with a large window that would let in the morning light. Elen-ai quickly heaved the still-warm body up and over the sill. She heard the thud as it hit the ground, muffled slightly by the rain.

Elen-ai left the room, taking her soiled clothes from the waiting Len-am and pulling them back on. The blood was starting to dry, making them stiff. "You went to inform Keela Rasatan of her son's death. She seemed wild with grief but screamed at you to leave so you did," Elen-ai instructed her.

Len-am didn't even hesitate before she nodded in reply.

They returned to the Queen's rooms in the silence, broken only when Elen-ai turned to Len-am. "You don't seem surprised," she commented.

In response, she was offered a knowing albeit weary smile. "I've been the chief servant to her Majesty for the whole time she has been on the throne. There isn't much that occurs that I don't at least know about. I know who you are."

Elen-ai wondered if Len-am knew about Latana and Zekken's relationship, but she did not ask. There were some things that were better left unsaid. The rest of their return to the Queen's rooms was undertaken in silence punctuated only by the patter of Len-am's footsteps.

Silence had settled over the room that held the Queen's body. Silius had joined Nikalus. Both were seated, their shock and disbelief etched into their postures. The Queen's body had been moved from its position slumped on the floor and instead laid on the couch. Erek's body had been removed. Elen-ai felt sorry for whoever had to handle the mundane details of this death; handling the corpses, or scrubbing the Queen's blood from the rug. Despite her familiarity with death, the prospect of cleaning the Queen's blood from the rug seemed somehow terribly sacrilegious. She hoped that the rug would just be burned.

Servants and guards moved quietly around the room. It didn't look as though there was any specific purpose to their movements. They seemed the actions of people desperate to have something to do rather than look at the body of their beloved Queen laid out in a terrible semblance of repose. Gidyon now stood at the window, lost in his own world. Something about the way he held himself kept everyone away from him – even Elen-ai.

The long slow tolling of bells began to sound from somewhere within the Palace compound. The length of each toll filled the air with a profound sorrow. Everybody in the room went totally still, waiting for the rest of Herran's bells to join in. It was only a few minutes later that the sound of all the other bells in the city could be heard. The last time the city's bells had sounded in such a way was sixteen months after Gidyon had been born when his grandmother had succumbed to a virulent winter flu. Elen-ai herself had been a relatively young child at the time, but she remembered the way the peals of lament had transformed the capital so suddenly, changing it from a vibrant and busy place to somewhere with sadness and mourning that swept through every corner, leaving no stone untouched by the weight of grief.

Gidyon stirred. He turned from the window. His eyes were red and tear tracks had etched themselves down his face. "We need to prepare mother for the funeral. Can someone please fetch the doctors?"

There was a rustle as though the room were awakening.

"I also want to speak with the Katan family," Gidyon added.

"Perhaps that can wait until the morning?" Silius raised his head to address Gidyon.

"I think not." Gidyon contradicted him with a firmness that gave no room for further discussion.

Silius did not try to push his nephew. "Where would you like to meet them? I'm not sure here is the best place," he said instead.

"The blue sitting room." Gidyon sounded so certain, so sure of himself. Elen-ai wondered whether he actually felt that certainty.

"Should you perhaps change?" Silius suggested, looking at Gidyon's blood-stained shirt, the red of the Queen's blood darker patches on the fine red cloth.

Gidyon glanced down. "No. Let them see. Elen-ai?" He swept from the room, not glancing at his mother's body laid out on the couch.

Elen-ai followed him silently. She did not ask if he was al-right. It was a preposterous question to ask. "Keela will not be a problem," she said instead.

"That's where you went?" was all Gidyon asked.

She nodded. He said nothing further.

They reached the sitting room. Gidyon did not sit. He re-mained on his feet, a stillness that concerned Elen-ai settling over him. A glassy look which spoke of thoughts far from the present flickered over his eyes.

The door opened and Silius and Nikalus came in. Focus came back into his eyes as the two men entered. When they crossed the room, his two uncles simply each rested a hand on his shoulder before selecting seats for themselves. Gidyon said nothing, but Elen-ai saw him work to swallow, and the sheen of unshed tears cross his eyes.

The knock on the door a few moments later signalled the arrival of the Katan family. They piled in, Liita, Enges, Halen, and of course, Serenah. All of them were in their nightclothes, and from the expression on their faces, it was clear that they knew but clearly did not believe what the toll of the bells was telling them. From Liita's gasp, Elen-ai assumed she had no-ticed the blood still on Gidyon.

Before any of them could say anything, Gidyon spoke. "Erek Rasatan killed my mother tonight."

Halen's eyes widened in shock. "What! Divine One around us."

Gidyon cut him off. "He came as part of your retinue, Halen. Tell me why I should not find you responsible."

For several moments, the man's mouth hung open in shock, elongating his face in a manner that would have been comical were it not for the circumstances. He shook his head slightly, sending his jowls fluttering.

"Your Highness," he began, but again, Gidyon cut him off.

"Your Majesty, you mean."

Halen looked at the boy before him who was young enough to be his grandson. The silent support of Silius and Nikalus and even Elen-ai in conjunction with the seriousness of the Queen's death left him totally dumbstruck. Elen-ai hoped he would refuse to recognise Gidyon's title so that Gidyon had a reason to arrest him. However, years of political nous meant that he was wily enough to not quite fall into that trap. "Of course. My apologies, your Majesty. If you wish to hold me responsible for Erek's actions, I understand but would ask that you do not punish my family for my lapse in judgment. Where is Erek now?"

"Dead." Gidyon's voice was flat. "I killed him in the struggle."

Again, he rendered Halen speechless. In this silence, Gidyon spoke again. "I can only trust that you would not have wanted harm to befall my mother or me in any way, especially given that you are our guests. Erek's madness is – was – his own and you cannot be blamed for failing to see it. None of us did. You are all more than welcome to remain in the Palace until the," he paused. "Until the funeral."

With Gidyon rescinding his threat, the entire Katan family visibly relaxed.

"We can't possibly impose upon you during this difficult time, we will return to our house in Herran in the morning." Halen's gently mournful tone had Elen-ai clenching her jaw. "I imagine this will be a difficult time for you. Your young years may find you lacking in some ways. I hope you will feel you can come to me for any advice you may need," the man added, his face a picture of sincerity.

Nikalus cleared his throat conspicuously, causing Gidyon to give a reflexive, empty smile. "I'll keep your generous offer in mind Lord Halen."

The silence that followed gave a clear indication that as far as Gidyon was concerned, the audience was over. The Katans departed the room in a silent awkward shuffle. Once they had left, Gidyon turned to look at his uncles and Elen-ai. She could see in his face that he was focusing on the matter at hand to keep himself together. It was heartbreaking. "He's unbelievable," Gidyon said quietly, running a hand through his hair, heedless of the dried blood still on his hands.

"He's unlikely to do anything now," Silius commented.

Gidyon pulled a face.

"Perhaps you should try and get some sleep, Gid," Silius suggested, his voice gentle. "We can discuss this at greater length in the morning."

This time, Gidyon did not disagree with his uncle. "Elen-ai?" He looked to her with vague, unarticulated uncertainty.

"I'm here," she reassured him.

Gidyon's uncles watched him with concern as he left the room, but both seemed at a loss for what advice or guidance they could give. Elen-ai could hardly blame them. She couldn't begin to understand how they were wrestling with their own grief while trying to discern what was best for the Queendom, and their nephew.

As they walked to Gidyon's rooms, Elen-ai thought that it seemed impossible that such little time had passed since they had ventured to back to his rooms after dinner. Latana had been alive only hours previously. Shock and disbelief hovered on the corners of Elen-ai's perception of the world, but she had the privilege of being familiar with death. Gidyon was not so accustomed to such things and it was his mother who had died. She knew that Gidyon was yet to be fully struck by what had transpired. When he finally did truly realise what had happened, it would be awful.

Once in his rooms, he finally washed his mother's lifeblood off him. He emerged in his bedclothes, looking no more refreshed. Elen-ai silently went into the bathroom, filling the tub with water and scrubbing at her own skin. She never ceased to be amazed at the way blood seemed to grind itself under even the shortest of fingernails. When she came out she found Gidyon simply sitting on his bed staring blankly at the wall.

"Do you need anything?" she asked.

Grief is a curious state of being. While two people can feel grief for the same person, more often than not they will experience it differently. For that reason, Elen-ai had always viewed grief as a feeling that was distinctly isolating.

"Do you think I should move rooms?" Gidyon asked rather than actually answer her question. "A ruler should have, I don't know, more grand rooms, don't you think?"

"I think you should have whatever rooms you feel most comfortable in," she replied, coming to sit beside him on the bed. "Will you be able to sleep, do you think?"

He shrugged, scratching his cheek with one finger. "I suppose I should try," he said.

"Whatever you want to do we'll do," she told him.

"This is my fault," Gidyon said, clearly not hearing her, too preoccupied with his own thoughts, his own grief, his own shock.

"No it's not, Gid." She was surprised by how vehemently she wanted him to believe her, to understand that he wasn't responsible for the crime of another man.

"If I hadn't made us go straight to her rooms –"

Elen-ai spoke over him. "He may have done something like that on another day. He was clearly not sane. You didn't see how Keela was with him. I can't imagine what it would have been like to be raised by her."

"Keela. She knows about mother and Zekken, you said." Gidyon looked down at the sheets with a frown on his face.

"I took care of it, remember?"

"Oh yes, so you did." He blinked.

"Look, I'll dim the lights. Try to rest, alright?" She stood and dimmed the flames that illuminated the room rather than extinguishing them completely, leaving a soft glow in the room. She did not want to leave Gidyon in the dark. Not tonight.

Rather than going to the cot in the room, she returned to the opposite side of the bed to him. After a moment, he lay down, and then she followed his action, lying back against the softness of the mattress. It was still a warm enough night that neither of them needed blankets. As they lay in the soft half-light, Gidyon's hand crept across the bed to find hers.

Elen-ai did not sleep that night and she could tell from his breathing that Gidyon did not either. The tolling of the bells was a constant note that endured through the night and long into the next day after they arose.

TWENTY ONE

The Queen's funeral took place on a spectacular summer day one week after her death. Elen-ai had barely left Gidyon's side through that week, from the morning he rose bleary-eyed from grief and the sleepless night, sitting through a series of discussions on the necessary actions to follow the tragedy, up to the funeral itself. It had been an awful week. The days had blurred into one another, filled with endless offers of condolences, decisions, and directives. This was all conducted to the background of numb shock, a sense that the world was somehow out of balance in some indefinably significant manner, and would never be right again.

The funeral procession wound its way through Herran's streets in the requisite showing of the body. The capital was still in shock, people thronging in a silent crowd to see for themselves that their adored Queen was actually dead. So profound was the people's grief that Gidyon had been required to order the bells to cease ringing two days after they had first sounded, otherwise it was likely they would still have been ringing as Latana's body was carried through the streets. Gidyon was dressed in mourning silver. The only splash of colour on him was the purple sash that cut his torso in two, denoting him as the ruler of the Second Country now. Silver was not his best colour, especially after several nights of little or no sleep. It served to emphasise the shadows under his eyes and the slightly jaundiced pallor to his skin. All things considered, though, he was doing a remarkable job of holding himself. He had only succumbed to true anguish once, on the third night after Latana's murder. The rawness of his grief, evident in every aching sob had been terrible to hear. Elen-ai had been the only person who had seen the true face of his grief. She had run a hand across his back as he cried, the only gesture possible to offer someone so profoundly grief-stricken; the reminder of 'I am here'.

In her own mourning clothes of silver, Elen-ai felt like some kind of fish, moving through the stream of the capital. She could pick out members of the Family at various points in the crowd, their inconspicuousness marking them out to her as though they wore some kind of sign. She knew they too saw her among the funeral procession, even though very few other citizens would have noticed her walking inconspicuously between Varl and Varlena Veertak, and Arlena Aadran.

The morning following Latana's murder, the Palace's messenger birds fastest messengers had departed for every part of the land. Members of the seven families had begun to arrive in the capital over the following days, coming to offer their condolences to Gidyon and prepare themselves for the funeral. The remainder of the Katan family had arrived mere hours before the funeral, coming by the fastest possible means, most of them having travelled through the nights in order to arrive in time for Queen Latana's funeral.

Elen-ai glanced at Varl as the procession passed the harbour's most scenic point. He was clothed in silver that somehow managed to clash magnificently with his white hair. Tears trickled unchecked down his wrinkled cheeks. Beside him, VArlena reached over and took her husband's hand.

There was something obscene about the beauty of the day. The harbour water was a brilliant blue, sparkling in the sunlight. Not a single cloud marred the sky, and the sun shining on Herran's buildings lent the city a particular radiance. Yet nobody was able to appreciate the magnificence of the day, for borne through the streets of the capital was Queen Latana the

Fourth, the most beautiful Queen ever to grace the Second Country.

At the city's merchant bank, Elen-ai glanced at the tall, stern building on her right. Arlena Aadran came into her view, walking as straight-backed as ever, the silver of her dress almost the same shade as the grey which coloured most of her hair. Elen-ai thought she saw a shadow of Gidyon in the arch of her brow, but then again, she could swear that Wenden Rasatan, Erek's father and Keela's husband, had the exact same nose as Gidyon. The man in question walked alone, whatever shame or personal grief he may feel at his son's crime and the apparent suicide of his wife, hidden. Gidyon had deliberated on banning him from the funeral but ultimately decided against it. The Rasatan reputation was already in tatters as a result of Erek's actions, and it seemed cruel to humiliate the man who had lost not only his wife and son but also his family's credibility.

A wheeze caught Elen-ai's attention and she saw Julyana Bertak struggling to remain silent in her efforts to keep up with the procession's pace. She wore a silver dress that looked as though it had been made for a far less substantial woman. Elen-ai somewhat nastily thought that the choice of a sleeveless bodice was an unfortunate one. Pink from the heat, her arms looked like two slabs of cured meat. Elen-ai gleaned a sliver of amusement from the fact that the woman's husband was a man of such slight stature that it looked as though she could squash him if she mistakenly sat on him. It was a welcome levity given the sorrow and concern that had weighed so heavily on her over the last week.

After the necessary rituals and prayers were performed in front of the city's temple to the Divine One, the procession made its way back to the Palace along a different route. Elen-ai heard weeping from among the crowd. The genuineness of the grief of the lowborn deepened Elen-ai's own grief. Despite her anger at the Queen for her reckless relationship with Zekken, like any member of the Second Country, she had held a love for her Queen that was intertwined with her love for her country. The Queen's untimely death was a profanity and the fact that she had been murdered simply extended the underlying shock and outrage at the fact that even Queens die before the time.

As they neared the Palace, the people lining the streets ceased to be the lowborn residents of the city and became the members of the seven families and their households gathered outside their city residences. Elen-ai glimpsed Rania among the Harete family, her pretty face stricken. Her parents walked in the procession, the pregnant Janyce supported on Timet's arm. Their acrimony was obvious to anyone who looked, her body bowed away from him despite the arm on which she leaned.

The procession passed the Aadran residence and Elen-ai could see Zekken standing with his other family members. He looked utterly devastated, his appearance barely presentable. His eyes were red and his face was puffy in the way that signalled he had shed a great many tears and was likely holding them back now. As the procession passed the Aadran family, his gaze flickered between Gidyon, the boy he believed to be his son, and the body of Latana, his adored lover, before he succumbed to sobs that he muffled poorly with his arm.

The procession re-entered the Palace compound, led by Gidyon and his two uncles – Kaine was unlikely even to have yet received word of his sister's death due to his diplomatic journey to the Fourth Country. The three men accompanied Latana's body into the incineration house. From a window in the Palace Elen-ai had watched the armfuls of wood being prepared for the fire that would consume the Queen's form in the early hours of the morning. When the sun set, the fire would be lit and the Queen's ashes would rise into the night sky and drift over her country. The funeral procession, the heads of the seven families and Elen-ai, milled in the yard that surrounded the little stone room.

It was mid-afternoon and the sun would not set for several more hours. However, tradition dictated that nobody was permitted to leave until the Queen's funeral pyre was lit at sundown. The Palace servants brought out water and Elen-ai gratefully drank. The walk had taken several hours, and the heat of the day had made it seem even longer. Chairs were also brought out, and several people gratefully sank into them.

The courtyard descended into the stillness of the vigil required by funeral custom. The sun lapped at the procession. Elen-ai could smell the salty tang of sweat as the gathered individuals perspired in the heat. She wondered whether it was hot in the incineration house and whether Gidyon had been offered a drink.

The hours passed slowly, punctuated with the occasional clearing of the throat or rustle as someone shifted in their seat. In different circumstances, Elen-ai might have enjoyed the extended period of silence, but today, surrounded by people whose boredom and grief were all a part of a game that left a sour taste in her mouth, Elen-ai wished she were in some other part of Herran, mourning the Queen in the noisy lowborn way. Finally, the sun dipped below the horizon and the Palace bells gave one single toll in recognition of the day's end. The door to the room opened and the men of the Royal family emerged. A flaming brazier was brought to Gidyon with a solemnity that befitted the moment. He took it, his hand steady, and turned back to the entrance of the room. Elen-ai glimpsed a small mountain of carefully piled wood before Gidyon touched the brazier to the nearest branch. The flame ran along the wood and out of Elen-ai's sight, but she saw the glow reflected on the room's walls which meant the fire had caught.

The heavy metal door to the incineration room was swung shut and firmly latched. Elen-ai looked up. Against the darkening sky she could see a trickle of grey smoke curling from the chimney. She wasn't certain, but she thought she could faintly smell the meaty, slightly sweet scent of burning flesh. It seemed almost impossible that in the stone structure before Elen-ai were the final remains of her Queen.

The funeral now complete, the members of the procession eased their stiff limbs and wordlessly entered the Palace. The funeral feast would be served following a short break to allow those who had been outside in the baking afternoon the opportunity to refresh themselves.

Elen-ai followed Gidyon to his rooms. He did not seem to have been particularly affected by the heat of the afternoon, but his air of malaise told her that his mother's funeral had, unsurprisingly, been deeply distressing. Once in his rooms, he exchanged his shirt for a fresh one and sat down on the couch, resting his head in his hands. Elen-ai changed her own tunic, carefully transferring all of her blades across into the new garment. She did not bother Gidyon with pointless conversation. If he wanted to speak, he would.

"I wish I didn't have to go to this dinner," he said softly, the defeat in his voice more upsetting than the sadness he exuded.

"One more night, then it will be done." Elen-ai did not seek to soothe or cajole, she simply sought to pull him through for one more evening. There may have been a time when she would have suggested he not go, but she knew him well enough by now to know he would never even entertain the notion. It was his duty to preside over the funeral dinner for his mother, so he would go.

He sighed. "I suppose you're right. Alright, let's go." He stood, his face slack with exhaustion and grief, and led the way into the banquet hall.

The immediate members of the seven families were in attendance at the funeral banquet. Elen-ai could hear the soft hum of their conversation as she and Gidyon approached the room. Outside the door, Gidyon paused. She saw his shoulders slump for a fraction of a moment then heard him take a deep breath and pull himself up straighter. He nodded to the guards and they opened the doors. With everybody wearing mourning silver, the room looked like a shimmering pool. Gidyon strode in, commanding the total attention of the room, the purple sash a contrast to the sombre tones. Elen-ai slipped in after him, as always, an unobtrusive footnote.

Everybody sank into a deep bow. Regardless of their allegiance to him as their ruler, he was nevertheless the reigning monarch, and a week ago he had lost his mother. Nobody would have dared fail to prostrate themselves before him. Even Elen-ai sank into a bow, although she kept a sharp alertness about her. She had failed the Queen one week ago, and she would not fail again.

The dinner commenced to a backdrop of music. The musicians played soft and gentle pieces which entrenched a sombre mood. Normally for a feast of this scale, the tenor of the music would be lively and cheerful, creating an ambience which urged diners to greater heights of cheer and merriment in a reminder of the fact that the Palace was able to hold the finest parties, amongst its other many points of authority. Tonight however, such cheer was out of place. As such, conversation never rose above a discreet murmur and no laughter sounded.

Elen-ai wandered over to the Veertaks, smiling at Varl despite the circumstances.

"My dear, I'm sorry we haven't had the chance to speak since we arrived." Varl returned her smile, his wrinkled face crinkling around the sadness that had settled on it.

"Gidyon's been very busy," she replied.

"Is he alright?" VArlena came to her husband's side, putting a hand on his shoulder. Without even seeming to realise it, he reached his hand up and across to cover hers.

Elen-ai gave a small shrug. "His mother just died. He is as well as can be expected."

"I do not envy him the task ahead, especially given the obstacles some may place in his way," Varl said, casting a pointed glance in the direction of Halen Katan and his wife, Lilyea, who were quietly conferring with Julyana and Aydrien Bertak.

"Have they no shame?" The little man practically vibrated with anger.

"My darling," VArlena's voice contained a note of warning.

"How dare they?" he uttered.

"You are not to go over there and berate them," VArlena told him sternly.

"I would never do such a thing," he protested, his eyes still on the little conference taking place on the other side of the room.

"You are a terrible liar and a good man. And I love you," she told him quietly. "But if you go over there and tell them off, I will have to stab you with a serving fork to prevent you from doing so," she added.

Elen-ai let out an amused breath. She actually believed that the dignified woman would make good on her promise in order to prevent her husband causing a worse scene.

Wenden Rasatan wandered over. His features were an echo of his son's, albeit without the striking good looks. Elen-ai wasn't certain if it was the haunted look he had adopted that made him so distinctively less handsome than his son, or if it was a slightly different arrangement of the component parts that meant that while he was good looking, Erek had been startlingly attractive. "Hullo Varl, VArlena," he said.

Elen-ai had noted the elliptical orbit of his path through the room, his momentum spurred on by the polite dismissals from anyone with whom he had tried to converse. Even the Veertaks looked mildly uncomfortable by his presence.

"Hello Wenden, how are you?" VArlena said, her question reflexively polite.

In reply, he spread his arms a little bit. "I could be worse I suppose." He gave a sad little smile that was surprisingly endearing.

"Are your other boys here?" Varl asked.

Wenden shook his head. "I thought it perhaps best if they didn't come. I'll head straight back tomorrow with..." He trailed off, although everybody present knew how that sentence would have finished. The bodies of Keela and Erek had been preserved for transport so that they could be appropriately sent off. While Keela would be given the traditional funeral by fire, Erek would, like all criminals, be buried. It was a twofold shame, to have a son who had committed regicide, but also whose resting place would be in the dirt with his final fate to be consumed by worms and rot. The prospect made Elen-ai shudder with revulsion.

The evening dragged on, a necessary unpleasantness to finish the formalities of the Queen's death. Gidyon departed at the appropriate time, not a minute earlier or later. She had watched him carefully avoid Zekken who tried to approach Gidyon several times throughout the night. On each occasion Gidyon had somehow managed to find someone else to speak with or somewhere else to be. She almost felt sorry for Zekken. He looked like a spectre of the man Elen-ai had met on the Tak estate. He and Wenden even seemed to resemble each other somehow, both men seeming lost as a consequence of their grief and shock.

In his rooms, Gidyon read over several documents that required his attention. Elen-ai sat silently watching him, preoccupied with thoughts of the horror of being buried and the look on Wenden Rasatan's face. The Veertaks had ultimately been kind to him, speaking with him far longer than anybody else, but even they had to consider their reputation. Being too friendly with the father of the man who had killed the Queen was not going to hold their family in good stead, so they too had extricated themselves from the conversation with haste. After seeing him, Elen-ai wondered how he had ever gained a reputation for being so ruthless and authoritarian. He had simply looked like an ordinary man to her.

Two days later, Gidyon paused in between his many meetings and turned to Elen-ai. She had never thought that the position of monarch would require so much work, but since Latana's death, she had been by Gidyon's side for meetings with various individuals who held positions that she did not even know existed, while he had read reports, and of course while he had listened to petitioners. He handled each of his duties with a dignity and calm that belied the fact that he was only about to turn seventeen and had just witnessed the murder of his mother by the man who might be his father.

"Elen-ai." From the way he said her name, Elen-ai knew that he was about to say something she wasn't going to like.

"I have given the matter of your contract considerable thought," he continued.

She frowned, uncertain of where he was going with this.

"My mother signed a contract with the Family to ensure it was safe for me to be able to ascend the throne. I have ascended the throne."

"Yes, but –"

He held up a hand to silence her, his face grave.

"You have fulfilled your contract, and I cannot expect or ask you to stay beyond the fulfilment of your contract."

Something that felt like panic bloomed in her chest. "You could take out a new contract with the Family," she suggested, hoping that she did not sound desperate.

He smiled, sadness in his eyes. "A contract to what? Protect me as ruler? You'd have to be with me for my entire life."

She opened and closed her mouth, uncertain of how she could respond. From the sad smile on Gidyon's face, he had apparently anticipated this. "I have arranged for the payment my mother promised to be made available for the Family to collect as they wish," he continued.

"I could stay just a little longer, just until things settle." She was starting to sound almost hysterical. Something about the prospect of leaving Gidyon alone, without her protection or companionship made distress secure itself in the pit of her stomach.

"Elen-ai, your contract is fulfilled." It seemed wrong that he was the one comforting her, but the gentleness of his voice made it clear that was exactly what he was doing.

"Gid." She was begging him, although she didn't know exactly what for.

"I've made my decision, Elen-ai," he told her. "Thank you. For everything. I am supremely lucky to have a friend like you." He embraced her. It was the first time that they had ever hugged.

She wanted to tell him that she was sorry she hadn't saved the Queen, that she was sorry for the fact that he was so terribly alone and facing the possibility that once the grief and shock of the Queen's death wore off the people may refuse to be ruled by a man. Instead, she held him close, feeling the slenderness of his form that gave away his age.

"It has been an honour to stand by your side," she told him, fighting to keep her voice from breaking as she felt tears threaten to fill her eyes.

TWENTY TWO

The Family's home was cool and dark, and a welcome sanctuary from the heat of the day. As Elen-ai stepped inside the familiar walls, she inhaled the slightly spicy scent that she simply knew as 'home'. It felt indescribably good to be back in the place where she had grown up, where everything was deliciously familiar. She could hear muffled noises coming from one of the rooms; probably a Mother or Father giving lessons to a group of the Family's children. She smiled at the familiarity, relaxing fully for perhaps the first time in a great many weeks.

The beautiful house was a mixture of timber – fine Harete wood – painted a dark colour and cool stone with high ceilings and floors that were heated ever so slightly in winter and somehow managed to remain cool even in the depths of summer. Despite having a great many windows, they were almost always covered by dark purple curtains, which meant that only a little light was let in by any one window. This created a row of thin rays of light punctuating the shadowy corridors. Elen-ai had always found it quite beautiful to walk along such corridors in the middle of the day, watching as motes of dust danced as they were caught in the beams.

She intuited rather than felt the appearance of one of her Fathers beside her.

"My daughter." Did she detect a hint of warmth in his voice, or was she succumbing to sentimentality?

"Father."

"It is good that you are back home with us." His face was totally impassive, as though he were making an idle comment about the heat of the day rather than bestowing on her an unusually high compliment.

"It is good to be home," Elen-ai responded, her own voice neutral. The calmness of being home, of being within those walls settled on her, smoothing away the excesses of emotion, of worry, anger, or sadness.

"I trust that you have not become lax during your lengthy time away from us."

"Of course not." Privately, Elen-ai worried that perhaps she had not done as much as she should have to ensure she remained in peak physical condition. She had made sure to do exercise every day, but it had often been done in whatever space was available to her and only within the time permitted.

The Father said nothing, he merely began to walk along the corridor. He did not have to tell Elen-ai to follow him. Any member of the Family who was away for an extended period of time was required to prove their capability upon their return. If they failed to demonstrate their competence they would not be permitted to take a contract until they returned to the peak of their abilities.

The courtyard felt particularly warm after the refreshing coolness of the inside of the house. The Father remained motionless by the door. "The roof," was all he said.

Elen-ai glanced up at the series of railings and ledges that were on the side of the house. There was an abundance of hand and footholds to get onto the roof from the ground, but the difficulty was not in finding ways to get up but in the speed that she was required to demonstrate she still possessed. She took a breath and launched herself at the wall, propelling herself up faster than a normal eye could follow. Within two breaths she had ascended the three-story building and stood on its roof, looking down at the suddenly small figure of her father. She saw his nod of approval and slipped quickly down the wall to stand back in front of him.

He directed her through several more exercises, forcing her to prove her speed, agility, silence, and then finally he stood in front of her, naked blade in his hand. She swallowed. Many who were required to prove themselves failed at this final stage. She did not want to be one of them.

She did not draw any of her blades. To do so would have been the mistake of an amateur. She did not know how the fight would progress and as such, she did not know which of her blades she would require. He came at her quickly. To anyone watching, it would look as though she simply swayed from one side to the other as she evaded his attacks, but she moved much faster than that. She kept her feet in place, refusing to give any ground. Another mistake made by many. She tried to sweep his arm aside with her forearm but he anticipated the move and came at her with his other arm, another blade appearing in his hand. Now she moved, having expected this tactic herself. He had taught her how to fight with knives, after all.

She spun on her foot, using the momentum she had generated with her forearm to pivot around him, now drawing a blade and thrusting it toward him. Anyone watching might have mistaken the movements of the two for dance, so graceful were they. In reply, he curved his body just out of her reach and he too spun. Elen-ai now drew a second knife, twisting herself in a counterpoint to his movement so that her knife came to rest at his neck when they both stopped. Their dance ended abruptly. Elen-ai held the blade there a moment longer to forestall any trick, lowering it only after he inclined his head in the tiniest of nods. She stepped back and he turned to face her. Something akin to approval flickered across his face. "You are a credit to your teacher," he told her, a shadow's smile on his face at the compliment he had given himself.

Dismissed, she went back inside the house, once more feeling the world outside the house recede as she entered its shadow. She navigated the stairs to the small bedroom that was hers. Members of the Family did not really own many possessions aside from their blades and perhaps a few clothes. There was no real need for anything else. As such, they could claim one of the narrow rooms furnished with a plain cot and blanket as their own, or move between them as they chose. Elen-ai was in the minority of the Family that chose a permanent residence for herself. She couldn't quite say why, but she liked the idea of knowing where she was going to sleep each night.

She slipped back into the routine of the Family as easily as though she was awakening from a strange dream, rising early to exercise, and eating her lunch on the roof with Mari-am on the days when she and her sister were both in the house. There was a comfort to returning to what she knew, a certainty of who she was and of what she was supposed to do. Contracts arose and she took them, escorting her targets to death. The summer wore on, the heat settling over the Second Country like a blanket. The wrongness to the world that had descended after Latana's death slowly receded – or rather, it became familiar enough that it ceased to be noticeable. A date for Gidyon's coronation was set, and the country began to consider the prospect of a man on the throne. Elen-ai heard all side of the argument as she passed through various residences, but it was as though she were hearing it from afar, unable to accept that these references to the boy King – or the imposter King – were in reference to the Gidyon that she knew.

Whispers reached the ears of the Family about the machinations of the seven families – the attempts of the Katan family to subvert support for Gidyon, and the fact that most of the families were hiring and training an unusually high number of people for their household guard. Regardless of whether or not individuals supported Gidyon, the people's unease about being ruled by a man was palpable, picked up in the myriad of conversations that were exchanged in places where nobody from the Palace would even have heard of. Rumours and reports even trickled into the Family of the increasing instability within the Fourth Country and the posturing of its leaders towards the Second and Third Country in an attempt to distract their population from this ongoing problem. However, the actions of people in power and the games played between them were no longer Elen-ai's concern. She put the reports that she heard to the back of her mind and focused on the simple and easy known parts of her life.

Around the peak of the summer's heat, she began to take part in training the Family's young children. It wasn't a task that she had done much before, preferring instead to take contracts, but now she found a curious satisfaction in walking through a group of children and correcting their grip on a knife, or coaching them through a particular flip, even weaving shadows around herself to show them what they may do in a few years' time provided they were able to find faith in the God of Shadows. It was disconcerting when they called her Mother, but something about it was natural, too. Many of her own brothers and sisters had already adopted the title of Mother or Father when dealing with the Family's youngest children. Perhaps it was time she joined them.

Even though on reflection it shouldn't have, she was initially surprised that what she had seen during her time with Gidyon was considered too valuable to the Family to remain only in her head. She was often asked to join the discussions in which the Family shared the information that their members had collected. Privately, she felt that she knew far less than was assumed, but she obliged the requests for her presence, contributing a comment here or there when she had something she could add. It was in one such meeting that the subject of Gidyon's marriage arose.

"The Haretes are apparently still hopeful that the Kingling will marry their daughter," one of the Mothers said.

Elen-ai could not contain her snort. It elicited the attention of the room's members, who all turned to regard her with expectant expressions. Elen-ai composed herself before she elaborated. "They can hope but Gidyon will not. He has pledged to marry a lowborn woman."

"Surely the support of one of the four largest families through a marriage would bring him enough strength to secure his claim to the throne," pointed out Wyn-et, one of Elen-ai's brothers.

The shake of her head was one curt motion. "Perhaps, but it breaks the neutrality that the royal family is supposed to maintain. He would never do something that would endanger the peace of the Second Country for his own immediate power."

Given the obviousness of what she had just pointed out, Elen-ai was surprised to see the expressions of surprise and confusion on the faces of the others in the room.

She received an explanation for the expressions only a few hours later. A Mother found her in the practice yards while she was going through a series of flips and twists as part of her daily practice.

"My child, may I have a word with you?"

With a shrug, Elen-ai jumped off the bar that she was on and landed noiselessly in front of her Mother. A vague sense of worry prickled in the back of her mind, but she told herself to cease being silly. She had done nothing wrong.

Her Mother led the way through the large house to one of the small rooms normally used for private meditation and prayer. With a gesture, she indicated that Elen-ai sit. Elen-ai did as she was bidden, descending to sit cross-legged on the floor in one fluid movement. Even though she had bested her Father at the trial upon her return, she was only now returning to the full extent of her capabilities and movements. Perhaps he had been gentle with her.

Her Mother sat too, facing Elen-ai. For a moment, the only sound was their barely perceptible breath. With the door closed, hardly any light came into the room, although that wasn't a problem for either of them. Finally, her Mother spoke. "The Family is neutral when it comes to the Royal Family aside from our interest in knowing what is about to transpire."

Elen-ai nodded. It was, of course, the most basic rule of the Family.

"But perhaps you are not quite so neutral in how you view the Kingling."

Despite the gentle tone, Elen-ai was stung. "Whatever my personal views on Gidyon, it does not mean that I do not share the Family's neutrality," she protested, a very real fear welling up inside her. She thought of those members of the Family who had left because they were no longer aligned with what the Family asked of its children. She did not want to be one of them.

Her Mother smiled at her. "I am not accusing you of anything, Elen-ai. This is merely an observation that has been made. It is not a shame to have your own opinion."

"But I don't want to leave," Elen-ai blurted out, horrified by her lack of self-discipline.

"Why would you leave?" A look of slight confusion crossed her Mother's face.

"If I don't share the Family's neutrality," Elen-ai replied. "It would be as if I wanted to have a child," she continued.

"My child, those who leave us do so because they wish to leave us. We have never made any of our children leave us, nor will we."

"Oh," was all Elen-ai could say. She had never really thought about it that way. She had always assumed that love with someone outside the Family was prohibited rather than perhaps being incompatible with wanting to remain a member of the Family.

"I will be frank with you, Elen-ai. The Elders have agreed that given the uncertainties surrounding the Kingling and his rule, we need more information on the goings-on of the Seven Families and the Palace."

Elen-ai nodded, privately agreeing with the assessment. People would always want to kill one another, ensuing coin aplenty for the Family. But it was a different matter entirely for the Family's position within the Second Country to be secure. If Herran looked like it may become a place of war, Elen-ai knew that the Family had contingencies to move to a safer area. The Family protected its own no matter what, and if their home was in the middle of a battlefield, safety could not be assured. But if they did not know where fighting was likely to occur, such measures could not be taken. If there was anything that Elen-ai had noticed at the meetings that she had been requested to attend, it was definitely that the Family did not know enough.

"Perhaps you could be persuaded to return to the Palace and find out what we need to know," her Mother said.

"But –"

She was cut off. "You want to help this Kingling. There is no shame in that. We need information so that we can keep our children safe. It makes sense."

Elen-ai shook her head. "I don't want to leave."

"Elen-ai," her Mother's voice was so gentle. "You do not have to accept."

"Surely if I did I would be taking a side, though," Elen-ai worried.

"You would not be there as a member of the Family."

Elen-ai raised a hand and pressed it against her cheek, trying to comprehend what was occurring. "Are you saying I should go back?"

"Do you believe that Gidyon should be King and that you can help him do that?" her Mother asked.

Elen-ai was silent for a long time. She had made a very deliberate decision to not ask herself such questions since her return. She was a member of the Family and her time with Gidyon had been in fulfilment of a contract. That contract had been completed, and she was obliged as a member of the Family to return home. Yet now that she allowed herself to consider the matter, she thought about Gidyon's desire to do right by his people, of the skill with which he dealt with the members of the seven Families. She thought about the grief that he had not allowed himself to feel for his mother because he had instead been obliged to attend to matters of state. Finally, she thought that at nearly seventeen, he was already a spectacular young man, and if he was given the chance, he might in fact be a great man and a great King. She looked up at her Mother. There was no judgment, no anger in her face, merely a serene acceptance of whatever Elen-ai chose to do.

"Yes," Elen-ai said. "I do."

ACKNOWLEDGEMENTS

Self-publishing is a particularly terrifying activity on which to embark. While there is a great wealth of 'how to' material, the varying and occasionally contradictory advice from these sources make the experience akin to diving into a body of water when you have no idea what lies beneath the surface. My thanks in particular must extend to Aaron Lamb, author of 'Pollen' and 'Stem', who was willing to take the time to sit with me and generously share his experience.

Closer to home, I have to give a huge thank you to my father, who not only built my website but also acted as a beta and proof reader in addition to, over the course of a great many lunches, supporting and encouraging me, even when I was filled with self-doubt. That encouragement and support was also forthcoming in extraordinary amounts from my mother, who quietly and consistently told me to be proud of the choice that I made to pursue this particular, terrifying, journey.

Ellen also deserves remarkable praise for a wonderful job with the cover artwork. The atrocities I did to her beautiful sketches with MS Paint cannot be spoken of, but she somehow translated squiggles and vague comments into images which inspired me to push through the final, torturous copyedit. I also must thank Marcus, for taking Ellen's work and making it into a cover which I love with care and originality.

Mitchell, too, deserves my eternal thanks. He is a sound-board, beta reader, provider of celebratory and conciliatory bottles of wine, and he encourages me to be kind to myself when I am very much not feeling so inclined. He is my muse, and I firmly believe that I could not write as I do without him.

Thanks must finally go to every single person who has offered me encouragement when I have been least certain. You are too many to name, although I must mention Jess for reading so much of my work and offering me necessary, brutal feedback, but also the most fierce and consistent encouragement. I feel remarkably privileged in being surrounded by supportive friends as well as my students, and the overlap therein. In so many ways, this book is for you, for your enthusiasm and love.

ABOUT THE AUTHOR

Alice Jane Boer-Endacott was born and bred in Melbourne, Australia, amid a home filled with books and cats. From a young age, she has worked to refine her prose (fairy princesses were a strong thematic element of her early work, in case you were wondering).

After finishing a few university degrees definitively not related to writing, Alice decided to return to her first great love, writing.

Alice enjoys a variety of leisure activities including eating, reading, woodworking, and deeply analytical discourses about contemporary media and politics with her three cats.

You can visit her website at: www.abendacott.com
Alternatively, you can follow her on twitter at ajendacott.
Or instagram at A B Endacott

KING OF THE SEVEN LAKES

Preview

ONE

Pulling her scarf more tightly around her in a valiant fight against the cold, the assassin hurried toward the Palace. She moved with lithe grace, habit pushing her to stay close to the shadows. The inclination to remain in the darkest, most unobtrusive part of wherever she went arose from the training instilled in her from the youngest of ages.

Elen-ai passed barely anybody as she ascended the hill to the Palace, where it occupied the highest point in the capital. Even now, despite months of living there, it felt strange to be climbing the broad street to the sprawling complex rather than winding her way through Herran's lanes to the Family's home. Opulence was all very good and well, but nothing could ever compare to the familiarity of home. But the information swirling in her head took precedence over any sense of being out of place. Despite the prowling sense of urgency in her stomach, she paused at a shrine to the Divine One decorated with coloured ribbons and flowers. It was the fifth shrine she had passed since leaving the Family's home. A year ago, there had been no such shrines in the Second Country, only the temple to the Divine One in the heart of the capital. Now, it was almost impossible to walk for five minutes without seeing one. Tensions between the Seven Families and the Royal Family had not yet led to any true instability within the Second Country. The roads through the Second Country were still reasonably safe to traverse, and there were no shortages of any food or material, but people were worried.

Some of the Seven Families, like the Veertaks, remained steadfast in their loyalty to the crown, but others had taken advantage of the recent political instability to try to subvert the authority of the Palace and increase their own wealth and power. Of course, while those seeking to gain – or at the very least not lose – power always had enough to eat and trained fighters to keep them safe, the lives of most others were less secure. Problems wrought by the squabbles of the powerful always affected those who lived at the pleasure of the wealthy. The lowborn were keeping a sharp eye on what transpired between the powerful families of the Second Country, and it was obvious that they were worried by what they saw. The concern the shrines represented in turn worried Elen-ai. People often turned to faith in their gods when faith in their leaders faltered, and when people no longer had faith in their leaders, they were often not particularly averse to seeing those leaders leave. Often bloodily.

It was one of the reasons the Family of Assassins would accept a contract on anybody of high or low birth, provided the client was able to pay: the Family did not discriminate. The only strict exception to that neutrality was an unwillingness to touch a member of the Royal Family. Their deaths would cause too much instability, and the Family liked being situated in a prosperous, war-free country. It was good business. The Family's home was in an area that straddled the less dangerous parts of the poor district and the residences of individuals whose wealth offered them some measure of comfort, where the buildings ceased to be made entirely from timber and the more sturdy construction of stonework crept into the designs. In some ways, the Family's home was situated in a space of perfect neutrality between the high and low born, echoing the Family's apolitical nature.

As Elen-ai progressed through the wealthy district, each shrine was grander than the last. Those erected by the poor were all hastily made from whatever materials could be spared – a sun clumsily carved from a piece of scrap timber, a wooden sphere painted yellow or orange, even a simple cloth banner with a sun symbol embroidered or crudely drawn on it. Not so the one outside the fencing arena of the Artisans Quarter. Some fortunate woodcarver would have received a handsome commission for the work. Even the arena, which was easily distinguishable by the height that enabled many people to crowd in to watch the match, was of better construction than those arenas in poorer parts of the city. This one was built mostly from stone and had a fresh coat of paint on the door. Elen-ai could easily imagine the wealthier members of Herran's society cheerfully coming here for an evening's entertainment. One of the favourite pastimes of the Second Country's residents was to watch several fencing bouts across an evening. A night's entertainment would start with matches in which contestants fought with dulled blades and were limited to touches, then progress to first blood as the determinant of victory, and then finally to unrestricted fighting when victory was only determined when one fighter yielded – or died. Those final matches were the most eagerly anticipated. Many a lowborn citizen had made a comfortable fortune from their prowess with a blade, especially those lucky few to be sponsored by one of the Seven Families looking to add a champion fencer to the things about which they could boast. Elen-ai wondered if the shrine was visited by the competitors before they came to fight. Not that a simple shrine to the Sun God would protect any of the contestants from a well-aimed strike, but people liked to believe that something larger than themselves watched over them. Elen-ai personally preferred to place her faith in quick wits and rigorous training.

Predictably, the Katan family's shrine to the Divine One outside their city residence was taller, wider, and more splendid than all of the others combined. Despite her desire to be out of the bitter cold, Elen-ai crossed to the other side of the street so she could better regard it. She snorted in amazement at the gold that covered the orb at the centre of the sun symbol and the gems embedded in the point of each ray emanating from the sphere. Such an extravagant display of wealth did not surprise her in the slightest. Halen, the leader of the Katan family, had aspirations for his granddaughter to be put on the throne. It didn't matter to Halen that Serenah was woefully inadequate as a potential ruler. He did not care that a ruler who had not been trained to possess the neutrality and even-handedness that was crucial when managing the delicate politics of the seven ambitious families, could be disastrous. The presence of a man on the throne following the brutal murder of Queen Latana was reason enough for Halen to justify the even greater instability he risked unleashing by trying to make his granddaughter queen. Though Elen-ai had only met the man once, it was a genuine pleasure to despise him. That vehement dislike was only compounded by what she had just learned about his actions. The rage that left a sick feeling in her throat fought with tense concern at what Halen's ambitions might mean. Taking one final look at the vulgar statement to Katan self-importance, Elen-ai continued on her way.

The ascent up the hill to the Palace offered progressively lovely views of Herran and the harbour around which it had been built. As she climbed higher, the city's rooftops fell together in a curiously harmonious patchwork of reds, greys and blacks, regularly interspersed with curls of smoke hanging softly in the cold air. With distance, even the ramshackle timber houses of the city's lowborn areas were beautiful. Elen-ai paused to turn and look back to the city. She swept her gaze along the crowded streets to the stone blue of the water in the harbour. In sunlight it would sparkle with unparalleled radiance. Today, however, the colour of the overcast sky was mirrored in the grey waves. She couldn't help but think that it suited her current mood.

Finally, she reached the Palace gates. Nearly the height of three people, the Palace's walls were an imposing sight, only rendered plain by the magnificent structure that rose behind them. Made from pale stone that glowed even in the lowest light, the immense complex was home to the Royal Family. Since the formation of the Second Country, its queens had resided within the Palace walls where they had managed the delicate power balance of the country's seven wealthiest families. Glimpses of the Palace could be seen from almost anywhere in Herran, but up close, there was something awe-inspiring about the elegant buildings.

Elen-ai wasn't sure she would ever become accustomed to so brazenly passing through the main gate. Her preferred method of entrance and egress was always the least noticeable one. Assassins who were spotted were not particularly successful in their trade, nor were they particularly long-lived. It was odd to realise that she even recognised the guards who stood on either side of the gates, nodding a quick greeting to them as she passed and receiving one in return.

For a moment, Elen-ai contemplated entering through the servants' door. The entrance was far less conspicuous than the grand doors of the Palace through which people of high birth, or high importance, entered. However, to enter through the servant's door would be more cause for attention given her place by Gidyon's side was well known. So, in defiance of every instinct she had ever cultivated, she gritted her teeth and ascended the stairs to the grand entrance. The door was opened for her and she walked out of the cold into the grand foyer. The foyer was its own testament to the wealth and power of the Royal Family. Several stairs and doors led away from it, hinting at the expanse of the Palace beyond. The foyer itself was huge. Every part of its walls was covered in murals painted by the most skilled artists of the time. Even the ceiling was painted: a blue sky, complete with clouds. Elen-ai had always found it odd to simulate the open sky while inside, but most people seemed to think it a stroke of the painter's genius. The first time Elen-ai had been in the space, she had been too curious as to why a member of the Family had been summoned by the Queen to actually notice the magnificence of where she was. Now, she had seen the foyer so many times that its splendour was almost lost on her.

Elen-ai made her way through the maze of breathtakingly beautiful corridors with a comfortable familiarity born from months of living there. Sadly, the stone out of which the walls had been built, despite the beauty it offered, held in the cold, encouraging swift passage through the building. Once more, Elen-ai thought wistfully of the Family's home. A clever system spread the heat from a fire throughout the home's walls. It meant that the whole building was a sanctuary from the chill of winter, unlike the Palace where one had to all but run from wing to wing in order to stay warm.

She was struck anew – as she always was – by the strangeness of being greeted by servants as she passed them. Never before had she been so recognised. Indeed, when she reached the council chamber, the guards at the door simply moved aside for her as they saw her approach. While there had initially been some element of novelty that made the experience somewhat enjoyable, she had never managed to shake the discomfort that such special treatment evoked. Anybody who was given immediate, unrestricted access to the most senior members of the Royal Family was uniquely privileged as well as uniquely conspicuous. It went against everything she knew to be at the centre of such attention.

At the opening of the doors, the room's occupants halted their conversation. Maps and charts pinned to the walls, with no regard for the plasterwork, all spoke of warfare strategies. However, the well-groomed and well-dressed men who were conferring inside seemed totally incongruous with war and fighting.

"Well?" The youngest of the group, handsome and authoritative despite his lesser years, seemed to recover himself first. He strode across the room to greet Elen-ai, who was privately delighting in the room's warmth.

Most people in Elen-ai's position would have bowed, faced as they were with their monarch. She did not. Gidyon and Elen-ai had been through too much for such formalities.

Every time she saw Gidyon, it seemed there was a further ageing in his face. At seventeen years old, it seemed hardly fair that the burden of ruling had been thrust upon him, let alone the burden of being the first male to sit on the throne of the Second Country.

His advisers, also his uncles, looked at her expectantly, waiting for the news that she had promised to bring. She remembered the hostility with which they had opposed her presence when Gidyon's late mother, their sister and queen, had engaged Elen-ai to protect Gidyon prior to the public announcement of her decision to make him her heir. Fearing violent reprisal for her boldness to go against centuries of tradition, she had engaged the Family, reasoning that an assassin would know best how another may try to take Gidyon's life. Elen-ai could still recall the suspicion and unease with which the Queen's brothers and advisers viewed the decision to have an assassin protecting the Prince. But their hostility toward Elen-ai had melted away in the face of Elen-ai's obvious loyalty to Gidyon. Perhaps a slight reserve remained, but she could hardly blame them for that. A member of the Family within the Palace was unprecedented. Then again, they were living in unprecedented times.

"The news is not good, I'm afraid," Elen-ai said. She made no effort to hide the grim tightness in her voice, or on her face.

A look of weary resignation flashed across Gidyon's face. He must have been very tired. Normally trying to discern what he was thinking or feeling was impossible. The duties and obligations of the throne not only robbed him of hours of sleep but weighed heavily upon him, too. Even Elen-ai, who was accustomed to very little sleep, would often take herself to bed long before him. It wouldn't be untrue to say that she worried about him.

"Let's have it then," Gidyon said. His face was totally impassive once more.

Elen-ai reported what she had learned at the Family's home: "From all accounts the Katan family is training a small army." She linked her hands behind her back while she observed the reactions of the men.

Silius, the oldest of Gidyon's uncles, displayed his anger in the tightening of his face and the flare of his nostrils. His two brothers, however, were less restrained, expressing their anger and dismay with muttered oaths and profanities. For his part, Gidyon absorbed the news with no visible reaction. After a moment, he let out a slight sigh.

"So it's for what we've been preparing," he said, his voice utterly even. He walked back to the table, Elen-ai falling into step beside him.

For a while, the five of them stood there in silence as the implications of her information were fully considered. During her walk to the Palace, Elen-ai had arrived at the conclusion that Gidyon and his uncles were no doubt drawing now: if Halen Katan would not be given the throne, it seemed he was willing to take it by force.